A MURDER IN THE GARDEN CLUB

Neal Sanders

The Hardington Press

Also by Neal Sanders

Murder Imperfect (2010)
The Garden Club Gang (2011)
The Accidental Spy (2011)

*For Betty, who thought I wasn't listening
when I came home and she said,
"You wouldn't believe what
happened to me today…"*

A MURDER IN THE GARDEN CLUB

1.
Wednesday

"*Chaos,*" Liz Phillips thought to herself. "*Sheer, unmitigated chaos.*"

Before her, thirty-five women and one lone man gossiped while balancing cups of coffee, cakes and fruit. Gaggles of three and four spoke together in animated tones while casting glances at other groups across the meeting room, eavesdropping even as they followed the latest installments in long-running human dramas.

"Ladies," Liz said in an authoritative voice designed to override the multiple conversations. "And Roland," she said, smiling at the lone man. "Can we get started? It's ten o'clock."

Dutifully, the group took their seats, like sheep successfully herded by a border collie using just the right bark. The Hardington Garden Club had been called to order.

Liz looked over her attendees. Thirty-five was a good number for a June meeting when many members had already decamped for summer homes on the Cape or the Berkshires. Plus five unfamiliar faces – potential members drawn by the three-paragraph article in the Hardington *Chronicle* extolling the opportunity to see Alicia Meriwether work her magic in floral arrangements using ordinary supermarket flowers. Alicia always drew a crowd and summer meetings needed appealing names and topics to attract new members to replace those who moved, dropped out or, as it was put euphemistically, 'aged out'. Liz hoped that Mary Giametti, her membership chairman, had already buttonholed these guests and pressed membership applications into their hands along with the promise of camaraderie and improved gardening appreciation.

The Hardington Garden Club meeting was really three meetings. The social get-together that had been ongoing since a quarter past nine, when the first members began trickling into the meeting room of the Congregational Church, was one. The business meeting that was about to begin, and the presentation that would follow, were the second and third. The trick to running a successful garden club was to keep this middle section as mercifully brief as possible. Most of what members needed to know was in the club newsletter, and Liz noted with appreciation that almost everyone had in his or her hands the newsletter over which she had labored the previous evening.

"Next month's meeting is the trip to Fuller Gardens," she said. "If you haven't signed up, this is your last chance. The sign-up sheet is on the table by the door. If you haven't paid your five dollars for the trip, you have to get your money to Fran before the trip. You can't pay on the day of the trip. Your seat will go to someone on the alternate list."

Liz had hoped that this brief announcement would pass without comment, but a hand was raised from the third row. "Why do we have to pay? What are our dues for?" The speaker was Delores Simmons, a seventy-something member who easily got her $25 per year dues just in the amount of coffee cake and cookies she took home in her cavernous purse each month.

It was a question that Liz has heard many times before. "Admission to the gardens alone is six dollars per person," she said smoothly. "The bus holds forty-five and we were given a price of $450. That means the club is subsidizing eleven dollars of the cost of every member who goes." The answer was technically true. Walk-up admission to the garden was in fact six dollars and the original quote from the bus company was $450. But Liz had negotiated down the bus company to $350 and the garden to $100 by buying a club membership. The club was still subsidizing the trip, but members now paid more than half the cost. The real reason for the charge, though, had been settled in the garden club board meeting months earlier. If the club didn't charge something, everyone would sign up, including the members who never showed up for the workshops and sales that paid the club's bills.

The answer seemed to satisfy Delores, and Liz quickly rattled through a dozen items, glancing at a sheet of paper she had printed out that morning. "We need volunteers for a summer cleanup at Paula's Place and there's a sign-up sheet on the table by the door."

This would be a tough sell. Paula's Place was a residence for people seeking cancer treatment and was near the Longwood Medical Center in Boston. Tending the facility's garden means enticing half a dozen members to make a dreaded trip into Boston, eighteen miles but a world away from Hardington. Liz knew that she could count on only two or three regulars to make the trip in addition to herself. She would be shorthanded, as usual.

"And, Sally has a few words to say about care of your sites for the summer." The Hardington Garden Club's true claim to fame was its care of two dozen roadside gardens at town intersections and traffic islands. The club's annual expenditure for annuals and perennials for these sites was more than $5000. Sally Kahn, who managed the roadside garden program, wanted to protect the club's investment in those flowers by stressing the need for frequent watering now that the heat of summer was here.

Liz looked around for Sally. She wasn't in the room. Come to think of it, Liz couldn't remember having seen Sally before the meeting, though that wasn't unusual. Several members invariably tackled Liz as soon as she came in, and she had made a point of spending time with the guest speaker.

"Has anyone seen Sally?" A few shakes of the head from members. "Well, Sally wanted to remind you that it's time to start using those jugs you've saved to water your sites," Liz ad-libbed. "If a plant wilts, it's stressed, and stressed plants don't flower. And, if you alternate with someone on your site, please make certain that you've agreed who tends the site on what weeks. Keep the sites weeded in June and it will make life easier in July. And if you need to replace any plants, let Sally know ahead of time. She won't authorize reimbursement for plants you just go out and buy. And water. Unless it rains an inch, lots of water." That was as much as Liz could remember from the board meeting speech Sally had given. Liz made a mental note to send out an email reminder that evening, and to gently berate Sally for having made Liz give her speech.

With the official business of the meeting dispensed with in a crisp twelve minutes, Liz introduced her speaker. At noon sharp, the meeting was over. She managed to greet two of the prospective members and get names. The other three had slipped out of the meeting as soon as Alicia had given away the last of the six arrangements she had made. Tired and a little thirsty, she made her way to the church kitchen where Roland Evans-Jones, the club's lone male member, was cleaning up the jumble of cups and saucers left scattered after the meeting.

"How did you get stuck with clean-up duty?" Liz asked.

Roland smiled. "I volunteered because I knew it was the only way you'd ever get a decent cup of tea. I'm making a pot so you get yours fresh. Earl Grey? Another meeting, superbly managed." He slid a cup toward her and poured a cup for himself and for her. "I love Alicia dearly, but she really ought to keep track of her jokes." He took a long sip and picked up a tea biscuit. "She used at least a dozen of those lines when she did 'container gardens to die for' last year. I mean, you're paying her – what – three hundred dollars? You'd think we'd get fresh stories." Roland was at least seventy, possibly even a decade older. But he had more energy than members decades younger and the sharpest tongue of anyone in the club. "Your recovery for our friend Sally was just wonderful. And no, she was never here."

Liz stayed another twenty minutes as Roland gossiped about members' comings and goings. Roland told her that four of the club's members – Eleanor Strong, Alice Beauchamp, Paula Winters and Jean Sullivan – were now "thick as thieves" in Roland's words, and continually giggled among themselves from the time they entered the church to the final round of applause for the speaker. "I can't imagine what they have in common," he said.

Liz listened but seldom contributed. Gossip didn't much interest her, but Roland's charm was his ability to weave tales, and his animation when he spoke was fascinating to Liz. Finally, she held up a finger. "I've got to run," she said, mostly truthfully. She quickly gathered together her papers. Another meeting in the bag.

She backed her Jaguar convertible – "the official car of the female midlife crisis," according to her husband, David – out of a quasi-legal spot near the church and nosed into Hardington's noontime traffic on Main Street. With David out of town again for the week, Liz was in no hurry to go home. Also, it troubled her that Sally Kahn, who never missed a meeting, wasn't there. She decided to stop by Sally Kahn's house with the excuse of dropping off a sheaf of British gardening magazines she had brought to the meeting.

The Congregational Church was in the center of town, an eighteenth century anchor on the Hardington town green. A picturesque glimpse of what Hardington looked like when it was an obscure farming community. Settled in 1660, Hardington flew under the radar of development for the first three hundred years of its existence. It was too far out of the city to attract suburban development in the first decades of the twentieth century and then overlooked when expressways and turnpikes were built elsewhere in the fifties and sixties. Now, those very qualities made Hardington eminently desirable. Eighteen miles was now 'close in' compared to the subdivisions sprouting in towns 25 and 30 miles distant from the financial district.

Commuter rail running along the right-of-way of the old Boston & Hartford line obviated the need for navigating those now-overburdened expressways. The fastest of the morning express trains made just four stops and took 34 minutes to get to

South Station. No wonder Hardington was filling up with what David called "hedge fund bonus babies", many of whose non-working spouses were now garden club members. Their homes sprouted like 4,500-square-foot mushrooms in former farm fields.

Hardington was changing, obscure no longer. The houses built in the sixties and seventies on acre-plus lots were now listed as teardowns, slated to be replaced by seven-bedroom "mansionettes" befitting the incomes – and the egos – of a new class of Hardington resident. The Victorians from the town's brief heyday as a manufacturing center – "the Straw Hat Capital of the World" – had been lovingly restored to their polychromed original look, only now with granite-countered kitchens and Jacuzzis for two. The surviving tiny, fragile homes from the colonial era were now enlarged into compounds. The original houses with their status-conferring year-of-construction plaque ("Bennett House – 1734") had long been overwhelmed by insensitive additions comprising master suites or indoor pools.

The signs of more recent change were everywhere. Liz was stopped at the traffic light at North Street where a cheese shop and decorator showroom had replaced Jenkins' Hardware, now moved to less pricey real estate on the north side of town. Taylor's, the town's "department store" for seventy years, still occupied one corner and did a brisk business, but its stock-in-trade was now Yankee Candles, expensive gift wrap and uniforms for various Hardington school athletic programs. In front of her at the traffic light were the two ubiquitous symbols of Hardington: a lawn service truck and trailer, and a Landini Brothers concrete mix truck. In a town where disposable incomes were high and free time was scarce, mowing a lawn was one of the first family routines to disappear. Of the eight homes on Liz's street, professional firms serviced seven.

The Landini Brothers truck was both the past and the future. The burgeoning suburbs between Routes 128 and 495, the two superhighways that arced around Boston, had turned the once-tiny sand and gravel company – actually located across the Charles River in Overfield – into a major player in concrete. Landini Brothers trucks were a constant presence through Hardington, slowing traffic to a crawl, belching diesel fuel and aging the town's roads at an accelerated pace.

Five minutes and a half a mile further along Main Street, Liz waited impatiently for the Landini Brothers truck to make its turn at Post Road, the acknowledged local's shortcut to neighboring Cavendish and then to Boston. As the truck waited for a gap in oncoming traffic, Liz had an opportunity to admire one of the club's roadside gardens. Main and Post or as Sally Kahn called it, "the Eastern Gateway." Eight hundred square feet of annuals and perennials, surrounded by a carpet of junipers. It was a beautiful design, a labor of love that had taken two years to install.

And definitely in need of watering, Liz noted. This was Sally's site and she was violating her own speech to the club – or, rather, the speech Liz had given on Sally's behalf. Liz knew Sally believed strongly in watering in the early morning, and chastised club members who ran sprinklers at midday. Main and Post had clearly not been visited that morning. The leaves on the recently planted annuals were drooped, their shallow roots in need of water.

The truck turned and Liz sped the last half mile to the Emerson Road turn that would take her to Sally's house. Sally was perhaps her closest friend. Though nearly a decade older than Liz, Sally was a true gardener in a world of people who were content to plant impatiens and rhododendron from Home Depot. She was also a dependable co-worker when others volunteered only if it was convenient. Sally spoke the Latin names of the plants in her garden as readily as she named her students from her days as a teacher. She was a kindred spirit, a woman with a passion for growing things and for thinking beyond the mundane.

Sally's street was, like Liz's, a cul-de-sac, though at the end of

Pequot Court and opposite Sally's house was a path that led down the hill to the Hardington middle and high schools. The street was deserted at noon.   Most mornings, Liz and Sally could count dozens of children using the shortcut.   At least it was good that they were walking to school, they agreed, an increasing rarity in a town where SUVs lined up to drop off students at the school's front entrance.

Liz turned into the driveway and gathered the magazines. Like most Hardington residents, Sally seldom used her front door, preferring to enter through the garage. Liz had seen Sally retrieve a key from under a pot many times and it was there, as expected. Once in the garage, Liz was gratified to see that Sally's Prius was in place. She had half-feared that Sally had been called away on an emergency.

Liz knocked at the door and listened for a response. She heard the radio – a WBZ 'traffic on the threes' report – from inside the house but no sounds of footsteps approaching. She rapped louder and was rewarded by the yapping of Chipper, Sally's Pekinese. Liz tried the door and found it unlocked. She stuck her head inside. "Sally?"

Chipper immediately jumped at her legs, pawing madly at her pants. "Hey little guy," Liz cooed. "Where's your Mommy?" Then, louder, "Hey, Sally!"

Liz looked around the kitchen where the makings of breakfast were all around. The scorched smell of coffee too long in the pot reached her nose, and she instinctively took the pot from its Mr. Coffee warming stand. It appeared that three-quarters of the coffee had already steamed away. "Sally!" she said again, holding the coffee pot.

Chipper had been circling her feet, whining. The dog clearly needed to be let out. But at the basement door, the Pekinese stopped racing and began a mournful howl. Liz glanced down the basement steps.

And dropped the coffee pot.

There, at the bottom of the stairs, was Sally. Her eyes and mouth were open. Her neck was at an angle no human could achieve naturally. "Oh, my God," Liz said and carefully picked her way down the stairs. Liz had never seen a dead person before outside of a funeral home. Gingerly, she touched Sally's cheek. It was cold.

She quickly retreated up the stairs into the kitchen. *Keep calm*, she told herself. Grabbing her cell phone from her purse, she dialed 911.

"Emergency services." A woman's voice. A statement.

"My name is Liz Phillips. I'm calling from 11 Pequot Court. I've just found…"

"In what town?" the operator interrupted.

"Hardington," Liz replied, making certain she used the approved, local pronunciation, "Hard'n'ton". An out-of-towner, or a Boston newscaster, would pronounce the "ing".

"I'll connect you." Then five seconds of silence that seemed like an eternity. "Hardington Emergency Services," a different voice said.

"I'm calling from 11 Pequot Court. I've just found the owner of the home in her basement. I'm pretty certain she's dead." At those words, Liz's voice lost its composure, and she began to feel tears welling up. "Please send someone. An ambulance, medics, police. Someone. Please." Liz took the phone away from her ear for a moment and did not hear what the operator said.

"I asked if you will please repeat the address," Liz heard the operator say.

"I'm sorry," Liz said, and repeated the address.

"Is there anyone else in the home with you?"

"No, I just got here a few moments ago and found her. Please send someone."

"The police and an ambulance are on their way," the

dispatcher said. "Can you give me the name of the person you found?"

"Sally Kahn." Liz started to feel the welling again. Sally Kahn was lying dead at the bottom of the basement stairs in her home. That was reality.

"Thank you," the dispatcher said. "Please wait there until the paramedics arrive." The line went dead. Liz stared at the phone for a moment, then her mind went back to work. The paramedics would expect to come in through the front door. The front door needed to be unlocked.

Sally's home had been built in the early seventies, as homes were starting to get larger, but long before the era of the behemoths being built today. She went into the living room and was stopped short, first by the unmistakable odor of animal feces. A newspaper was lying on the floor and, on it, a neat pile of Chipper's feces. Sally instinctively picked up the newspaper. Yesterday's *Globe*. From the teeth marks, Chipper had apparently pulled the paper off of the coffee table in order to conduct his business. A well trained dog, indeed.

That was when she saw the beer cans. Two of them. On the floor. *That's odd*, Liz though. *Sally doesn't drink beer and she would never leave empty cans in the living room.* She started to reach for one with her free hand but thought better of it.

Something's wrong, she thought. And then found that the front door was already unlocked. *Sally never leaves her front door unlocked. She unlocks it if someone comes to the front door, she locks it when they leave.* Twelve years of widowhood had made her aware of her vulnerability. Twelve years of being moderately wealthy had made her wary, period.

Retracing her steps back into the kitchen, she attempted to put the scene into a timeline that made sense. Sally was making breakfast. Sally had gone downstairs. Sally had fallen, perhaps she had tripped over Chipper. *Chipper*, she thought. The poor dog was whimpering again. Sally opened the slider from the kitchen to the deck to let him out. The back door, too, was unlocked.

As her mind was wrestling with these incongruities, she heard the sirens. A moment later, an ambulance came to a stop on the street in front of the house. Liz was at the front door before the paramedics, and was in time to see a Hardington police car pull up.

The next several minutes were a blur – paramedics descended the stairs and then emerged to fetch equipment and, ultimately, a stretcher. A policeman observed, spoke with the paramedics and made notes. Liz stood to one side, looking on. A second police car arrived bearing a uniformed officer and a man in a sports jacket and tie.

The man in the sports jacket pointed and spoke with the paramedics and the other officers. Several times, he glanced in Liz' direction but said nothing to her. Finally, he nodded his head to the paramedics and policemen and walked over to where Liz was standing.

"You made the 911 call?" he asked. Liz nodded. "This must be awful for you. Mrs. Kahn was a friend?"

"Yes," Liz said, not wanting to break down as she had on the phone. "She was a friend. I was dropping over some magazines for her. She missed a club meeting this morning…" Liz stopped, grasping why her friend had missed the meeting, and feeling ashamed that she had thought ill of Sally for not being there to give her pep talk or for not watering her site.

"You are Liz Phillips?" He read from a notebook.

"Elizabeth Phillips, yes. I go by Liz."

"And you live here in Hardington?" Liz noticed that he used the out-of-town pronunciation. His was more of a Boston Irish accent. *Dorchester*, she idly thought, though she knew no one who lived there and could not have placed Dorchester on a map.

"Yes. Number 8 Old Schoolhouse Road." The man in the sports jacket nodded in a way that said that he knew Old

Schoolhouse Road. She shifted uncomfortably.

He noticed the shift and nodded in the direction of the dining room. "Perhaps we could talk away from all of this."

Settled in a pair of dining room chairs, he continued. "By the way, I'm Detective John Flynn. I'm sorry we have to be meeting under such circumstances, Mrs. Phillips, and I'll try not to keep you very long. Mrs. Kahn has a dog. I saw the dishes on the floor in the kitchen." It was a statement rather than a question but Liz nodded. "Small dog?"

Now that she had a name to go with the voice, she regarded Detective Flynn. Not too tall, maybe five-nine. A stocky build under the sports jacket, but no fat around the neck. An athlete, possibly a runner. Close-cropped brown hair with the first flecks of gray on the side. A kind face, she thought to herself, but with sad eyes.

"Pekinese. Chipper." Liz responded. "I let him out a few moments ago. He apparently really needed to go. He had – well, he had made a mess in the living room."

"Do you think that's why Mrs. Kahn fell down the stairs? She might have tripped over the dog?" He tapped his lips with a pen, peering intently at her.

"I suppose," Liz said. "Chipper is one of those dogs that lives to eat. He's always running around at mealtime."

"You have a dog?"

"No, a cat, actually." Liz was embarrassed by this admission. Cat Lady. Always a bad sign.

"Do you know how the coffee pot ended up on the floor?"

"That was me," Liz said, feeling the color drain from her face. "When I came in, the first thing I noticed was that the coffee was scalding. I was holding the pot when I... when I saw her."

"I'm pretty sure I would have dropped the coffee pot too, Mrs. Phillips. By the way, I don't see evidence of a Mr. Kahn. Was your friend married?" It was the first time Liz had heard Sally referred to in the past tense.

Liz shook her head. "Widowed. Twelve years. Charlie, Charles." Liz repressed a smile. As long has she had known Sally, it was always, 'my Charlie'. "My Charlie never took up golf." "My Charlie always told me I looked good in yellow."

"Children?" The question snapped Liz out of her reverie.

"Uh, a son and a daughter. Both grown. Carol lives in Atlanta. Tim – he lives in Boston. I think Sally said Allston or someplace like that. They're both in their thirties." Carol was fine, married with two children. Tim had dropped out of college and basically done nothing since except be a worry to Sally. Who was going to tell him?

"Brothers? Sisters?"

"No, just the two of them," she answered, half thinking about how to track down Tim. And people in the garden club needed to know…

"I meant Mrs. Kahn. Did she have any brothers or sisters? Living parents?"

Liz thought for a moment. Sally had buried her parents long ago. A brother? She couldn't be sure. "I don't think so, but I'm not certain."

The detective nodded. "Do you know how to get in touch with her children? Did Mrs. Kahn have a phone list of some kind?"

Liz looked around, memories jumbled together of Sally looking for phone numbers. "There's a bedroom upstairs that she keeps as an office. You'll see a computer, printer and some other equipment. There's a print-out of important numbers. She keeps it in a red binder."

The detective nodded and closed his book. He started to rise, but then sat, a puzzled look on his face. "Oh, Mrs. Phillips. I forgot to ask. How did you get in?"

Liz grew red in the face. "Sally always uses the garage door.

She keeps a key under a pot. I've seen her use it hundreds of times." She had consciously used the present tense.

He nodded. "A fine old New England tradition. That one I ought to have figured out." And he stood up.

Liz did not. "Detective Flynn, I take by your questions that you assume this was an accident." This time she did not phrase it as a question.

He thumbed through his notes. "We'll have to investigate before we make any conclusions, but yeah, I mean, an older lady with a dog gets up one morning, the dog's yipping around while she's making breakfast, Mrs. Kahn starts down the basement steps and the dog runs between her legs. It's tragic, but it's an accident."

Liz pursed her lips. "The front door was unlocked. So was the back door. Sally never kept her doors unlocked. And there are two beer cans in the living room. Sally would never leave beer cans lying around. Also, she doesn't drink beer."

"You didn't mention any of that."

"You didn't ask any of that. You wanted to know what kind of dog she has."

The detective sat back down. "Mrs. Phillips, we're going to have a look around. We're going to make certain that we know exactly why and how your friend died. Thank you for telling me about the beer cans and the unlocked doors. In fact, thank you for all your assistance. I will get back to you if I need anything else. And I know how upsetting this can be. If you'd like someone to drive you home, I'll be pleased to arrange it." He handed her a card with 'Hardington Police' in bold relief.

More than anything else, Liz hated to be patronized. And, she thought to herself as she drove herself home, *Boy, am I being patronized*.

* * * * *

John Flynn sat at his desk and wondered, as he had every working day of the past month, why he hadn't been content to take his Boston Police Department pension and retire to Florida like everyone else he had worked with. Thirty-five years with the force, the final twenty-four as a detective. A stellar record for closing cases and a reputation for dogged determination. Enough close calls to feel he had earned his pension and the thanks of a grateful city.

And now, here he was in Hardington, a town that needed a detective the way – how did the old feminist thing go? – the way a fish needs a bicycle. A town where crime sprees consisted of bored teenage boys bashing mailboxes with baseball bats. In a month, his detective duties had consisted of organizing thirty years of case files, during which he had learned that Hardington had been the scene of exactly two homicides. Both were domestic violence cases, neither went to trial. A dozen burglaries and half a dozen rapes had been serious enough to warrant intense investigations. The perps had invariably been from Boston. There were drug busts, another symptom of bored children with access to money and a lack of common sense.

Apart from the two homicides, there had been roughly fifty death investigations. A couple of drug overdoses but the preponderance of the deaths was routine. Victim fell from roof after apparently suffering heart attack. Victim severed artery with power tool while working alone. Lives ended prematurely, but lives ended by accidents. In Hardington, you might electrocute yourself trying to install your 64-inch LED-LCD high-definition wall television system, but you weren't going to get murdered in your home.

His predecessor marked time for ten years and then jumped at the offer of a chief's job at a town on the Cape. He had left behind a meticulous set of notes for Flynn, a who's who of Hardington perps, such as they were. Who dealt cocaine and grass from out of Washington Gardens, the Section 8A project on Washington Street. Which teenagers were the ones to watch in case of a B&E.

It was all here, how to be the Hardington town detective in a dozen single-spaced pages.

So, why was he here, he thought to himself, again?

Because he hated Florida, he thought. And he hated Arizona. And he hated golf, and fishing, and everything else that awaited him in retirement. Because at 56, he wasn't ready to retire. And he wasn't ready to spend his days trying to get interested in some damned hobby that had failed to capture his imagination for the preceding five decades.

And, when he got right down to it, he wasn't ready to spend every day at home trying to come up with something to say to Annie. They got along, such as they got along, because he routinely volunteered for twelve-hour shifts, weekends and overnight stakeouts. They got along because, on average, he could expect to be home and awake for perhaps ten to twelve hours a week. He had enough safe conversational topics to fill a dozen hours, but any more and there was likely to be trouble. Bliss was coming home to find a note on the refrigerator that Annie was at her sister's house.

So, Hardington was a place of refuge, a holding action that could keep him out of the house all day. It had been made clear, though, that here in Hardington, his was a forty-hour work week without possibility of overtime or weekends, unless he wanted to put on a uniform and direct traffic at a road construction site. Chief Harding kept to a budget. Chief Amos Harding, the fifteenth Harding to be a Hardington policeman or police chief. The town bore the name of his ancestors. So, too, did the police department. Chief Harding proudly spoke of his family's long line of service as a mark of distinction. After a month, Flynn had concluded it was more like a lack of ambition.

Before him were all the elements of an accidental death, but decades of intuition and police work told him it was not an accident, though it was not his practice to say so at so early a stage of an investigation. It was also not his practice to say such things to friends of the deceased who would inevitably twist his words as they repeated them as gossip.

Yes, sixty-something-year-old women got tangled in their dogs' feet and fell down stairs. And a fall down a flight of stairs could end in a broken neck. But such an outcome required that the individual take no action to break the fall – not grab for a railing or put arms out to cushion the impact. For Sally Kahn to have broken her neck in a fall down the stairs and still be an accident, one of two conditions was required. Either Mrs. Kahn be so drunk when she fell that she was heedless of the danger, or be unconscious at the time of the fall.

The first theory fit none of the facts. He had walked through the house when the EMTs had left and found Sally Kahn to be as Liz Phillips had described. She had been a meticulous housekeeper and well organized individual. There was none of the randomness or disorganization that came with someone who drank to excess, secretly or otherwise. Sally Kahn had not been drunk when she fell. The second theory – that she was unconscious – had promise and he held it aside to examine later.

But the larger alarm in his mind was the physical evidence. The EMTs had noted that state of rigor mortis was all wrong for an accident that had taken place six or seven hours earlier. If she were making breakfast, the logical time of death would be between five o'clock and seven o'clock this morning. At one o'clock, the time the paramedics arrived, Sally Kahn should have been in full rigor. Instead, the paramedics noted she was passing out of it. That put the time of death sometime before midnight. Say, as early as nine o'clock and probably not more than two hours later. Who makes breakfast before going to bed?"

He started scribbling notes.

Forensics. Here was the problem. Hardington was not equipped to survey a possible homicide scene. He was starting with nothing. For an official autopsy, he would have to call in the State Police, considered by Boston PD to be incompetently run and staffed with lifers who couldn't get a job with 'real' police departments if their lives depended on it. And, once he called them in for an autopsy, he would have these incompetents horning in on the opportunity to pursue an interesting homicide – interesting because it wasn't Yet Another Drug Deal Gone Bad or a domestic violence. Not a ground ball.

Tim Kahn. The son. Sally Kahn's desk had yielded an address and a phone number in Allston. He noticed Liz Phillip's body language had shifted perceptibly when she provided his name, something she had not done when mentioning the daughter. She didn't like him or there were some very bad associations. Who lives in Allston? People who lived there all their lives, college kids who couldn't afford someplace closer to their school, twenty-somethings fresh out of school and saving for a 'real' place – and people with a drug problem. He tried to picture Elmore Street, the address in Sally Kahn's address book. Shabby and anonymous.

He picked up the phone and dialed a familiar number, a Boston PD detective with whom he had worked for more than a decade.

"I need a couple of small favors," he said after a few minutes of pleasantries. "I've got a suspicious death and I need an autopsy. And I need to keep this as far away from the staties as possible. Next, I need a house dusted and inspected, low key but thorough. Third, I need a rundown on a person of interest. Timothy Kahn, 114 Elmore Street, Allston. Just surface stuff from whoever in the precinct might have run across him."

He listened to protests, he parried with lists of favors, personal and professional, done over many years. A compromise was found. He put a check next to 'forensics.'

Next, he called Tim Kahn's number and crossed his fingers. An answering machine. Flynn had just bought himself a couple of hours. He left a message asking Mr. Kahn to contact him at the Hardington Police Department, saying it was important, but not providing the reason. Flynn consciously did not give his cell phone number. He had made the required call and made it promptly.

The next call went to the daughter in Atlanta. Twenty-four years as a detective came into full play as he told the woman that her mother had met with an accident. Carol Kahn would be on a plane as soon as she could arrange for someone to care for her children.

He then called the son of a friend, twenty years old, aching to get a slot on the Boston PD, and willing to do menial work to beef up his law enforcement résumé and get a reference from a detective. "I need an exterior babysitter for a house that may have been a crime scene. The job starts immediately and lasts until I say otherwise. You stay out of sight unless someone tries to go in. Then you make a polite interception." The son of the friend readily agreed.

He made a final call, hoping not to get an answering machine, and was rewarded with, 'Hello'.

"Mrs. Phillips, this is Detective Flynn. I have some follow-up questions and hoped you would be home this afternoon." He got a satisfactory response. "I'll be by in about half an hour," he said.

Flynn got up and knocked on Chief Harding's door. Harding looked up from the Boston *Herald*.

"I want to brief you on the Sally Kahn death," he said, keeping his tone flat and casual. Harding invited him in and motioned to a chair.

"Sally was a real fine woman," Harding said. "New people, but good people. Here about – what – thirty years now? She took care of the flowers out in front of the station for about five years with the garden club. Never let a weed creep in. You know she also use to teach up at the high school. Very popular teacher. That's a real shame."

Flynn had suspected Chief Harding and Sally Kahn would have known one another. He chose his words carefully while keeping the casual tone. "It appears accidental," Flynn said. "She fell down the basement steps, probably tripped over her dog. Broke her neck. I'm still trying to nail down the time of death. I'll try to have a full report tomorrow. I've called the daughter. She's flying up from Atlanta in the morning. I also called the son and left a message."

Harding shook his head. "Tim Kahn. I haven't thought about him in years. A real bad egg. Used to get in a lot of trouble. Mixed up in – what – drugs? Alcohol? Where does he live now?"

"Boston," Flynn replied, leaving out the specifics.

"Well, I hope he turned himself around. That kid was a pain in the ass."

Flynn nodded. "I'll keep you posted." And he left before Chief Harding had time to develop any more questions.

Back at Sally Kahn's house, he chalked everything he thought would be of value for fingerprinting and tagged items that crime scene investigators would carry out. He hoped that his plea for discretion wouldn't get lost in the relaying of messages from one individual to another.

Fifteen minutes later, he turned the corner for Old Schoolhouse Road. *Money*, he thought to himself. In Hardington, wealth translated into property. A lineup of colonial-style houses on steroids, each on at least a two-acre lot, each with manicured lawn and tennis court or swimming pool. Houses with three-car garages and annual property tax bills equal to the size of a compact car, and he would bet a week's pay that not a one of them had voted in the last town election or been to the annual town meeting.

It wasn't hard to spot Liz Phillips' property. Instead of manicured lawns, a pool and a tennis court, it was manicured flower beds stretching the width of the property and then bordering the driveway. *Nice*, he thought. *And it probably takes an army of Guatemalans to keep it looking this way.*

* * * * *

The reality of Sally Kahn's death did not strike home until Liz put down her purse. *Damn it*, she thought to herself. *I forgot to leave Sally the gardening magazines.* Which is when she realized that Sally would never see those magazines or speculate on whether manure or chemical fertilizer was being used to create such gorgeous dahlias in the photos.

Sally Kahn. Friend, fellow gardener, fellow tea lover. Health nut, golfer, confidante. One of the few people with whom she could truly open up. Someone for whom the truth was not something to be packaged.

Sally Kahn… tea lover…

What in the hell was a coffee pot doing being plugged in? Sally *hated* coffee and only kept a coffee maker for the occasional guest or neighbor who drank the stuff. She would never put on a pot for herself.

And, something else was out of place. She mentally went over the rooms she had just seen. The kitchen – the makings of breakfast. A melon waiting to be sliced, a bowl, cereal, a banana… and the antique sugar bowl. *Sally pulled out that sugar only when she baked or had company. Sally, the health and fitness freak, would no more have put sugar on her cereal than she would have put salt on it.*

Which meant just one thing. Sally wasn't alone this morning.

For reasons she could not fathom, Liz found her hands shaking. Assume, just assume, that Sally was making breakfast for two, and that the second person was the one for whom the sugar and coffee were intended. Where was that person? Why didn't they call the police?

Put that together with the unlocked doors and the beer cans.

Whatever happened to Sally Kahn was no accident.

The detective's words were also still in her mind. *"We're going to make certain that we know exactly why and how your friend died."*

Yeah, right, Liz thought. *You condescending asshole.* She picked up the phone.

"Roland, it's Liz. I'm afraid I have some horrible news. Sally's dead." The first part was easy. The balance – saying that she had found Sally, was infinitely harder, and Roland was both sympathetic and probing. It took ten minutes to get to the questions she wanted to ask.

"Roland, you saw Sally yesterday, didn't you?"

"We have lunch almost every Tuesday. You know that."

Liz chose her words carefully. "Was she worried about something? Did she act strangely? What did you talk about?"

Roland paused. "Are you suggesting…"

Liz cut him off. "I don't know. Some things don't add up, but I don't want to say anything until I know more. So, what did you talk about?"

She heard Roland's sigh. "If you tell someone else 'what doesn't add up' before you tell me, you'll never hear the end of it, Missy. Mostly, we talked about the club and about Tim. Tim has been bugging her every other day. Tim needs money to get his car repaired. Somebody stole Tim's television and he needs a new one. Tim needs money to go to Arizona where a friend is going to get him a job. Tim lost the rent check. Sally was very distraught."

Liz knew well about Tim's insatiable need for money because it was also an occasional part of her and Sally's private conversations. Tim was almost certainly a drug addict, and a lazy, lying man-child who blamed everyone else for his problems and who expected his mommy to bail him out. Sally had confided to Liz that he was undergoing treatment for Hepatitis C, a condition that was an invariable consequence of drug use. Sally saw in Tim her failings as a mother, coupled with Tim's inability to get over his father's death. Liz saw a monster who manipulated and tortured his mother, and she had said as much many times. And Sally kept writing checks.

"Was he coming out to Hardington?"

"Oh, yes. She wanted to make him dinner, but he said he had a job interview and couldn't get out until later. Job interview, my Aunt Fanny. I told her, for probably the two-hundredth time, that it was time to cut him off. He's never going to get better as long as she plays the enabler."

"Roland, I've told her the same thing. She won't listen." Liz stopped and choked on her words. *I'll never talk to her again. We'll never have those conversations again.*

"I know what you're thinking," he said, gently. "We'll get through this."

Liz comported herself and breathed deeply. *Keep it together*, she thought. "Was he driving out?"

"Nooooo. He was going to take the 'T' and call her from the station, I think. Or take a cab. Remember, Tim's car broke down. If he didn't sell it. If he ever had one in the first place."

"Did you talk about anything else?"

"Oh, lots of things. She was all excited about some new day lilies she found at Weston Nurseries. Excuse me, *hemerocallis*. My god, you would have thought that woman grew up speaking Latin. For the first two minutes, I thought she was talking about finding some kind of hand cream. She was all over Landini Brothers because one of their trucks ran over her site or something, and they practically threw her out of their offices when she went there to complain. We talked about Charlie, and what a good man he was. We talked about the club and what a great job you're doing, and we talked about you."

"Oh, god. Why did you talk about me?"

"Sally is afraid you're going to move. You're going to sell your house because Sarabeth is married and David is never home and it's too big a place to take care of. And if you move, she said she'd lost the only friend who knew more about plants than she did."

Sally was right, Liz thought. *The place was far too large...*

"And I guess you may as well know this," he sighed. "Sally had made up her mind that she was going to 'out' Irina at the meeting today. She was very mysterious about what evidence she had, but she said she finally had 'got the goods', and she was going to tell everyone Irina was a thief."

"Oh, god, no," Liz said, bewildered. "Why didn't you tell me this? Why didn't *Sally* tell me this?"

"Because we both knew you wouldn't stand for it. Because you'd make the two of them sit down and work it out. You'd be on Sally's side but you'd be very even-handed. And Irina would write the club a check for about fifty dollars and that would be the end of it. Until next spring and then she'd do it again."

Liz slumped in her chair. The petty business of running a club. Sally ran the roadside garden project with its two dozen sites, and managed its $5000 budget. Each site manager submitted an annual estimate to replace plants and to add annuals. Most members were meticulous about the number of plants they requested. Many paid for additional plants from their own pocket. Irina Burroughs, nee Dupree, nee Volnovich had, in three years, annually submitted receipts for hundreds of dollars' worth of plants that never made it to her site. Two dozen premium geraniums for which the club was billed a hundred dollars would miraculously morph into six scraggly plants that could be purchased at Lowes for two dollars each. The previous program manager had tolerated Irina's excuses that the plants must have been "stolen". Sally was livid that a member of a group performing a public service would steal from it.

She and Sally had talked it through several times. Liz had, three weeks earlier, spoken privately with Irina, who protested her innocence and would admit to nothing. Liz's solution was to propose giving maintenance of Irina's site to another member. No more opportunities to submit bills, no more opportunity to steal. Sally, though, wasn't satisfied. She wanted Irina to be shamed in front of the club. Liz had said that, without proof, nothing could ever be said publicly. But in point of fact, Liz didn't *want* to say anything publicly. The garden club was supposed to be about harmony and working together, not about pointing fingers of blame.

"...I notice Irina didn't show up for the meeting," Roland was saying.

Liz's mind snapped back to attention. "I'm sorry, Roland. What did you say about Irina and the meeting?"

"I said, Missy, that our little Russian mini-mobster didn't come to the meeting because she probably caught wind of what Sally was going to do."

"How would she have known that?"

"Oh, because Sally doesn't just confide in me. She would almost certainly have told Mary Giametti or Rose – you know, felt them out about whether it was a good idea. Chances are, one of them would have dropped a hint, and Irina decided to stay away for the duration."

"You said Sally had – what did you say – 'got the goods'. Did you mean Sally had proof? What was it?"

"Oh, she was very mysterious. She just said, 'I've finally got the goods on her, and everyone is going to see for themselves tomorrow.'"

Liz sighed. "Roland, you know how I feel about this. Why didn't you tell *me*?"

Roland sounded sheepish. "I just thought it would be great drama. You know, *j'accuse'* right in front of the assembled membership. Maybe big blow-up photographs of Irina's yard down in Mattapoisett with little arrows pointing to plants that belong at the corner of Washington and North. Summer meetings are always so dull."

Liz rubbed her temples. She had other people to tell. She was going to need help. Roland was the perfect bearer of the news. "Can you call some of the members for me? Just tell them the facts, though, not the stuff about Irina. And *please* don't say that I have my doubts. If I hear that back from anyone, I'll never speak to you again."

"You have my word as a gentleman and an antiques dealer, Liz. Paul Revere will tell the facts, and just the facts. And I'm very sorry to hear about Sally. I'm going to miss her very much."

"Me, too, Roland. I'll talk to you later."

Liz looked at her watch, it was almost four o'clock. She wanted to call David and tell him. They had talked, as they did every morning when he was away, at six. It was a morning 'hello' and an exchange of schedules. What had he said about today? Customer meetings? His life was an endless series of meetings with banks, employees and customers. He would fly home Friday night, drained by another eighty-hour week.

She dialed the number in Pittsburgh and got his secretary. He was on a conference call. Would she like to leave a message or to go to voicemail? Liz said, "Just ask him to call."

Liz made half a dozen calls to people whom she had known were close to Sally. Each one wanted to commiserate, each one to say that they were sorry that Liz had been the person to find Sally. To none of them did she voice her suspicions. She had just completed a call when the phone rang. The caller ID said, "Hardington PD." She picked up the phone and was surprised to hear Detective Flynn on the other end of the line.

A half an hour later, there was a knock at the door.

2.

John Flynn had built his career as a detective by forming theories that carefully fit available facts, and then scrutinizing each new fact to determine whether his basic theory still held. His basic theory of Liz Phillips had been formed by ten minutes of conversation at Sally Kahn's home and his awareness, based on reading through police reports, that people who lived on Old Schoolhouse had money. Because she was at a club meeting in Hardington on a Wednesday morning, Liz Phillips did not work – at least not full time – therefore, she was a Lady Who Lunched. She was trim, therefore she spent hours at a fitness club. She was blonde and wore her hair relatively short and in an expensive-looking cut, therefore she had idle hours to spend in a salon. She was involved in a garden club, so she was directed toward the kind of useless, time-filling activities that the well-to-do preferred. She appeared to be about fifty, although she might be two or three years younger. Any children would either be in college or out on their own. She wore a wedding ring with a big, carat-plus diamond, so her husband would be a portfolio manager at one of the downtown financial firms. This was his theory of Liz Phillips.

She greeted him at the door, a mixture of coolness toward him for reasons he could not discern, coupled with an eagerness to tell him something. He accepted the offer of a glass of iced tea and was led into what he had learned was called in such houses, 'the great room.' A 'great room' would have been called a family room in an ordinary house, but in this house the family room was a massive glass-walled space, two stories high with skylights to provide additional natural light. Flynn mentally judged the length at about forty feet, the width at just under twenty feet. He observed sourly that, taking off the garage, his three-bedroom home in Roslindale would just about fit in this space.

Flynn quickly took in the room. He noted the massive stone fireplace and the oak floors with their polished shine. On a credenza against one wall was a group of wedding photos including one large one of a bride, a younger version of the woman who now sat opposite him.

"Your daughter?" Flynn asked, gesturing at the center photo. Women loved to talk about their children and about weddings. It was his sure-fire opening.

"Yes, it's my daughter," Liz said. "And, under different circumstances, I'd be pleased to tell you all about the wedding. But a good friend of mine died today, and the more I learn about the events of the past twenty-four hours, the more I'm convinced that her death may not have been an accident. So the choice is yours. Would you like to hear what the bride wore when she walked down the aisle, or would you like to hear what I've learned about Sally's day, and what I observed at her home?"

Flynn immediately scratched out a major part of his original theory of Liz Phillips.

"Please tell me everything you know, and everything you suspect." Flynn took out his pad and his pen. He was surprised by the contriteness in his voice.

"Let's start with the basics," Liz said. "Someone was in Sally's house. Sally doesn't drink coffee. Sally doesn't drink beer. And Sally doesn't use sugar except when she bakes. Yet, all those things were in her house this afternoon. Sally may have put those things out for someone else, the coffee, for example, but it doesn't make sense that she would have those things out for breakfast.

"Also, Sally never watered her site this morning – she has the wayside garden at Main Street and Post Road. She usually is out there before six every morning and she always waters before breakfast. I've done a lot of dawn walks with her, and she never puts out the makings of breakfast and then comes back. She has a routine." Liz took a breath, organizing her thoughts.

"Is there more?" Flynn asked, writing as quickly as he could.

"I already told you about the front and back doors being open. She didn't leave those doors open. Ever. She feared burglars. And, I mentioned her son this morning. I spoke with a friend who had lunch with her yesterday, and he said…."

"What's your friend's name?"

"Roland Evans-Jones – Evans-hyphen-Jones. He lives on West Street. His telephone number is 5078." Flynn noted that she used the "townie" convention of conveying telephone numbers using just the last four digits, assuming everyone has the same prefix and area code.

"Roland said Tim was coming out to Hardington to see Sally last evening. I don't know if he ever got here or how long he stayed but, as of noon yesterday, he was coming out. Of course, Tim isn't the most reliable person on the face of the earth, but he was hoping to leave with a check, so the odds of his turning up were pretty good."

"Tim does that a lot? Asks for money from his mother? Flynn felt a mental click of a tumbler falling into place.

"Sally supports him – supported him. I don't think Tim has ever had a real job."

"Mrs. Phillips, was Sally Kahn…" Flynn chose his words with care, "…comfortable? You told me she had been widowed about twelve years. Was she provided for after her husband's death?"

Flynn saw Liz pause. She, too, was choosing her words carefully. "Sally's husband was a technology company executive. He left Sally well cared for. Yes, she was 'comfortable'."

Flynn nodded, the pieces of a puzzle coming together…

"What have you learned about her death, apart from what I've told you?" Liz asked.

Flynn was snapped out of his thought process. "I really can't go into that," he said. "It's far too early."

"Bullshit, Detective Flynn. I can find out more things in an afternoon that you can in a week, because I knew her and I know the people she knew. If you throw some police crap at me, then I'll keep asking my questions of the people she knew, and I'll take that information directly to the Mass Bureau of Investigation, starting the minute you walk out that door. I'm sure they'll take it seriously, and they'll do a competent job of investigating. And besides, don't the state police investigate all homicides?"

Flynn felt his face redden and he involuntarily clenched his fists. "What I'm trying to say is that I don't want to speculate on something I'm not certain of. And I don't call in the state police until I'm certain we're dealing with a homicide."

"Then we have nothing further to say to one another, Detective. I hope you understand that I've got to…"

"All right," Flynn said. "Sally Kahn didn't die this morning. She died last night. Probably between ten and midnight. And the way she died suggests that it wasn't an accident."

"What do you mean, 'the way she died'?"

"I mean that I've been investigating deaths for a very long time, and I can tell when someone goes down a set of basement stairs like a sack of potatoes. Sally Kahn didn't try to break her fall. She didn't take the fundamental step that every living being does when they fall. That makes the death suspicious. Suspicious enough that I have a crew going over her house, and when I leave here, I'm going to meet a medical examiner who is going to do a very unofficial autopsy."

"Hardington's finest is going to do a crime scene investigation? Not the state police?"

"No. The state police do some things very well, but investigating suspicious deaths is not one of them. This crew is from Boston PD. They're very good. In fact, they're the best. They're doing it because I asked them, and because they owe me a favor." He watched with satisfaction as she nodded appreciatively.

"You are taking this seriously." Now it was she who sounded contrite.

"Yes, Mrs. Phillips. And now, let's go over the details again. Let's start with what you saw in the driveway when you arrived…"

An hour later, Flynn fought his way across still unfamiliar back roads to get to Framingham and the MetroWest Medical Center. In the hospital's morgue, he found that a Boston PD pathologist was already well into an examination.

"Surprise number one," the pathologist said, turning Sally Kahn's head to one side. "Somebody slapped her around before she died. Hard slapping – open handed. Someone who was almost certainly right-handed. Broke some capillaries in the process. Can't say if the person doing the slapping was male or female, but I can say your victim was probably seated when it happened."

The pathologist continued. "Second surprise. She died about eleven last night. Internal body temperature confirms what the EMTs said about rigor. Certainly not after midnight. Probably not before ten. I haven't gotten to her stomach yet, but I suspect I'm going to find an un-digested dinner."

"I'll bet there's more," Flynn said.

"That's the third surprise," the pathologist said. "She was pushed down the stairs, backwards, and hard. Two hands against her shoulders. Never had a chance to grab the railing because she couldn't see it. Her shoulder blades hit the stairs. Gravity and the initial force did the rest. She continued rolling and her neck caught the full weight. Death was within seconds. I've drawn blood and fluids, but you've got your basic story."

Flynn peered at her neck. "Was someone trying to kill her, or could it have been an accident?"

"There's no body bruising, so she wasn't beaten up," the pathologist said. "Her hands and feet weren't tied. She wasn't gagged. But the slapping was hard. It was intended to hurt, and she was crying – there's residue of tears on her face. I have no way to nail down the precise time between the slapping and the push down the stairs, but it was less than ten minutes because of the minimal bleeding in the capillaries. Did somebody know that she'd break her neck? Not likely, though I've seen cases where someone finishes the job manually. They usually get it wrong and rotate the neck the wrong way. But this was the result of the fall. It's no less than manslaughter, in my professional opinion."

Flynn looked over the body, especially the bruising at the shoulders. "Any chance of physical evidence? DNA?"

"I've taken swabs. We may get something off of her face. Nothing under her fingernails. Nothing defensive. My guess is that either she knew the attacker or she was very afraid of the attacker."

"Then I guess this visit is official," Flynn said. "Do it right. Write it up. I'm going to talk to the son. The daughter will be in town sometime tomorrow morning. Welcome to the suburbs."

"What about the staties?"

Flynn paused, weighing his words, knowing he was about to cross a line. Under long-established precedent, only two police organizations were authorized to investigate murders in Massachusetts: the state police and City of Boston detectives. Suburban police departments had it drilled into them that upon finding a body their first action was to call the nearest state police barracks. But the staties' reputation for screwing up murder scenes was legendary. Their closure rate was pathetic. Flynn has personally closed hundreds of cases. Tough cases. He wasn't about to watch this one from the sidelines.

"What they don't know won't hurt them," Flynn said. "I'll call them when the time is right."

Outside, Flynn sat in his car and rubbed his eyes. He had a murder on his hands. The first genuine murder in Hardington in more than a decade.

He called the Hardington police department and found the desk sergeant. "Chief went home about half past four," the sergeant said. "He's talking to the seniors tonight. Safety. That sort of thing."

"I'll fill him in tomorrow," Flynn said, avoiding any details.

Flynn's original plan had been to drive into Allston to speak with Tim Kahn. Now, that meeting would have to be far more carefully choreographed. "Did Tim Kahn call?"

"About an hour ago."

Flynn thanked the sergeant. He very much wanted to talk to Tim Kahn, but first, he wanted to speak to his Boston PD contact, even if only to confirm what Liz Phillips had told him. His contact gave him the name of a detective at the Allston precinct and Flynn dialed the number.

"Oh, he's a beaut," the detective told Flynn. "The guy's got a hundred-dollar-a-day habit, easy. He's got at least a dozen plead-outs for possession. If he were any brighter, he'd be in jail. He fancies himself a con artist. He's always pitching schemes that involve some small, upfront investment. Trouble is, he's in the wrong part of town and he's too lazy to get on the bus. We know him. We keep an eye on him."

"Do you think he'd push his mother down the stairs if it meant scoring a couple of mil?"

"If he was coked up enough, he'd do it for a fix."

Flynn thanked the detective. He thought for a few minutes. To catch a fish, you set a lure, he thought. He needed to set an irresistible lure for Tim Kahn. He found the number in his notes. This time, Tim Kahn answered the phone.

"Mr. Kahn, this is Detective John Flynn from the Hardington Police Department. Thank you for returning the call earlier, and I'm terribly sorry to be getting back to you at this hour." Flynn looked at his watch. It was a little after seven. *Keep it obsequious.* "Mr. Kahn, I'm afraid I have some terrible news. Your mother is dead. She apparently fell down her basement stairs this morning. She was found this afternoon."

He waited for the reaction. How well would Tim have rehearsed?

"Are you sure?"

Now there was a dumb question. Are you sure we have the right Tim Kahn? Are you sure she's dead?

"Your mother lives at 11 Pequot Court in Hardington. Is that correct?"

"Yes."

"Then I'm afraid I'm sure. We've called your sister. She'll be up sometime tomorrow. You and she probably need to speak as soon as possible about funeral arrangements." It was interesting that the sister hadn't called Tim. Was he that useless, or did she suspect?

Flynn continued. "Because we don't know when she will arrive, it would be very helpful if you could come by the station in the morning. There are a lot of details to go over with you, and a fair amount of paperwork. I suspect your sister is overwhelmed with trying to arrange for someone to take care of her children. I think you could be of great help both to us and to her." *Make it irresistible.* "The sooner we can get the paperwork done, the sooner you'll be able to start putting her financial affairs in order."

The last bit did it. "I could be in Hardington by nine if that's reasonable." *Took the bait. Took the bait hard.*

Flynn assured him that nine o'clock would be very reasonable.

He drove back to Hardington, his mind setting scenes and traps for Tim Kahn. With the right trap, he could extract a confession in one session. Kahn wasn't very bright. Kahn considered himself a con man. Use that to advantage. Start by catching him in a lie, then work from there.

At Sally Kahn's house, two unmarked Crown Victorias were in the driveway. Inside, Flynn found the team at work. Based on his conversation with Liz Phillips, he had the crew bag and remove the sugar bowl, Mr. Coffee, and beer cans. He also ordered a special fiber sweep of the kitchen floor where Sally Kahn's assailant might have slapped her.

With them was Billy Toole, the friend's son he had asked to watch the house. "You ought to be outside, Billy," Flynn said gently.

"I just came in when they got here. I'm set for the night. I've only ever seen a crime scene worked one other time."

"Then stick around and watch the pros. Anyone else come by?"

"Hardington cop, black guy, about half past eight. We showed him ID and he left. A woman was here, too. A little after five."

"Describe her."

"Tall, blonde. Older – about your age. Slender build. Drove a green Jag. I got the license plate."

Liz Phillips, he thought. "What did she do?"

"Went in by the garage door. I was trying to stay out of sight. I was on my way to ID her when she came back out. She wasn't in there thirty seconds. Then she went next door and was let in by the woman there. Then she left. You want a written report?"

"Not unless something happens during the night," Flynn said. "You did well."

By eleven, the house was secure and thoroughly documented. All physical evidence was removed and a chain of custody established. Flynn was assured that prints would take no more than two or three days to run. Tired but pleased that his investigation was under control, he started for his home in Roslindale, hoping that Annie would have already gone to bed.

He wasn't disappointed.

* * * * *

Liz noted that Detective Flynn had never used *the* word. He said "suspicious". He said, "probably not an accident." But he didn't say *murder.*

Liz was firmly convinced it was murder. Someone had set up the makings of breakfast to throw off the apparent time of death. Someone who didn't know Sally or her habits. Someone had broken her neck. Someone killed her.

Who? Why?

She paced the house. Abigail, her orange tabby, had gone into hiding as soon as a strange man appeared at the door. Now, the cat peered down from the stairs. Was the coast clear?

"Who would murder Sally?" Liz said aloud, which the cat took to be an invitation. Abigail circled her feet, sniffing her legs, apparently not liking what she smelled. The cat then walked over to its food dish and then looked back at Liz.

"Oh, my god. Chipper," she said. She quickly gathered her purse and keys, and was out the door in seconds. On the drive over, she continually turned a phrase over in her mind. *Tim Kahn killed his mother.*

Tim Kahn was many things. Thief, addict, liar. But murderer? The mental image, though upsetting, had to be viewed frame by frame. Tim went to the house last night. He argued with his mother. He wanted money, Sally said no. He pushes her down the stairs and checks to make certain she is dead. He then sets up the kitchen for breakfast and leaves the house.

It didn't make sense. Tim was weak. Not physically weak, though the last time she saw him, the debilitating effects of hepatitis, drugs, and god knows what else had taken their toll. He was gaunt, his skin pock-marked. He had once been a good-looking boy, but now... No, Tim was emotionally weak. Even if he had pushed his mother down the stairs, he could not have cold-bloodedly left her there. He would have panicked, called for an ambulance and come up with a story about her falling. And he wasn't smart enough to think about setting up for breakfast.

And besides, Sally would have given him the money.

"Was she provided for after her husband's death?"

God knows she was provided for. "My Charlie always said he'd look after me... My Charlie was always smart about those options..." Charles Kahn had been an executive at EMC, a big technology company out in Hopkinton that sported a then-astronomical share price. He had a heart attack in the spring of 2000. He had a lot of options and they vested upon his death. Against the advice of accountants and brokers, Sally immediately cashed in the options. Against even more vehement advice, she had bought treasury bonds. Charlie also had insurance and Sally took the proceeds and bought even more bonds. Liz knew for a fact that Sally was sitting on a nest egg of more than four million dollars generating more than six percent interest. Sally's complaint was that she – literally – couldn't spend her income. And so she gave generously to charities... and to her children. Sally would have given Tim whatever money he needed.

Which meant that someone else had murdered Sally Kahn.

Liz arrived at Sally's house but saw no sign of Chipper. She let herself inside and found a forest of yellow post-it notes and chalk lines. Sensing this was Detective Flynn's directions to the crime scene investigators, she backed out, being careful to touch nothing. The dog, she concluded, had likely been taken in by a neighbor.

She knew none of the homeowners around Sally. The lot to the left of her house had, until a few weeks earlier, been the site of a smaller Dutch Gambrel colonial. Then, in a scene that was becoming an increasingly familiar one in Hardington, a bulldozer had razed the house in a single day. Every trace of the old house had been carted away in dump trucks, even the foundation. Now, a new foundation had been poured for a house with a footprint twice the size of the old one, and set back more generously from the street. Only a few older specimen trees remained as evidence of earlier occupation.

Liz knocked on the door of the house to the right of Sally's.

Liz introduced herself as a friend of Sally's and was invited in. The neighbor, a woman in her thirties with two pre-schoolers, had seen the arrival of police cars and ambulances earlier and had surmised that something awful had happened to Sally. "They didn't seem to be in any hurry to get that ambulance out of here," the woman observed. "That's a bad sign."

Liz asked about Sally's dog and was told that the animal control van had been by about two hours earlier. Because the woman seemed observant, Liz asked if she had noticed anything going on at the house last evening.

"I think I saw her go out about 7:30," the woman said. "It's a cul-de-sac and so you tend to notice cars, especially when they start their engines. Anyway, it was during *Jeopardy* and I think she came back before eight because I heard her garage door go up. I saw lights from one or two other cars after it got dark, but they might have just been lost."

The woman did not remember seeing Sally's son or anyone else walking on Pequot Court. That was the problem with family rooms, Liz thought. Everyone is in back of their house so no one sees what's going on in the street. Fortunately, the weather was still mild and people had not yet sealed their houses for the air conditioning season, so they at least heard noises.

It occurred to Liz that, if people were in their family rooms, that the house behind Sally's might be a better place to ask questions. She thanked the woman and drove around to Hill Street, judging which house was most likely to be the one that backed up to Sally's. The homes in this area were all on at least an acre, but the house behind Sally's had been built toward the back of the lot, giving it a clear view of the Kahn home.

"I think she had someone over," a woman just coming home from work told her. "I only know her to wave 'hello' when we're both in the yard. I'm reasonably certain I saw her moving around in her kitchen as well as upstairs. You just notice these things, but there's no pattern to them. Later, after dark, I saw what looked like more than one person - I couldn't tell if there two people or more – and they seemed to stay in the kitchen. All I could really see were shadows because she has curtains. I went to bed a little after ten and her lights were still on both upstairs and down. I thought that was a little odd because I know she's up very early most days, and it's usually 'lights out' before ten."

The information was useful but not conclusive. Sally went out and came back before eight. Other cars may have been on her street, and one or more people were in her house later on. Liz didn't want to pry further and so she let it be. But she did do one thing that was unusual for her. She asked that, if either woman thought of something else, that they call her.

Liz had one more responsibility before going home. Rush hour was starting to wind down along Main Street, though the westbound river of cars and trucks along the two-lane state highway was still a steady stream and would remain so until after seven o'clock. The bumper-to-bumper congestion had eased and merging traffic at Post Road was down to two or three cars at a time. An hour earlier, twenty cars might be lined up. Now Liz was able to ease her Jaguar onto the side of the road without annoying anyone.

She surveyed the site. Apart from the need for water, Sally's maintenance was excellent. Because of the site's prominence, the town had, several years earlier, run a tap from a nearby hydrant, ensuring that whoever cared for the garden did not need to bring along jugs of water. Liz retrieved a watering hose under a bush out of sight of cars. As she watered, she noted a need for deadheading and that one area of annuals seemed ragged and spotted, unlike the others. She made a mental note to return with plant food and gloves.

For now, though, her mind was distracted by a different to-do list. First, finish the conversation she had started with Roland

Evans-Jones. Draw out the additional details she had missed when they first spoke. Second, talk with Mary Giametti – someone else, according to Roland, in whom Sally confided. And, third, track down Irina Burroughs and see how she reacted when the subject of Sally's death was raised.

Her cell phone rang, startling her out of her thoughts. It was David.

"Sorry it took so long to get back to you," he apologized. "I only just got the message. What's up?"

Liz took a deep breath. "Sally Kahn was murdered last night. Unfortunately, I was the one who found her body this afternoon." It was the first time she had articulated the reality of what had happened. *Murdered.*

"Good god," David said. "Are you all right?"

Thank you David, she thought. *At least you are thinking about me first.* "I'm OK," Liz said, honestly. "At first, everyone assumed it was an accident." And she explained what she had found, and what Detective Flynn's suspicions were. They spoke for fifteen minutes and promised to resume the conversation when he got back to his hotel.

Roland Evans-Jones was delighted to see Liz at his door. "And I'll bet you haven't had dinner, and probably never had lunch. You need a drink and something to eat." Liz didn't protest the offer, but insisted on helping. Roland's kitchen was large and well stocked, as though he was forever expecting someone to unexpectedly drop in for dinner.

"You'd be surprised at the number of guests who drop by at supper time," he said after she commented on the quantity of food on hand. "The garden club and the historical society are where all the widows go to pass the time. I think my role in life is to make certain they get enough to eat."

"Was Sally a frequent guest?" Liz asked.

"Almost every Wednesday night. I cooked one week, she

cooked the next."

Odd, Liz thought. She knew Sally and Roland lunched on Tuesdays. The Wednesday evenings, she had always thought, were spent – what? – playing bridge? Oh, well.

"So, this would have been your dinner night with Sally…"

"I'm afraid so," he said, quickly and sadly. "You interrupted quite a little pity party, with yours truly as the guest of honor."

"Roland, there's almost no question but that Sally was murdered. All of those breakfast makings I saw in the house were just to establish a different time of death. She was killed sometime last evening. The police detective says she went down the stairs, in his words, 'like a sack of potatoes'. She didn't fall – she was either pushed or she was thrown."

"Which makes Timmy the Monster the most likely candidate."

"I'm not so sure," Liz said. "Why would he do it? Sally never turned him down when he asked for money. She would have given him whatever he wanted. And besides, he's not smart enough to have tried to throw off the time of death. He would have panicked and called the police and said it was an accident." Liz waited for Roland to nod agreement. Instead, Roland shook his head vigorously.

"Liz, you live in a sheltered world. Tim is an addict. Tim lives from fix to fix and the more money Sally gave him for those fixes, the more he needed. It took Sally years to realize that fact, but she was learning to say no. I told her it would be dangerous…"

"Wait a minute, Roland… I never had any conversation like that with her…"

"Because Sally was ashamed and didn't think you'd ever understand. You raised the perfect daughter. Sally raised a daughter with more quirks than a pretzel and one monster. Sally compartmentalized. I'm sure she told you things about her life she'd never tell me. Well, I got the part about Tim. When we had lunch yesterday, she was looking for specific advice about how to handle Tim. She needed a pep talk. She needed hand-holding because she was going to stop writing those checks."

"Why you?"

"Does it matter, Liz? I had a partner with a drug problem. I lived with it for a year and then fixed it. Sally knew that and came to me for moral support. She trusted me."

"So you think Tim could have killed Sally?"

"Liz, I think a man who needs a fix and who has a habit as bad as Tim's might either do something stupid or else decide it was time to take a shortcut to his inheritance."

"What about Irina?" Liz asked.

"Our little Ninontcka? Because Sally was going to embarrass her? Oooh, I don't think I'd rule that one out. But Tim's your man."

"Roland, you said she was very mysterious about her evidence. If she told you all about Tim, why wouldn't she share her evidence?"

"It wasn't that she wouldn't tell. It's that we got interrupted. We were at Zenith, having a wonderful lunch. Sally was telling me about getting thrown out of Landini Brothers…"

"When did that happen?" Liz asked.

"Oh, Monday morning. One of their trucks ran up over the curb and onto her annuals while she was watering. In the process, it sloshed some of whatever gunk those trucks carry. Well, Sally said she was through putting up with that kind of hooliganism, and she got in her car and followed it to Overfield. She marched right into the main office and demanded to speak to whoever was in charge. Well, whoever was in charge came out, took one look at her, and then demanded that she get off their property. She was very upset and still more than a little angry…"

"So what about Irina?"

"I was coming to that. She told me she had concrete evidence that Irina was stealing – and that was her word – stealing from the club. She was just getting to the good part when some people sat down at the table next to ours. You know how Sally feels about crowds. She said she'd tell me later. There never was a 'later'."

Liz nodded. "Do you know what she did for the rest of the day?"

Roland thought for a moment. "No idea."

Much relaxed, but with little more information than she had when she knocked at Roland's door, Liz was home before ten. *About the time Sally died*, Liz thought to herself. She called David at his hotel and brought him up to speed on the events of the day.

As they ended the conversation, David said, "I'll bet Chief Harding is going to go through the roof on this one. I don't think there's been a murder in Hardington in at least ten years. There goes his perfect record."

Liz pondered the thought. Small town. Small *peaceful* town. Small peaceful town where everyone is comfortable with the doors unlocked and no one fears for their safety. Yes, Chief Harding was definitely going to go through the roof on this one.

3.

Thursday

"What in the hell do you think you're doing?"

The scream could be heard by everyone in the Hardington police station and likely carried over to the fire department next door. Flynn gripped his hands behind his back and told himself, *take it easy, let him vent.*

Chief Amos Harding, however, was still working his way up to his full decibel level of outrage. The first call had been merely perplexing. Doc Simmons had called him last night at home to say that, when he went to sign the death certificate, he was told by the morgue attendant at MetroWest Medical Center that Sally Kahn's body was unavailable and that some doctor from Boston had taken care of the formalities.

The second call was more unsettling. Reading the overnight patrol logs, the morning dispatcher noted that a Hardington police car observed two Crown Victorias outside of the home of Sally Kahn. Investigating, the police officer – a naïve twenty-three year old new to the force – had been intercepted by persons displaying Boston PD badges who said they were conducting a crime scene investigation at the request of Detective John Flynn of the Hardington Police Department. A third, younger, individual who also claimed association with the Boston PD was also present, though he produced no identification. Alert to anything that was out of the ordinary, the dispatcher had called Chief Harding at home, disturbing his breakfast.

The third call put him over the edge. The Boston PD medical examiner's office had called requesting an email address to "send a PDF of the ME's handwritten notes". Chief Harding had a difficult time with this request because he did not know if, indeed, there was an email address for the police because he did not know how to use a computer. There was one in his office, of course. It was untouched since its installation four years earlier. He further did not know what a 'PDF' was and, when he asked and was told that a PDF was a 'portable document format', he remained unenlightened. Diligent questioning, though, yielded that the ME's office wanted to send over the preliminary notes on the Kahn autopsy.

Flynn had made the mistake of walking into the station as Chief Harding hung up with the Boston ME's office.

"It's a murder investigation, Chief," Flynn said, coolly. "I used the best resources I had available to me."

"It wasn't a murder investigation yesterday afternoon," Chief Harding screamed back. "You said it was accidental and all you had to do was establish the time of death."

"I said it *appeared* accidental. I was very specific about it. The EMTs said her body was starting to pass out of rigor mortis, which didn't jibe with a death yesterday morning. The ME confirmed the EMTs' observation, and also said that Mrs. Kahn had been pushed down the stairs backwards. That means someone went to a lot of trouble to make it *look* like an accident that took place yesterday morning. Someone assumed that Mrs. Kahn's body wouldn't be found for a day or more, and that the breakfast makings would establish the time of death, rather than the physical evidence."

"And so you just invited in your old pals from Boston to start investigating murders in Hardington?" Chief Harding's tone was less a scream now than a bellow. What Flynn was saying was sinking in.

"I had to move quickly. I have a lot of favors owed to me by people in Boston. I called in some of those favors. Every hour counts in an investigation like this. You know that far better than I do."

Up to that point, Flynn had stuck meticulously to the truth. By now, however, he was convinced that Chief Harding would no more have known how to conduct a murder investigation than he could have conducted the Boston Symphony.

"You don't have any favors owed you by the state? That's who you're supposed to call when there's a suspicious death." Harding's voice was still elevated, but he was beginning to understand.

"Chief, with all due respect, do you want me to turn over evidence to the same guys who took three years to run DNA on a prime suspect in that murder-rape out on the Cape? If we're going to find out who killed Sally Kahn, we've got to do it ourselves and do it quickly. The idea of some patronage buddy of the Speaker of the House being in charge of running DNA matches on a murder in Hardington is not something I want to rely on."

Harding sat back in his chair, his fury short-circuited by facts. "You have a suspect?"

"Tim Kahn. I know he was supposed to see his mother Tuesday night. He's coming in here this morning. He thinks it's to start the process of claiming his mother's estate. I'll question him at that time."

The concept of a murder in Hardington began to sink in on Chief Harding. "My god, we haven't had a murder here since nineteen...." He closed his eyes, remembering dates. "Nineteen ninety seven. Joellen Coombs. On Riverside. Her husband shot her. Called the station to say he had done it. Then some damn fool Boston lawyer tried to get him to plead 'diminished capacity'. What a mess. Ralph Coombs did eight years at Cedar Junction. What a mess." His attention shifted back to the present. "Tim was a bad apple, but he doesn't seem the type. How certain are you?"

"I did some checking," Flynn said. "Tim Kahn has been sponging off his mother for the past fifteen years. He's a junkie with a first-class habit. Mrs. Kahn may not show it, but she was left a lot of money by Mr. Kahn. My theory is that Tim decided to take a short cut to his inheritance by pushing his mother down the stairs. Whoever killed Sally Kahn also slapped her around pretty good first, which also fits."

"He slapped her around?"

"That was part of the ME's findings. Before she was pushed, Mrs. Kahn was slapped in the face by someone right handed. He did swabs. He didn't guarantee there would be usable DNA, but he said that was the best chance. Mrs. Kahn had no defensive wounds. She never scratched her assailant, she never fought back. That would tie to a family member. Even though, in the back of your head, you think your son is going to hurt you real bad, you don't hurt him back. It shows you're a bad parent."

"Won't Tim need an attorney?"

"Not the way I want to play it," Flynn said. "This is family stuff. Assuming he did it, he's carrying a load of conscience, even through that drug-addled brain of his. I want to give him an opportunity to get it all off of his chest. By the time he gets his Miranda, he's going to be relieved that he's not having to keep it bottled in. My guess is that he'll waive. I've done it dozens of times." Flynn spoke confidently, drawing on more than two decades of experience breaking down perps. By the time he was finished, Tim Kahn would thank him for allowing him to confess his guilt and expiate his conscience.

"When is Tim coming in?"

"Nine o'clock. Here's a thought, if you want to help put him at his ease, come in and pay your respects, then excuse yourself."

Chief Harding shook his head. "The last time I saw Tim was at his father's funeral. The time before that was when I was running him in for drug possession. I'm not exactly a friend."

"Suit yourself. It was only an idea."

At nine o'clock, Flynn had arrayed the station's conference room with a dozen Dunkin' Donuts in assorted sugary glazes, a gallon of coffee to go, a stack of whatever forms he could find around the station house – mostly motor vehicle accident reporting forms – and a cassette recorder with two backup microcassettes.

Tim Kahn entered the station at five minutes after nine. Flynn would have known him anywhere. Eyes darting left and right by dint of habit. This was hostile territory. Sallow, pock-marked skin, a sure sign of the jaundice that accompanied the hepatitis. Dockers that hung loosely on his waist. These were clothes from a time when his body had greater muscle tone. A corduroy jacket suitable for September or October, and probably the only jacket he had not pawned or lost. And nothing ironed. Certainly not the once white, tie-less shirt. Tim Kahn was a short-timer. If he was current with his Hepatitis C treatments, he might hold out another year or two. But, if he was still doing IV drugs, then his liver was going to fail before Christmas. Tim Kahn might have a very short time to enjoy his mother's inheritance – and the state's hospitality.

Flynn took all of this in and then made a great show of greeting Kahn before the man had time to inquire at the dispatcher's desk.

"You must be Mr. Kahn," he said, deferentially. "I'm John Flynn. I called you last night." Flynn guided him into the conference room before Kahn had the opportunity to fully register *police station*. "I'm sure you'll want to spend as much time as possible with your sister, so I'll try not to keep you. I apologize that I haven't had breakfast. Please help yourself if you like."

Tim Kahn saw the food and reacted with an almost feral instinct. In under a minute he had reduced two chocolate glazed donuts to crumbs, washed down with sweetened black coffee. He was working on a third when Flynn picked up the stack of forms and held them in his hands.

"We have a lot to go over, but before we do, can I ask how long it's been since you've seen your mother, and have you thought about funeral arrangements?" Two questions, one easy to answer, one very hard.

"Uh, about three weeks ago. She invited me out for dinner."

Lie number one, Flynn thought. *Now why does he need to tell a whopper right off the bat?* "It must be very difficult getting away from work, Mr. Kahn. "Hardington isn't the easiest town to get to on mass transit." Actually, there were twelve trains a day, four of them expresses. But it sounded sympathetic. "You're in Boston, I think."

"Yeah, Boston." A jelly-filled donut disappeared from the box. Flynn was still working on his first cruller.

"I need to go over the circumstances of your mother's death with you, Mr. Kahn," Flynn said in a sympathetic voice. *Lower the boom. Lower it slowly.* Your mother appears to have fallen down the stairs sometime yesterday morning. She probably tripped over her dog, a Pekinese, I think.

"Yeah, one of those little yappy dogs. She got it after Dad died."

Flynn nodded sympathetically. "I had hoped you might be the person we need to speak with to close out the case and, in a way, I'm sorry it wasn't you at her house last night."

"What do you mean?" Kahn was alert now, though the sugar also dulled his senses.

Flynn leaned across the table. "Your mother went out about eight o'clock yesterday evening. She brought someone home with her, according to her neighbors. We don't know when that person left, but there were several beer cans in the living room indicating that they stayed awhile. We don't want to go to the trouble of dusting for fingerprints if we can find who that person was…"

Kahn looked confused. Connections were being made in his mind. "Mom put those in the recycling bin," he said.

"Excuse me?"

"You said there were beer cans in the living room. When I was there, I had some beer, but I saw my mom throw the cans in one of those blue bins."

Flynn reached for the pen in his pocket and started to write, then stabbed at the paper. "Stupid pen," he said. "It's out of ink. Do you mind if I record what you're saying. It may take me forever to find that pen."

"Sure, go ahead and record. Whatever." Those were the first words that appeared on the recording.

"Thank you, Mr. Kahn. "You think that the beer cans we found in the living room may have been the same ones you saw your mother throw away when you had dinner with her three weeks ago."

"Uh, no. That was last night. I thought you meant the last time I saw her before last night." His reptilian brain was taking over, adapting to new circumstances. If it was helpful to have been there last night, then he was there last night.

"Then that helps us a great deal, Mr. Kahn, and I'm sorry for misunderstanding your earlier answer. So, your neighbors said your mother was gone about twenty minutes. Did she pick you up at the train station?"

"Yeah, at the train station."

"Did you stay the night with your mother or go back into the city?"

"I went back into Boston. On the train."

Another lie. The tremor in the voice gave it away.

"That would have been the 10:50. The last train from Hardington." *And easy to check since it carries about three passengers.*

"Yeah, the 10:50. Can we get to the paperwork?" Kahn eyed the stack of papers.

"Just as a matter of curiosity, Mr. Kahn, no one remembers your mother leaving the house after eight. How did you get back to the station?"

"I took a cab."

Holy cow, Flynn thought. *This guy is getting in deep. Why the lies? Or does he just do it as a force of habit?*

"Thank you, Mr. Kahn. That's very helpful. I think someone said they remembered seeing a cab on the street a little after ten. That certainly clears up those open questions. Mr. Kahn, did your mother give you a check last evening?" *Here we go.*

Kahn paused. The questions weren't making sense. "She may have."

Crime Scene had called him at close to midnight. Sally Kahn had written a couple of checks that day off of her Rockland Trust account, though none to Tim Kahn since April. Because they were very thorough in their work, they also noted that three checks were missing from the back of the checkbook.

"Does she usually give you a check when you come to see her? I think that's very caring on her part."

"Yeah, she was very caring." Tim Kahn shifted in his chair. "Actually, I think she gave me some cash."

"Cash, not a check?"

"Yeah, I'm pretty sure it was cash. You know, cab fare. A hundred dollars. Something like that. I said I didn't need it. She insisted." *Deeper and deeper.*

"Tim, I'm sure you loved your mother, so what I'm going to say is going to come as a large shock to you." *The switch of tone. No more "Mr. Kahn". From now on, it's "Tim".* "Tim, we're pretty sure your mother's fall wasn't because she tripped over the dog. We're pretty sure someone fought with her and pushed her down the stairs."

"No! What do you mean?"

"Tim, it may have been an accident. It probably was an accident. Whoever did it probably never meant to hurt her. But we can't close the case until we know. We can't help you settle her estate until we know. The insurance people – they'll go bonkers. The banks – they'll keep her accounts zipped shut. I've got to close the case. And Tim, you were the last person to see your mother before she fell."

Tim Kahn's face was now ashen.

"Tim, were you there when your mother fell down the stairs?"

"No!" Tim shouted. "I wasn't there and I didn't stay all night. You said she fell down the stairs in the morning. I was out of there by ten."

"I may be wrong about the time of her death. These things are never exact." Flynn leaned further across the table. "Tim, you acknowledge that you were the last person to see her. I ask you again. Were you there when your mother fell down the stairs?"

"I want a lawyer. I'm not saying anything until I see a lawyer."

For the next several hours, Flynn would keep coming back to that final vehement 'no' from Tim Kahn. The guy had lied from the moment he scarfed down his first donut. But in that one instant, Flynn believed him.

* * * * *

Liz Phillips habitually rose with the sun every morning. The problem was that, in mid-June, sunrise was a few minutes after five and her bedroom was filled with light twenty minutes earlier. Therefore, at a quarter after five, and having already had breakfast, Liz was already at work in her perennial beds, weeding and deadheading. Beside her, a forty-gallon cart was filling with the detritus of the summer garden.

And she was thinking.

"A man who needs a fix and who has a habit as bad as Tim's might either do something stupid or else decide it was time to take a shortcut to his inheritance... Liz, you lead a sheltered existence..."

Liz reconstructed Tuesday evening yet again. Tim is coming for dinner. Tim wants money. Sally is going to say, 'no more money.' Tim needs a fix. Tim wolfs down dinner, or maybe never even has dinner, just some beers. Tim demands money and Sally stands her ground. Tim goes out of his mind with rage and pushes his mother. She goes down the stairs, breaking her neck in the process. Tim feels for a pulse but there is none. He is certain that he is going to be charged with her murder. He thinks quickly. Sally's body may not be found for a day or more. Let people think she died the next day. Pull out china and the makings of breakfast. Put on a pot of coffee. Sneak out the back door and go home.

It fit, up to a point. But how could Tim be both out of his mind and so calculating as to think of pulling out breakfast foods? How could he have the presence of mind to put on a pot of coffee yet leave beer cans in the living room?

It didn't add up. Had Sally written a check? If she wrote a check, then why did he become enraged? He could get any kind of fix he wanted.

She needed more information.

Irina Burroughs bothered her. Irina bothered her in a way that was unsettling. There were two stories about Irina. One was what she told about herself. The other was the story other people swore was true.

"I come from Russia in 1996," she always said. *"I am just twenty. Communism gone and I want my freedom. I come to America to find freedom. I marry a good man, but he drink. Soon he start to beat me. I love him but I must divorce him. Then I meet Peter and I fall in love with Peter. He makes me very happy and we buy house in Hardington. Peter do very well at Putnam and we buy house in Mattapoisett. But Peter cheat on me. I love him, but what can I do? Now I am alone and barely able to make ends meet. I hope I find a good man who will love me."*

It was a swell story. This sweet young thing, now thirty-six, with two tragic marriages in her past, just hoping to find love.

And at least half a dozen people had told Liz it was so much crap.

Irina Volnovich Dupree Burroughs, Liz was told on great authority, was one of the original Russian mail order brides, except that she was already pushing thirty when she arrived in the U.S., and it was 1992, four years earlier than her professed timeline. Dupe Number One was duly judged to be desperate but financially solvent. In four years, Irina cleaned out Alan Dupree, purportedly stashing half a million dollars in safe deposit boxes and then taking Mr. Dupree for half of his remaining net worth when Irina showed Polaroids of herself with bruises and a black eye. How anyone could know this with certainty was beyond Liz's comprehension, but it did not stop those who told her this story from saying that they knew their facts were straight.

The Dupree nest egg was depleted after a post-divorce, multi-year spending spree, but it set up Irina to go after Peter Burroughs, who was newly widowed and slightly off balance as a result. That had been three years ago. Irina went after Peter like a Russian Wolfhound and married him in six months. Three months after that, they purchased a five thousand square foot McMansion in Shady Oak Estates, and Irina was spending money like there was no tomorrow. It took Peter two years to come out of his coma, but he had finally done so and realized that his jointly held Merrill Lynch portfolio was shrinking like the polar ice caps.

Peter sued for divorce, painting Irina as a voracious weasel fully capable of supporting herself. A judge agreed. Irina kept the properties – and their mortgages. Peter Burroughs moved to Arkansas where he hoped never to hear a word of Russian again in his life. The last part was something Liz knew to be true.

Now, Irina was, while not destitute, running out of time. Her plan following the divorce had been to move to Miami, where there were lots of aging millionaires. To that end, both houses were on the market, and had been so for more than six months. It wasn't just the $1.7 million asking price for the Shady Oak Estates property that scared away buyers. It was also the over-the-top decorating that Irina thought "revolutionary" and prospective buyers found "revolting". Home buyers, especially in the current, depressed market, were unwilling to pay an extra half million for someone else's decorating mistakes, and so Irina was on her third broker.

In the meantime, weekly trips to day spas in Wellesley were now being supplemented by botox injections, or so said those in the know. The myth of being thirty-six was, if not completely shot, dependent upon a target being several sheets to the wind. That last remark, while catty, was also on target, Liz thought.

Irina had joined six venerable Hardington organizations upon moving to town. Part of establishing her bona fides, Liz assumed. Why Irina was still in the garden club now that she was divorced was beyond anyone's comprehension, except to check on the vital signs of members to see if any looked to be in failing health, or could be pushed in that direction, thus freeing up a potential Dupe Number Three.

Irina's position was becoming precarious. Scandals were rare in Hardington and they usually involved adultery. Getting called on petty theft in front of the assembled garden club membership could conceivably be the last straw for Irina Burroughs's chances for that wealthy husband, at least from the local pool of available men. What happened in clubs reverberated in strange ways in towns like Hardington, and were remembered for a very long time.

Would she murder for it?

Liz sketched the scene in her mind as she continued deadheading. Irina learns that Sally is going to publicly humiliate her at Wednesday's club meeting. She doesn't call and demand a meeting. Then, she leaves her car elsewhere and sneaks over. Shady Oak Estates and Pequot Court are three miles apart. She sees Tim there, but Tim is leaving. No sooner is Tim out the door than Irina is in, demanding the evidence. Sally hangs tough. Irina, seeing that Sally is going to be her undoing, shoves her down the stairs. Now, we've got a cold, calculated murder on our hands. Irina sets the scene for breakfast. And, just in case the police aren't bright enough to go through the garbage, Irina retrieves some beer cans and anything else she can think of that might have junior's prints on them and plants them in plain sight. She leaves via the back door and sneaks home. If Irina were attempting to establish her alibi for Wednesday morning, she was probably at an early morning workout at Curves where she could be seen by dozens of people. She would be at the garden club meeting, telling everyone how tight her schedule was for the day…

Except that Irina did not show up for the meeting. While she might otherwise have missed the meeting for any number of legitimate reasons, someone attempting to be seen by as many people as possible would have made a point of being there. Instead, Irina's absence hinted that she feared what Sally might say or do at the meeting, meaning Irina didn't know Sally was dead. Or, Liz thought, was she just over-analyzing the situation?

The evidence, such as it was, still pointed to Irina. It required that Irina fear Sally's wrath enough to commit a murder. And commit it in such a way that blame fell on someone else. Irina had to be willing to do things that would send Tim Kahn to prison. But, would she do all of this over a hundred dollars worth of flowers?

Liz made mental notes. Play the theory off of Roland, and then visit Mary Giametti to see if indeed someone had given Irina a preview of what was going to happen at the meeting. Then, go see Irina to see how she reacted. Then, if everything held up, go see Detective Flynn, and hand him his case.

Promptly at six, the cordless phone clipped to her belt chimed. "You're not outside already, are you?" David asked. "Outside" meant out working in the gardens that bordered and framed their house.

"I've been out here for over an hour. To be honest, it helps me think."

"About Sally?"

"About Sally. Roland says I'm naïve and don't understand the real world."

"And I think Roland knows more about antiques than he does

about either you or the real world."

"That's sweet, but I've been thinking about Irina." Liz provided the short version of Irina's motive.

"You don't think murdering someone over a hundred dollars' worth of flowers is a bit far-fetched?" David asked.

"Weren't you the person who told me after the Garden Party that you felt like Irina was running a mental net worth check on you while the two of you chatted?" The Hardington Garden Club held an annual wine and cheese party in March for the benefit of spouses. David had remarked afterward that, 'that Russian lady did everything but take out my wallet and count the twenties.'

"But murder?"

"Someone did it, David. Someone killed her. Someone had a motive strong enough that they killed Sally." The words sent an involuntary shudder through Liz's body. *Someone had a motive....*

"And the smart money has still got to be on Tim," David said. "That doesn't mean you're naïve or Roland is some kind of psychological *wunderkind*. It just means that it takes a powerful motive to kill someone. Families have that kind of motive. The tension builds for years – decades. Russian divorcees need to have a lot to lose before they start pushing people down the stairs."

Liz was quiet, digesting David's words.

"Are you going to be on the four o'clock flight tomorrow?"

"Come hell or high water."

"I'll have dinner waiting."

Liz worked steadily for another two hours, formulating her plan, rehearsing her lines. Central to her plan was holding a memorial service for Sally. Lord knows one was merited and few people in Hardington would think of organizing one. Before ten o'clock, she had spoken with the secretary of the Congregational Church and made preliminary arrangements for Friday evening. Then, she alerted half a dozen of the most competent garden club members and asked them to take on specific tasks. She arranged with two to meet at the church later that afternoon.

By ten, she was en route to Shady Oak Estates. If Old Schoolhouse Road represented a degree of wealth that made Hardington natives uncomfortable, Shady Oak Estates was irrational exuberance writ large. Forty homes plopped like toadstools into forty acres that were cow pasturage until 1998. Forty homes, each of at least 5,000 square feet, vying for the most styles in a single development. It wasn't just Palladian windows on oversized Colonials, an all-too-common *faux pas* that set Roland's teeth on edge. It was Spanish haciendas next to half-timbered Tudors across from faux Norman chateaus. Worse, the developer had landscaped the homes using nearly identical trees and shrubs. The effect, augmented by lawn maintenance firms that piled garish red cedar mulch on everything, gave the overall impression of a temporary subdivision that had been put up overnight, and that would return to pasturage as soon as the farm's owner had need of the acreage or the film company left town. It was the only group of homes in Hardington whose value stubbornly refused to rise. Prospective buyers new to the Boston area were driven through Shady Oak Estates and they invariably said, "show me something else."

The "For Sale" sign in front of Irina's house was from a Cavendish realtor. After two Hardington-based firms failed to sell the property, the town's other realtors had declined the listing. The house itself was modeled on an antebellum Southern plantation. It including a garden shed disguised as a privy, complete with a large crescent moon on its door. Three cherubs peed into a fountain in the center of the circular driveway.

Liz had not called ahead. Rather, her plan lay in the element of surprise. She believed that calling and asking to meet would result in layers of excuses as to why today was impossible. She rang the doorbell, the chime inside sounded the first ten notes to, "Lara's Theme". Moments later, Liz saw Irina peering at her through the glass panels on either side of the front door, a look of astonishment coupled with apprehension. A key turned in the lock.

"Liz? Why are you here?" It was about the level of greeting she expected. The door was open about three inches.

"I'm sorry to drop in on you, Irina, but I wanted to discuss a memorial service for Sally…"

"Memorial service?" Irina looked puzzled. The door remained open just enough to show part of Irina's head.

"If you'll let me in, I'll explain."

Irina pondered this for several moments. If it had been a telephone call, and if Irina had not been screening calls using Caller ID, this is where the brush-off would have come. Instead, Irina's look changed to one of resignation, coupled with the same wariness she had first displayed. Irina wordlessly opened the door and gestured Liz inward, looking outside to either side of the lawn as if to see if anyone else was going to rush the door.

"Thank you so much, Irina." Liz was at her most gracious, but she had also chosen an authoritative-looking linen suit. They were standing in a marble foyer. Ahead, a twin, winding staircase ascended to a landing above. Irina had decorated the foyer with modern art in the style of Kandinsky and Chagall. "Is there someplace we can talk?"

Irina glanced left and right and finally settled on what Liz assumed to be the media room. The room was dominated by a mammoth, flat-panel television with a six-foot screen. Irina gestured to a chair. "I don't have much time. I was on my way out." It was a half-hearted lie. Irina was dressed in a bathrobe and slippers.

Liz launched into her rehearsed appeal. "Sally's daughter, Carol, is flying in today, and she's going to be overwhelmed. I thought we could help her out by arranging a memorial service at the Congregational Church. I want to make it for tomorrow evening. That will allow Carol to plan the funeral for whenever she can get the family together without having everyone wondering what they can do to help. I was hoping I could count on you to do the flowers. And, could I get a drink of water?"

"My coffee pot isn't working. I'm sorry." Irina had clearly been working on that excuse, but she anticipated the wrong question.

"I didn't ask for coffee, Irina. I just wanted to know if I can have a glass of water." Irina realized her mistake and sighed. She got up and Liz followed her into the kitchen. "You're so good with flower arrangements, Irina. I can't think of anyone else who could do three or four large arrangements in a day and a half."

Irina was busying herself with the water, and so Liz continued. "Actually, it isn't so much Carol getting the family together – I think it's just her and her brother. It's more a matter of when the police are going to release the body, what with the autopsy and all…"

Irina whirled around. "Autopsy? Why they do autopsy?"

"Oh, hasn't anyone told you? The police suspect foul play. They don't think it was an accident. They think Sally was pushed down her stairs." Liz didn't have to wait long for a response.

"Who do such a thing?"

"That's what the police are going to have to find out. They're going to be questioning everyone who knew her, wanting to know where they were and what they were doing."

"They ask garden club people?" Irina had the glass of water in her hand, but had not offered it to Liz. The water vibrated as her hand shook.

"Oh, I think they'll especially want to know about us. Anyone who had a disagreement with her. May I have that water, please?"

Irina looked down at the water, appearing to have forgotten why she had drawn it. "Why they ask us? We ladies. Ladies not kill each other." The Russian accent, usually well under control, was becoming thick. Her English was disintegrating.

"Because someone killed her," Liz said, smoothly. "There's no logical suspect, so the police have to check everyone's alibi. They've already questioned me quite thoroughly." The last bit was a lie, but it sounded good.

"I not have problem. I am at gym. I work out. I sign in. I sign out. Many people see me."

Liz noted that Irina's explanation for her whereabouts was the same that she had surmised for Irina hours earlier.

"But that's no good, Irina. The police wanted to know where I was Tuesday evening."

"What you mean, Tuesday evening?" Irina now had a desperate look in her eye. "Roland say Sally die yesterday morning?"

"The police apparently think differently. I said I was home and they said they'd check my phone records. I think they're really serious."

Irina was breathing hard, the water glass shaking. "They want alibi for Tuesday night?"

"That's what it looks like, Irina. We're all going to have to be able to prove where we were Tuesday evening."

"But I here. I alone." Irina's English vocabulary had degenerated to the point of monosyllables. Her brow was creased, her mind working furiously.

"But I'm sure you made phone calls, or you were on the Internet. That's all the police will need. If you made calls, they'll just check to see that the times match. If you sent emails, they'll just check the time stamps, or even just look at web sites you visited. It's all time coded. I'm sure you have nothing to be concerned about." Liz's voice became soothing.

"Phone calls? They want to know who I make phone calls to? And where I go on Internet? That not illegal?"

"The police will just want to know that you can account for

where you were," Liz said. "And it may not even come to that. I'm sure they'll catch whoever did it and we won't even be bothered." Liz smiled her disarming best.

Irina forced a smile. "We see." An enigmatic response. The worried look was still very much on her face, but there was more now. She was starting to think ahead. She was formulating a plan. "I must get dressed now. We talk again."

Liz found herself being herded toward the door. While most of her suspicions had been confirmed, she still had one question. She stopped at the door. "Irina, why did you miss the meeting Wednesday?"

Irina, so close to having an unwanted visitor out of her home, was again caught off guard. "I miss meeting because I not want... I miss meeting because..." She paused again, this time with a thought fully formed. "I forget it is Wednesday. I stay too long at gym."

And then Irina added, "I not sure I be here Friday. I may need to go visit sick family. You find someone else, Liz."

And then Liz was out of the house and trying to assess what she had learned. Irina could not account for her whereabouts. Irina seemed frightened of any investigation. Irina intimated that she might be prepared to leave town rather than answer questions.

Irina might well have killed Sally Kahn.

4.

For at least the tenth time, Flynn played back the last two minutes of the Tim Kahn interview.

"Tim, were you there when your mother fell down the stairs?"

"No!" I wasn't there and I didn't stay all night. You said she fell down the stairs in the morning. I was out of there by ten."

Flynn had questioned suspects for three decades. He had been lied to repeatedly during this interview. He knew a dozen ways to tell when a perp was lying and Tim Kahn, who apparently was a habitual liar, had exhibited nine of them over the course of an hour. But in that final minute before he demanded a lawyer, Tim Kahn may have spoken the truth.

Tim Kahn now was consigned to the Hardington Police Station's conference room. He said he didn't want a public defender. He also said he couldn't afford a lawyer but would ask his sister to pay for one when she arrived. With the question of a lawyer at an impasse, Kahn had been asked to stay in the conference room and given the balance of the box of donuts and coffee to keep him company. When last seen, he had been sound asleep.

Chief Harding, though, heard the same tape but arrived at a far different conclusion.

"You got your guy, John. Hell, the kid is lying through his teeth. He changed his story five times. This guy was trouble for ten years when he lived here and now he's gone off and killed his mother."

"I've got a lot of facts to check, Chief. It's too soon."

"I don't think you understand, John. I've got three selectmen screaming at me that this is going to blow up and we're all going to be on the six o'clock news with some damn 'horror in Hardington' lead. This town doesn't need that kind of publicity. The state police are going to hear about it and demand to know why the investigation wasn't handed over to them. Plus, I've known this kid since I first dragged him in for shoplifting when he was nine. He's trouble. He was there. He had plenty of motive. And he's a damned hophead. He was probably coked out of his skull when he did it."

Flynn couldn't remember the last time he had heard anyone use the word 'hophead'.

"Chief, the guy's sister will be here in a little while. Let's see what she wants to do and whether she has anything to add. Tell the selectmen that you've probably got the guy – and I mean *probably* – and that they can stop worrying about property values. But let me do this right. Let me finish the investigation."

Chief Harding was slow to agree. "You do what you have to do, but you do it quickly. And if you don't make the arrest, I will." With that, Chief Harding executed a military-style about-face and left the room.

Flynn spent the next half hour marshalling his meager resources. A patrolman was dispatched with Tim Kahn's photo to canvass the 8A project on Washington Street to see if Kahn had been there last evening. A second patrolman was sent to track down the conductor on the last train from Hardington to determine whether Kahn had been aboard. Calls were placed to expedite the crime scene unit's analysis of Sally Kahn's home.

Finally, Flynn reached for the phone. He hesitated, then punched a number.

"Mrs. Phillips? This is Detective John Flynn again. I need your help."

Twenty minutes later, he was back in Liz Phillips' great room.

"Mrs. Phillips…"

"Please call me Liz. I think we've been formal long enough."

"Liz, I'm just getting to know this town. You've lived here –

what – all your life?"

"Actually, about twenty-five years with a few off for good behavior. That makes me practically a newcomer."

"You know the town. I don't. You apparently understand the dynamics. I'm still carrying around a slip of paper with important names on it. I've got a murder investigation in a town where people aren't supposed to get murdered. You knew Sally Kahn well. To me, she's only a name. I need someone I can trust. Are you that person?"

Liz was slow to respond. "I'm not nearly as well plugged in as someone like Roland Evans-Jones – he has an antiques shop on Main Street – you've probably seen it, Rare Treasures. It's like gossip central. Roland hears everything."

"You talk to Mr. Evans-Jones. I'll talk to you."

"Why me?"

"Like you said yesterday, you can find out more things in an afternoon than I can find in a week. If fact, you remind me of my last partner back in Boston. You never stop asking questions."

"Are you open to theories?" Liz asked.

"I wouldn't be here if I weren't."

"Then try this one on. Tim Kahn didn't kill his mother. He may have been there to beg for money and maybe to steal, but he's not smart enough to have set it up the way it was done. But there *is* someone who is smart enough, and who just may have had a motive, however petty it seems to you and me."

"Then I think I need to fill you in on my conversation with Tim this morning and some evidence that has come to light since we last talked," Flynn said.

Liz Phillips made lunch while Flynn talked. An hour later, he had eaten a satisfying grilled cheese sandwich, and Liz Phillips had a long 'to do' list.

* * * * *

Carol Kahn was in with her brother when Flynn got back to

the police station. Flynn quickly introduced himself and said he would be at his desk, that she should take her time. "We have a lot to discuss."

Two reports were waiting for him at his desk. No one had boarded that last train at Hardington on Tuesday night. And Tim Kahn was a periodic visitor at one Dwayne Jones, a resident of Washington Gardens Apartments, Hardington's grudging answer to the state's requirement for affordable housing. Unfortunately, no one could be certain if Kahn was there Tuesday evening. Dwayne Jones, according to the twelve-page dossier left by his predecessor, was a small-time drug dealer who had caught the attention of the Hardington Police, but had never done anything so flagrant that he merited arrest. Dwayne was strongly suspected of selling small quantities of cocaine, marijuana and other drugs, but he sold only to people he knew and he stayed away from the schools. Thus, in the eyes of Hardington, he was just far enough under the radar to avoid being rooted out. The theory was that the dealer who took his place might be considerably worse.

Flynn called his contact at Crime Scenes.

"That ain't no friendly town you got yourself hooked up with, Flynn," his contact told him. "It'll take until tomorrow to process everything, but I can give you a couple of highlights. First, your buddy Mr. Kahn is in the system and his prints are all over, including on those two beer cans. I'll email you the full run of prints tomorrow morning. The problem is, those beer cans appear to have been consorting with yogurt – a nice big smudge on each can. And, because there was yogurt in the garbage can, a reasonable person would conclude that those cans were fished out of the garbage by person or persons unknown. You're going to have a fun time putting together that puzzle."

His contact continued, "We got nothing off her face by way of foreign DNA, so that's bad luck. There are fingerprints on the coffee pot and sugar bowl besides Mrs. Kahn's, but they're not in the system. At least not any system that we've gotten a match on. Lots of hairs and fibers and we're classifying them now. We also found concrete dust in the rug."

Flynn recalled the area. "Yeah, some big house going in next door. There's a new foundation."

"That would explain it. Also, some mulch. We took samples from outside to see if it matches."

Flynn asked, "Is there anything at the scene that would rule out a woman as a suspect?"

His contact paused. "Nothing, really. In fact, the whole thing with going through the garbage can, the slapping rather than bare-knuckled hitting, and setting up for breakfast has a kind of a feminine feel to it. That's a personal rather than scientific observation."

Flynn thanked his contact and rang off. He looked up to see Carol Kahn approaching his desk. He stood up to greet her. She looked neither teary-eyed nor distraught. Only tired.

"Ms. Kahn, I'm very sorry for your loss. Do you have a few minutes to talk?"

"Kahn was my maiden name. It's Carol Driscoll." Flynn noted she appeared to be about forty, which would make her the older sister. Her black hair was flecked with gray and she had pasty skin, as though she never went outside.

"Your husband and children are on their way up?" Flynn asked.

She nodded. "Tom and the boys will be here tomorrow morning. Tom Junior is seventeen, Scott is fourteen. They took the news pretty well. I'm not sure how they're going to take learning that their uncle killed Nana."

"Unless he said something to you in there, there's no proof that he did it."

"Oh, he denied it up and down," she said, bitterness creeping into her voice. "Said he was just there to borrow some money.

He's been denying things all his life. He's never done anything wrong. He didn't wreck the car when he was fourteen and he was framed by the police for shoplifting. He didn't break into any of our neighbors' houses and he has no idea why stuff kept disappearing from our house. How long of a list would you like, Detective Flynn? He flew down to see us for a few days last year. He managed to 'lose' three sets of tickets – two paid for by Mom and one paid for by me. I finally told him I didn't care if he showed up or not. And when he did show up – two days late – he managed to get himself beaten up twice. That was probably when he was out buying drugs or pulling some scam."

"Oh, and when he left, he took a little something extra with him. Three checks from the back of our money market account checkbook were missing. We didn't find out about that one until we got a statement showing that he had cashed one for two thousand dollars. He told me he didn't do that, either. In fact, he swore to me on Dad's grave that he didn't take those checks. He had no idea who did, but it wasn't him."

Flynn listened carefully to the sister's account. He especially noted the swearing on his father's grave.

"Let me tell you what we know," Flynn said. "Your brother was in your mother's house Tuesday evening. He acknowledges that. He says he left around ten. Sometime after nine o'clock, but before midnight, someone slapped your mother several times. Within a few minutes of that slapping, that someone pushed her, backwards and hard, down the basement stairs. Your mother's neck was broken in the fall. Death was instantaneous or nearly so. Then, someone set up the kitchen for breakfast in an apparent attempt to make the time of death look like Wednesday morning."

He let that information sink in before continuing. "Your brother said he took a late train back into Boston. We know he did not do so. He may have visited a small-time drug dealer here in Hardington later that night. We can't establish his whereabouts at any time Tuesday evening or up until the time I reached him at his apartment Wednesday evening. There are also a couple of odd things, like some unknown fingerprints in the house, for example, on the items that were set out for breakfast. There is also an indication that the beer cans we found with his fingerprints on them may have been retrieved from the garbage. That's puzzling, and I can't explain why that would have happened."

Carol Driscoll had been listening intently, nodding in several places. "I can probably help you out with one gap, Detective. You'll want to pay a visit on Joe Haskell. I assume he still lives on Pine Grove. He was one of Tim's drug buddies when they were in high school, and they're still quite close. Tim and Joe have a lot in common. Neither one has ever held down a job. They both think the world owes them a living and that each day should start and end by getting high. I wouldn't be surprised if shoving Mom down the stairs was Joe's idea, because he's been living off of his parents' estate since he was about twenty-five. His are probably the other set of fingerprints." Her voice was becoming angrier as she spoke.

"Your brother is going to need an attorney, Mrs. Driscoll. He has asked for one and we can't question him until he has one. Tim apparently has no money. Would you be willing to pay for one?"

"So that someone can get him off on a technicality?" she said angrily. "So that someone can show that Tim was a 'victim' and it wasn't really his fault? No thank you, Detective Flynn. My brother killed my mother. I'm going to have to live with that for the rest of my life. Please don't ask me or my poor, dead mother to bail him out one more time."

Flynn kept his voice even and cordial. "I'm very sorry, Mrs. Driscoll, but I had to ask. You should also know that -- do you know a friend of your mother's named Liz Phillips?"

She nodded. "She's one of Mom's closest friends. They're both gardening fiends." There was a little laugh at the end of the statement.

"Mrs. Phillips is organizing a memorial service for your mother for tomorrow evening. I need to also tell you that we can't release your mother's body until after the autopsy is final. I would also ask that you not stay at your mother's house. If you'd like to go in, I'd appreciate it if you did so with a police officer. It is a crime scene. Incidentally, Mrs. Phillips asked me to pass along to you that she would be pleased to put up you and your family while you're here. I've seen her house. She certainly has the room."

Carol nodded again. "I hadn't thought about any delay in the funeral. I'd like to get this done as soon as possible for everyone's sake. If you can help…"

"I'll do everything I can. I have a few more questions. First, has your mother ever spoken about someone named Irina Burroughs?"

Carol smiled, fleetingly. "The lady from Russia who goes through husbands like disposable diapers."

"Do you know about any disagreements between your mother and Mrs. Burroughs?"

Carol nodded vigorously. "Like, she puts in for plants she didn't buy or charges the garden club for plants that end up at her house? Mom was livid. It's been going on for years." Her brow furrowed. "Is she a suspect?"

"We need to cover all the bases," Flynn said. "What you just said confirms something else I heard. How about Landini Brothers?"

"She hates them. I mean, everybody hates them. She said their trucks are tearing up the streets and running over the garden club sites. Mom's kind of an environmentalist."

"Did she ever mention anyone in particular there?"

Carol closed her eyes for a moment. "She's talked about Frank Landini. I assume he's one of the owners."

"Is there anyone else with whom she has had any strong disagreements?"

"Are you looking for another suspect?" Carol pointed at the conference room. "The person who killed my mother is in the room right over there."

Flynn nodded and spoke reassuringly. "If you want to think of it in a positive light, let's say that I've got to rule out everyone else who might have had a motive. If your brother goes to trial, his defense will have a much stronger case if it turns out that we didn't look under every rock."

Carol concentrated. "Like I said, Mom cares – cared – about the environment. She was also very disturbed about the new house going up next door. She even offered to buy the property in order to keep the developer from tearing down the Robinson's house. She hated the idea of some monster house going up in her neighborhood."

"Do you know who she argued with about that house?" Flynn asked.

"Oh, a lot of people. She was livid at the Robinsons for selling – she matched the bid from the developer, but they turned her down. She was convinced the developer – Mulroney or something like that – must have paid extra money under the table. She was after the town for allowing the new house to be built so far back on the property. She really fought that house."

"I see there's a foundation in place," Flynn said. "Is it over with?"

"Not by a long shot. She told me she was hiring a lawyer to stop the construction."

"Was your mother.... an angry person? Was she mad at a lot of people all the time?"

Carol shook her head. Her eyes were becoming moist. "No. She was usually a very gentle person who got along with everyone. But like I said, she cares about Hardington and especially about our old neighborhood. She watched the Robinson's house get torn down and she said it made her sick inside. She doesn't think people with money and power ought to be able to do whatever they want. Which is pretty ironic because, well, my dad left a lot of stock when he died, and Mom pretty well cashed it out at the top of the market." Her face turned glum again. "Which gave my brother a couple of million motives to push her down the stairs."

"Did your mother ever say 'no' to him when he asked for money?"

"She attached conditions. 'I'll give you a check when you show me that you've enrolled in a substance abuse clinic.' So he'd sign up. Two weeks later he'd be back for more money and the clinic would have burned down or the program would have him on a wait list. It was always something."

"This last question may be the hardest, Mrs. Driscoll. Did you ever see Tim as a violent person? Did he ever abuse your mother?"

Carol was quiet. Now, for the first time, Flynn could see her blinking back tears. "My brother is weak, Detective Flynn. Not physically weak. Call it spiritually weak. I think he started smoking pot when he was about twelve and, by the time he was fifteen, he was what we used to call a 'stoner'. I mean stoned all day. I went off to college and every time I came home you could see it was worse. Mom refused to see it, even after Dad died and it got much worse. When you're stoned like that, you're not violent. You have no energy to be violent. All you're thinking about is how to get high again, and where you can get money to buy some more stuff."

"Your parents were an obstacle to what he wanted?" Flynn asked.

"No," she said. "For Tim, Mom and Dad were simply an annoyance. They had the money he needed. But instead of just giving him the money, they made him think up excuses – other reasons why he needed the money. And that meant work – thinking up some cock and bull story about the car needing new tires or the airline tickets getting stolen. And that was annoying.

So I think Tim got tired of having to think up some new, creative reason, and he pushed Mom down the stairs. I think pushing her down the stairs was easier than thinking up an excuse."

Tears were streaming down Carol's cheeks. "I'd tell Mom over and over that she had to cut him off. But she said that as long as she was alive, she'd take care of Tim. She was the only one who cared and the only person who could change him." Carol was crying as she finished and Flynn pulled a Kleenex from a box on his desk.

"I'm terribly sorry, Mrs. Driscoll. I'm starting to understand how hard this is on you."

"Maybe I realize it was only a matter of time. Maybe I could have done a lot more to help her with Tim."

Flynn gave her home and cell phone numbers for Liz Phillips and offered her the use of a desk for phone calls.

* * * * *

Liz's first call was to Mary Giamatti. The garden club's gregarious membership director used caller ID to greet friends by name.

"Hello, Liz! I was just thinking about you. I hear you're the one who thought of organizing a memorial service for Sally tomorrow night."

"Word gets around fast," Liz said. "I was calling to ask if you could help spread the word."

"You haven't checked your email. I've gotten, like, six messages and three phone calls already. There are a group of us doing flower arrangements tomorrow afternoon. Rose has come up with a program. I hope you know you're speaking."

Liz didn't, but elected not to say so. "Mary, I have what probably seems like an absurd question. Did you and Sally talk on Monday or Tuesday?"

Mary said, "hmmmm" for several seconds. "We had a long talk on Monday evening and a brief one Tuesday afternoon.

Why?"

Liz ignored the question. "Did Sally tell you about, well, about what she was going to do at the meeting on Wednesday. About Irina?"

Mary was more guarded in her answer. "She may have."

"Did you say anything about it to Irina?"

"Oh, Liz, you're not saying that Irina had anything…"

"No, no, no… I'm just asking if Irina knew in advance. If that's why she wasn't at the meeting on Wednesday."

"Irina said she had already heard about it," Mary said. "She said Sally was imagining things and every plant was accounted for."

Bingo, Liz thought. *Keep the conversation moving.* "What else was on Sally's mind when you talked to her? Was anything upsetting her? It could be important, Mary."

"Well, she told me her son, Tim, was coming over for dinner Tuesday night. Do you think the police should know that?"

"They already do. In fact, I know they've already spoken with Tim." Liz was careful to avoid saying Tim was a suspect. "What else?"

"Oh, she was upset about her latest run-in with Landini Brothers," Mary said. "They told her they'd press charges for trespass the next time she showed up on their property. She was a little – what would you call it – melancholy – about Charlie. It was twelve years in April since he died and she said she misses him more today than ever. She hates that the house next door got torn down, and that had her both angry and sad at the same time. Those are the highlights."

"If you had to think of one thing that was most on Sally's mind – the one thing that she was worried about – what would it be?"

"Tim. And a dozen years without Charlie. Sally said she was starting to feel old. You know she was sixty-five in April. Her knee is bothering her but she doesn't want… I'm sorry. She didn't want surgery. She worried about what would happen to Tim if something happened to her. Oh, Liz, that's horrible. Tim may have done something to her."

"We don't know that, Mary. Sally's daughter flew in this morning, and I think things will start to get a lot clearer. I'm hoping Carol and her family will stay with me. They can't stay at Sally's because it's…" Liz almost said, "a crime scene", but stopped in time. "Too sad a place."

But the police say it wasn't an accident," Mary said.

"Who told you that?" Liz asked, wondering how widespread the information about the investigation had become.

"At least three people. It's all over town. Sally was pushed down the stairs."

Liz switched the subject to the flowers, making suggestions but generally going along with what the 'flower committee', as they called themselves, proposed.

Mary said, "The reason I was thinking about you when you called was that, just before you called, Rose came up with the suggestion that we might re-name the Eastern Gateway site, 'the Sally Kahn Garden.' Rose wondered what you thought of the idea and if you'd take it up with the town. We thought that we could all chip in for a sign."

"Mary, I think that's a lovely idea. I'll get to work on it." Liz made some notes to herself. The memorial service was clearly in good hands. She had just finished her notes when the phone rang.

The caller ID said "Hardington PD." Liz was about to answer, 'Hello, Detective Flynn' but thought better of it. A moment later she was relieved she had not done so because the caller was Carol Driscoll. Liz immediately offered her condolences.

"The detective said you're putting together a memorial service for Mom. That's wonderful…"

"And I need to fill you in on the details, which I can do when you get here," Liz said. "We've also got to arrange to get Chipper out of the animal shelter. He's OK there for a few days but he's going to need a home, whether with you or with someone else."

"The detective also said you had offered to put us up for a couple of days. It's a kind offer, but I'd rather be alone right now."

"Carol, there are no hotels within ten miles of Hardington that you'd want to stay at. There are people you're going to want to see here and arrangements to be made. Are you sure you want to be doing that from a hotel room? I've got three spare bedrooms that are ready for company."

They spoke for several minutes and ended the conversation agreeing that Carol would stay at a hotel that night, but that the offer of rooms for her and her family would remain open.

Liz sensed Carol's feeling of being overwhelmed by events. Afterward, Liz checked the guest rooms, in case they were needed, including the one set up for Sarabeth for her infrequent visits home. This was not the house Sarabeth had grown up in and she felt little connection to it. Sarabeth's friends, too, had moved away, lessening the reasons for making the long journey east. Since her marriage two years earlier, her daughter had been back to Hardington just three times, and one of those was really a business trip for her company. The calls were still frequent – two or three long chats a week - but her daughter was now a woman with a husband and career. Her childhood was growing increasingly remote, her childhood home now occupied by strangers. Liz seldom came into this room. On a day like today, the reason was abundantly clear.

The bedroom that had been earmarked as David's office was a similar, unused shrine. In the beginning, David had expected to be on the road at most one to two days a week, working from home the rest of the time. That had been part of the decision to buy the house when they returned to Hardington and David decided to go into business for himself. There was ample room for a consultant working from a home with all the trappings of a successful career. Instead, David had found that "hands on" was the only policy that worked, and his days on the road stretched into months-long stints, with only brief hiatuses between assignments. The "office" had not been used for its intended purpose in over three years.

In reality, Liz realized, she occupied just three rooms of the house when David was not home. Only the kitchen, the great room, and the master bedroom were used. The formal living and dining rooms were entered for purposes of cleaning. The door to the library was opened only when a particular book was sought. An entire wing of the house was effectively sealed off, unused, as was an attic *au pair* suite. It *was* far too much house, too much upkeep. Liz cherished her gardens but their maintenance now stretched to as much as twenty hours a week.

She shook off the creeping feeling of despair. *Not now. People need you. Sally needs you.* She gathered her purse and keys and headed for the door.

* * * * *

Flynn had two visits on his agenda. Joe Haskell and Frank Landini. Haskell merited a paragraph in the twelve-page dossier Flynn had received. He was listed as living at 240 Pine Grove. Pine Grove, in turn, was in Metacomet Park, a 'white-flight' 1960s-era subdivision identical to ones that sprang up in almost every suburban town around Boston. Their owners were the former residents of Hyde Park, Jamaica Plain, and Roxbury who had fled the city when court-ordered busing appeared imminent.

The quickly and cheaply built houses of that era in many Boston suburbs were now deteriorating into substandard housing. But in Hardington, those one- and two-acre lots were prized far more than the houses that sat on them. The Dorchester natives who bought $18,000 Metacomet Park houses with no-money-down VA loans were now sitting on $350,000 lots and nobody gave a damn if the kitchens still featured the original aquamarine Formica countertops. When the O'Briens and the Shaughnessys sold, pocketed their untaxed capital gain and headed for a warmer climate, the new owners brought in wrecking crews.

No one had to tell Flynn these facts, he had grown up with them in Dorchester. He had remained in the city only because busing did not affect Catholic Memorial where he lettered in football and track. His neighbors moved out in droves to be replaced by people who were decidedly non-Irish and usually non-Catholic. Two years at Holy Cross taught him to his satisfaction that he was not 'college material', even if an athletic scholarship meant he could have taken an additional two or three years to fully absorb the lesson. The summer after his sophomore year, he took the bus from Worcester back to Boston and never looked back. A year later he was a rookie cop walking his first beat. He had finally found his role in life.

Flynn thought these things as he sized up 240 Pine Grove. *There but for the grace of God go I.* Had their son not been on that varsity track team, Sam and Rosemary Flynn would have certainly uprooted their brood when the neighborhood began to change. But instead of the luck of the draw and landing in Hardington, the family Flynn would almost certainly have gone no farther than Quincy or Dedham and secured the blessings of an all-white, but decidedly inferior school system and a home destined to develop dry rot.

The residence of Joe Haskell looked as though it had received no capital investment in the form of gutters, shutters, or paint in at least a decade. The split-level home was hidden behind evergreens that now obscured windows and were threatening to envelop what remained of the sidewalk. It was a developer's dream. It was a neighbor's nightmare.

The dossier described Haskell as a 'disaster waiting to happen,' a thirty-five-year-old teenager whose adolescence was extended into perpetuity by drugs and the ability to pay for a continual high. Haskell's parents had died a decade earlier when their car was demolished by a speeding Pepsi delivery truck. The insurance settlement ensured that Joe Haskell need never worry about the mundane requirements of life such as finding employment or contributing to the community.

Haskell, according to the dossier, lived in a perpetual drug haze. He was suspected of, though never arrested for, introducing select members of the Hardington middle and high school population to drugs and of supplying them with 'starter' bags of marijuana and pills. The homes of those to whom he was believed to supply drugs also had a greater propensity to be subjects of unexplained thefts. Fingers perpetually pointed back at Haskell as a source, though there were no convictions to show for these suspicions. Haskell was smart enough to choose his clientele carefully and leave behind no incriminating evidence.

Flynn knocked on the back door, the front door showing no signs of having been used in the new millennium. It was two o'clock, about the time most druggies would be coming out of their narcotic-induced slumber. After about five minutes of insistent pounding, he heard footsteps and low muttering. The back door opened and a gaunt man in filthy jeans and a fraying Aerosmith tee-shirt stood, blinking in the sun.

"Top of the morning to you, Mr. Haskell," Flynn said and walked past the still-blinking man. "'Tis a fine day we're having and I'm here to share a bit of the luck of the Irish with you." The exaggerated accent served only to further confuse Haskell, who did not know this person and only vaguely thought of himself as Irish.

"I've been having a bit of a wee talk with your pal, Timothy Kahn. Mister Kahn says that you and he made a fine night of it on Tuesday, and I wanted to check that your story and his were the same. By the way, in case you're not keen on calendars, this is Thursday."

"Who the hell are you?"

"Ah, saints be praised. We've not yet been formally introduced, even though you might be me own flesh and blood.

I'm Constable Flynn, your local guardian angel." Flynn had pulled up an ancient aluminum and plastic stool, the seat of which had long ripped to show filthy cotton batting.

"Tim Kahn?"

"Ah, the lad has his wits about him. Yes, of course, we're speaking of young Timothy Kahn. Who may not be Irish but who has the luck all the same. Now, when did our Tim come to see you and did the two of you stay indoors, as it were, or did you venture out into that grand evening?"

Haskell scratched his stomach and eyed the refrigerator. Flynn positioned his chair between Haskell and his source of energy – or delay.

"Yeah, he came by around – what – eleven o'clock?"

"Are ye asking me or telling me, Joseph, me boy?"

"Eleven. Maybe a little later."

"And the two of you had a little party? Did young Timmy bring his own or were you a proper host?"

Haskell didn't like the question. "I don't have to answer that kind of question. What the crap did you say your name was?"

"Father O'Malley from the church of the true confession. We're not here to grant absolution or to point fingers. We're only interested in the coming and goings of Tim Kahn. Now, did Tim come bearing gifts?"

"Yeah, he got some coke and some poppers. I thought you said you're a cop?"

"And did any young ladies share your company that fateful evening?"

"Two. I don't remember their names."

"And when did you and Mister Kahn go to see the lad's mother?"

Haskell looked confused. "We didn't."

"That's good enough for now, Joseph. And when did our Mister Kahn take his leave?"

"About two or three. Just about this time yesterday."

"And the young ladies. Did they stay?"

"Naw, they were gone when we got up."

"And was the visit a surprise, or did Mister Kahn let you know he would be coming to share his bounty?

"He called Tuesday. I don't know when."

"That's a fine lad. Well, you'll be wanting to have your breakfast, I suspect, so I won't be holding you up." Flynn went to the back door. "A final question, though. How did our friend Mister Kahn describe his visit with his mother?"

Haskell shrugged. "He said it was the usual bullshit."

"Ah, a man of few words. We will see you soon, Joseph Haskell."

"What the hell did you say your name was?"

Flynn did not bother to answer.

As he drove toward Overfield, he assembled his facts. Tim Kahn had apparently left his mother's around ten. He had walked to the 8A projects on Washington where he visited a drug dealer and procured cocaine and methamphetamines. He had then walked to Joe Haskell's for a pre-arranged party, with Haskell supplying girls, probably in barter for a cashless high. If Tim Kahn had walked directly from his mother's home to Washington Gardens, effected a quick transaction for drugs, and then walked to Haskell's, the elapsed time would be 45 minutes or less. Haskell's dimly remembered, *"Eleven. Maybe a little later,"* was worrisome and would need to be further checked.

Tim Kahn had awakened in the early afternoon and most likely taken the train into Boston. Allowing for connections on the T, he would probably not have arrived until after four or five, too late to have cashed one of the checks he had stolen from his mother. Kahn had called Flynn around seven o'clock, leaving only two or three hours unaccounted for.

It did not rule out Tim Kahn as the murderer of his mother.

But it made for an improbably blasé one. The routine of hitting up his mother for money, buying drugs, and then partying at his old drug buddy's house was unchanged. A murder, either planned or accidental, would have shaken someone as weak as Tim Kahn. His sister's protestations aside, the weight of circumstantial evidence began to point away from Tim Kahn.

Landini Brothers Stone, Gravel, and Concrete was readily visible as Flynn crossed the Charles River on the state highway. The core of the business was a massive gravel pit, the product of glacial activity ten thousand years earlier. The gravel pit alone covered more than ten acres, massive piles of rock and stone, sorted by size, occupied as much space again. A dozen trucks lined up outside a tower that apparently dispensed ready-mix concrete. A pathetic, dust-covered group of boxwoods, many of them brown, spelled out LANDINI BROS at the entrance.

Flynn quickly found what appeared to be the main office and parked in the handicapped spot. It was unlikely anyone in a wheelchair would be placing an order in person anytime soon.

It was a pleasant day outside but the office was sealed and chilled, most likely to ward off the dust.

"How can I help you?" asked the receptionist who looked to be about twenty. She wore a Johnny Damon Red Sox jersey. A streak of her hair was dyed fuchsia.

"You are aware that Mr. Damon played for Boston two or three teams ago, including an unforgivable stop in the Bronx?"

"Yeah," she said. "But he's still cute. What can I do for you?"

"You can find Frank Landini. Tell him Detective John Flynn from the Hardington Police Department is here to see him."

The receptionist reached for the kind of old-fashioned microphone that was once found in principal's offices at elementary schools around the country. "Frank to the office. Frank to the office. You have a visitor."

"Hasn't the world pretty much gone to those walkie-talkie cell phones?" Flynn asked.

"Uncle Frank likes to hear his name over the loudspeaker, I guess," the receptionist said. "Also, this place has really terrible cell coverage."

Flynn let it drop. He looked around the office as he waited. He counted no more than half a dozen desks or offices. It seemed too small an office staff for such a large business, on top of which none of those other desks were occupied at present. Also, computers were noticeably absent. Police departments may have come late to the information technology revolution, but they had converted wholesale in the mid-90s with a dramatic impact on productivity. Ten years later, the Landinis were still using adding machines and Selectric typewriters. Nothing illegal, of course, but it spoke of a mindset. By contrast, the fleet of trucks, he noted, all appeared new or nearly so.

Ten minutes later, a forty-ish balding man, twenty pounds overweight and dressed in a plaid shirt and khakis barged in the door.

"Karen, I asked you to take care of the little stuff today. We've got…" He noticed Flynn, who had positioned himself off to one corner, out of immediate sight of whoever came through the door. "And you would be?"

"Detective John Flynn. Hardington Police Department." Flynn handed him a card. Landini looked at it with suspicion.

"Do you have an appointment?"

"Yes, and I'll be late for it if we can't wrap this up fairly quickly." Flynn grinned, waiting to see if Landini got the joke. He didn't. "Can we talk in your office?"

Wordlessly, Landini walked toward a small office at the corner of the building. It was plain, furnished in cast-off desks and chairs, and the top of the desk was covered in paperwork. On the walls were pictures of ten or so Little League teams.

"How can I help the Hardington police? If you're hitting me

up for a PBA pledge. I really don't have time. Karen will give you fifty bucks out of petty cash."

"No, I'm here about Sally Kahn. Do you know Mrs. Kahn?"

"Yes, and she's a pain in the ass. So are half the people in Hardington."

Are you aware that Mrs. Kahn died Tuesday evening?"

Landini started to answer, then stopped. "Maybe you want to ask why she's such a pain in the ass."

Flynn noted that Landini had sidestepped the question. "Go on."

"Karen!" The girl was in Landini's door a few seconds later. "Get me the Kahn file."

"The woman who got killed?"

"Yeah. That Kahn file." When Karen was out of earshot. "Jesus Christ." He looked at Flynn. "You got any nieces or nephews?"

"About a dozen."

"Well, don't ever hire one. You hire one, you own them for life. God damn it."

"Your niece doesn't strike me as incompetent."

"Well, that's my problem, not yours."

Karen was back a minute later with a manila file folder. "Check on Bruce and find out when those god damned trucks are going to be back. They should have been here half an hour ago."

Landini opened the folder, which contained several dozen slips of paper. "Each one of these is a visit by that bitch. Each one of these is a complaint. Each one of these is twenty minutes or half an hour out of my time, my foreman's time, or my office staff's time dealing with her. Mrs. Kahn was a giant pain in the ass. She followed our trucks in to report them speeding. She gave us the license number of trucks that went over curbs or drivers who dropped cigarettes out of windows. Let's see what else we have here." He sorted through some of the slips of paper. "Oh, here's a good one. "March 30. Complains driver Alan Jones passed over double yellow line on Main Street, Hardington.'"

"She knew the drivers by name?" Flynn asked.

"No, she would always bring in the license number. The secretary matched them up with the truck assigned to that driver on that shift."

"And what happened Tuesday morning?"

"Mrs. Kahn shows up here at half past six in the morning screaming her head off that one of our drivers ran up over the curb at her precious bunch of flowers at the Post Road cutoff. She demanded to talk to the driver. I told her to get off the property once and for all. We got the biggest job in our history and she wants to shut the place down to chew out somebody because they ran over some pansies. I told her this is private property, I've offered to pay for the flowers, I'm sick and tired of seeing her, and if she shows up again, I'd call the Overfield cops and have her dragged off the property feet first. That's what happened. OK, you satisfied? I gotta go back to work."

"May I have a copy of the file?"

The request appeared to catch Landini off guard. He thought for a second. "Sure. Why not? Have a ball." Landini rose from his chair, handed him the file, and made for the door.

"One last question, Mr. Landini. Did you ever go over these complaints with the drivers involved."

Landini laughed. "Sure, whenever we needed a good yuck. 'Now, Tony, Mrs. Kahn caught you throwing a cigarette out the window of your cab. Don't you do that anymore'." He laughed again and left the building, still chortling.

Flynn waited until Landini had been gone for about fifteen seconds before approaching the receptionist. "Karen, Mr. Landini said it was OK for you to make a copy of this file."

"I heard. It's a small office."

Flynn stood beside her at the Xerox machine while she arrayed the slips of paper on the glass. "What's the big job? He said it was your biggest ever."

"Some sewage treatment plant out in Milford. It's like, a million yards of concrete or something like that."

"Why does Mr. Landini dislike you so much?"

"You're a smart guy," she said. "You figure it out." Flynn thought for a minute. He figured it out. *You can't jump your own niece. It looks bad in the family.*

"Whose idea was it for you to work here?"

"My aunt. His wife." *Exactly.*

"You going to school?"

"Framingham State." She did a little 'whoop-di-doo' twirl in the air with her finger. She made the last copy and handed him about a dozen sheets of paper.

"Which one of these is the report for Tuesday morning?"

She took back the sheets and riffed through them. "Huh, I wrote it up but it isn't in here."

"Do you remember the details?"

"It's what he said. He wasn't lying."

You were here?"

"We open at half past five. I got here right before she did and I have to be here at 6:30, which is why I know the time. We need to have loads at sites by seven."

"Who was the driver?"

She thought for a moment. "Joey was driving – here, I'll write it down. Joey LaRusse was the driver. Do you want to know who else was in the truck?"

"Sure, why not?"

"Mike Pastore and Dan Sypek."

"Three guys in a cement truck. That must be a tight fit."

"Well, this isn't a cement truck. It's a big flatbed."

"Oh." Flynn took the papers. He was full of questions, but didn't want to overstay his welcome or raise suspicion.

He drove back over the Charles River and stopped at a boat ramp on the Hardington side of the river. He pulled out his pad and pen and began to write.

Landini project: what Milford sewage plant – where?

LaRusse, Pastore, Sypek. Record? Prints?

Milford is west. Why were they coming from the east?

Why coming in at 6:30 a.m.?

Why three people?

Flynn drove back to the station, ready to start making calls. Instead, the dispatcher said he was urgently needed in Chief Harding's office.

"He's under arrest, John. He confessed. I did it myself." Chief Harding was dressed in his formal uniform, the one he wore when he went out to talk to civic groups.

Flynn was stunned. "Maybe you want to take me through this."

"You left here for God knows where. I'm getting calls from the Boston stations saying they're working on a story about a Hardington widow being murdered in her home. Apparently one of *your* friends likes to talk to reporters. I told them we're investigating, and they said they'd like to send out a crew. I tell them it's too soon but we have a suspect. They want to know who the suspect is, and I tell them we can't release that information. They want to know if they can interview me. I tell them it's too soon. They tell me they're sending out a crew to do a report from Sally's house, and they'll call me when they're done to see if I want to comment. So I decided to talk to Tim. The damned public defender lady hasn't shown up, and Tim is in the conference room."

"You know Tim had asked for a lawyer. You can't question him after that."

"I know that. I just wanted to talk to him. He was kind of rattled from talking with his sister. So we talked. And he confessed."

"You read him his rights before he did this?" Flynn asked.

"Of course I did."

Flynn was incredulous. "How exactly did he confess?"

"In his own handwriting." Chief Harding crossed his arms and looked smug.

"I had a tape recorder, it was on my desk. Did you use it?"

"Didn't need it. Got it in writing."

"May I see it?"

"No reason why not." Chief Harding took a single sheet of paper from his desk. A Xerox copy of the original that appeared to have been written on a lined yellow pad.

My name is Timothy Kahn and I reside at 114 Elmore Street, Allston, Mass. I am writing this of my own free will. On Tuesday, June 9, I went to see my mother, Sally Hickman Kahn, at her home at 11 Pequot Court, Hardington. I told her I needed $5,000 for car repairs and she refused to give me the money. I had several beers and became drunk. She told me I was wasting my life and that I was dependent upon drugs. I told her I would get off drugs if she would give me the money. She told me she would not give me any more money until I showed her I was clean for at least a month. I told her I needed the money to get clean and she said I needed to get a job. We argued. I became very angry that she wouldn't give me any money. She finally gave me $300 in cash and said I should use that money to start over. I got really angry because it was not enough money and I told her so. She said it was all she would do for me until I got my act together. I said is that all I get and she said come back when you've made a start. I didn't want to hurt her but I was very angry and drunk. I pushed her down the stairs into the basement. I am responsible for her death. I have written this of my own free will.

Timothy Kahn

Flynn clenched his teeth, his hands squeezing the sheet of paper. He looked up at Chief Harding, who continued to look smug and content. "That's what you got? 'I pushed her down the stairs into the basement.' No detail, no anything."

"It's all we need," Chief Harding said.

"And there were witnesses when this was written?"

"I was there. I witnessed it."

Flynn worked to control his temper. "And you helped him write it?"

"It's in his handwriting, you may have noticed," Chief Harding said testily.

"And you think this will stand up?" Flynn realized his face was turning crimson.

"God damn it, John, I got his confession. It's your job to make it stand up. You've got all the probable cause you need, and I can tell the TV folks that there's no story. The kid did it in a moment of anger. He'll plead to manslaughter and that will be the end of it. And you and your goddam friends from Boston can pack up their evidence bags and their medical examiner and their computer P-D-whatevers and leave us alone. And I don't ever want to see anything like that in this department again. You need help, you go to the state police. You need a death certified, you call Lester Simmons. And you get my permission before you do any of that. Do you hear me? Because I don't want people in this town to be afraid that there's some murderer on the loose, and I don't want Channel 7 news telling the world that old ladies aren't safe in their homes in Hardington. And if you disagree with any of that, you're welcome to clean out your desk and go somewhere else."

Flynn swallowed his instinct to lash back in kind. Instead, he said, "I understand you perfectly, Chief." And then he said nothing.

Chief Harding waited for the counterblow that would give him the authority to fire Flynn. He was unprepared for the acquiescence. After a moment, he said, "Well, what are you going to do now?"

"You made clear when you hired me that I'm paid for a forty hour week. It's five o'clock. I'm going home. Tomorrow, I'll start sorting out the evidence."

Half an hour later, five news crews were on hand to see Tim Kahn do the "perp walk" from the front of the Hardington police station to a waiting Norfolk County Sheriff's van. Chief Harding did a stand-up in front of the station in his dress uniform. He said that good police work had led to a swift conclusion that this was a family argument that had ended in tragedy and that Tim Kahn was a troubled young man who needed society's assistance as much as he did its condemnation.

5.

Liz spent an hour going over arrangements with Patricia Allerton, the secretary of the First Congregational Church. Sally Kahn had been an active and vocal member of the church for more than 30 years, her tastes in music were well known as were her thoughts about 'appropriate' decoration. Over the course of the hour, Linda Tenzer and Barbara Desmond joined the group, each with checklists of things accomplished or to be done. This was the heart of the garden club board. These were people who, given tasks, needed little direction because no one dithered. Linda had already drafted a program and needed only to drop in specifics about music and speakers. Barbara had culled photos taken at garden club events, scanned, and enlarged them.

Liz was ready to leave when she had a thought. "Did any of you see or talk to Sally on Tuesday?"

Patricia and Barbara had not, but Linda Tenzer said she had spoken with Sally in the afternoon – "around four o'clock."

"She called me about my site," Linda said. "She said she had found some new daylilies that would work well with the other colors and, if I wanted them, she would pick up enough for my site when she bought some for her own."

"Anything that wasn't about the garden club?" Liz asked.

Linda thought for a moment. "She said she had to run some boys from out of the new house foundation next door. She said that for the past several days, some boys coming up the trail from the school would go down into the foundation and they'd stay in there for hours. She was afraid they were going to hurt themselves, and so she had to excuse herself to chase them off the property."

"Did she sound upset? Did it seem like there was a serious problem?"

"Just that it seemed to be the same boys every day and they're at an age where respecting adults isn't high on their agendas. She said the young ones would take off, but the older ones just – you know – flipped her the finger. I think she was also concerned that something illegal might be going on."

Liz mentally filed it away, then was seized with an idea. "You have everything under control here. I've got to go home to write my talk for tomorrow." She looked at her watch. It was just four. They might still be there.

Liz parked her car in front of Sally's and walked to the house foundation, where she heard whispering and laughter.

"I need your help," she said with authority when she was at the rim of the foundation. Inside, five boys – the youngest probably twelve or thirteen and the oldest perhaps two years older – were sitting in a semicircle on the basement floor looking at the screen of an iPad, their backpacks arrayed around them. Several were smoking cigarettes. They instantly looked up and the two youngest stubbed out their cigarettes. "Who was here on Tuesday?"

"Who are you?" the oldest of them asked, flipping down the computer's cover.

"Someone who doesn't care what you're doing right now, but who needs to know if you were here the day before yesterday."

"Is this is about the old bag who croaked?" the oldest boy asked.

"It's about Mrs. Kahn, the woman who lived next door. Which of you were here Tuesday about four in the afternoon when she came out?"

The five boys quickly looked at one another. The oldest said, "It wasn't us."

"That's strange. The description she gave matches you perfectly, right down to the color of the backpack."

This gave the oldest boy pause. "What about it?"

"She asked you to leave here. What I want to know is, how

many of you came back later, and how late did you stay?"

One of the younger boys scrambled up, grabbed his backpack and ran for the basement stairs. Liz moved around the lip of the basement and intercepted him.

"You let go of me! My father's a lawyer and he'll sue you for everything you've got!"

"I'm a lawyer, too," Liz lied, smoothly. "And my husband is a judge. And I think your father would thank me rather than suing me." She pointed him back down the stairs. "Now, which of you came back and how long did you stay?"

With their exit blocked, the boys stood in one corner. "I came back after dinner. So did Kyle," said one boy, who appeared to be their leader.

"How long did you stay?"

"Until it started getting dark."

"Did you see Mrs. Kahn drive out and back?"

"Yeah."

"What kind of car was she driving?"

"The funny shaped one."

"Prius," whispered another boy, apparently Kyle.

"Prius."

"And was she alone when she left?" Liz asked.

"Yeah."

"And when she came back, was she still alone?"

"There was some guy in the car with her."

"And what did they do?"

"The garage door went up, the car went into the garage. The garage door went down."

"Did anyone come back out?"

"Not while we were here," the boy said.

"How much longer after she drove back were you here?"

"I don't know. Until dark. Then we went home."

That would have been about nine, Liz thought. "Did you see

anyone else, either in a car or on foot?"

"Guy walking his dog. Couple of cars came down the street and then turned around in the circle. Like they were lost."

"What did the cars look like?"

"It was starting to get dark. Just cars."

"There was a woman," Kyle added. "She came up the path from the school."

"You saw her," the other boy said quickly. "I didn't see her."

"She came up the path and went to the side of the old lady's house," the younger one said. "Then she went back down the path."

"What did she look like?" Liz asked.

"It was getting dark. She was kind of short."

"How do you know it was a woman?"

The boy started to say something and then looked embarrassed. He held his hands cupped in front of his chest. "You know."

"I understand. Tell me anything else you can about what she did."

Kyle thought for a moment. "She was, like, sneaking around. She was trying to stay in the shadows. She went up along the hedge and disappeared around the far side of the house. She was back in less than a minute. She went back down the path."

"And Kyle didn't say anything to you about her?" Liz asked the older boy.

"I was kind of occupied."

Liz didn't want to know what constituted "kind of occupied" to a twelve- or thirteen-year-old boy.

"Kyle, I'm going to need your full name and address." She nodded at the older boy. "Yours, too. A policeman will probably want to talk to you. He isn't going to care what you were doing here, either. He just needs to hear what you told me."

Both boys provided full names and addresses. Liz did not tell them that Detective Flynn would question them in the presence of their parents and that, while the police would not care what was going on in the foundation, their parents might feel otherwise.

Liz went back to her car and was making notes when her cell phone rang.

"Mrs. Phillips, it's Detective Flynn. I want to bring you up to speed on some developments. Could I impose on you…"

"I'll meet you at my house, and I thought I told you that you should call me 'Liz'."

* * * * *

It was the third item on the six o'clock news on Channel 7, behind a fire in Somerville and a gruesome car crash on Route 128. Liz and Flynn had spent the past hour comparing notes, sketching timelines, and exchanging theories. Liz looked up at the TV in the great room to see Tim Kahn being led, head down and in handcuffs, from the police station to a Norfolk County Sheriff's Office van as a crowd watched.

A voice-over intoned, "Hardington police today announced the arrest of Timothy Kahn, thirty-five, of Allston, in the death of his mother, sixty-five-year-old Sally Kahn. Police say Kahn, who has a history of substance abuse, confessed that he pushed his widowed mother down the basement stairs of her Hardington home Tuesday evening in a dispute over money."

Chief Harding, in dress blues, spoke in front of the police station. "This is the first homicide in Hardington in fifteen years. We have a very peaceful town and a very law abiding town. I knew Tim Kahn when he was growing up. He had all of the advantages Hardington has to offer, including the best public schools in the Commonwealth and a supportive home environment. It's sad to see a tragedy like this."

Sally Kahn's house appeared behind a blonde, blue-eyed reporter in a yellow, skirted suit. "Chief Harding told me that, although she lived modestly in this affluent community of sports stars and financial moguls, Timothy Kahn's mother had been left a multi-million-dollar estate by her husband, a high technology company executive.   Tomorrow, Kahn faces arraignment in Norfolk County Superior Court, the probable charge, manslaughter."

The two co-anchors clucked their disbelief that such a sad thing could have happened, then moved on to the drowning of a Lowell man.

"I don't believe it," Liz said. "That's it? Case over and done with?"

"As far as Chief Harding is concerned, it is," Flynn said. "He has a 'confession', he solved the case in the only acceptable way, which was death at the hands of a family member. The fact that the confession – even if it is admissible – won't hold up, and that the facts don't make sense is beside the point. Harding has his peaceful little town back and everyone will stop bugging him. The worst part is that Tim Kahn is the kind of guy that juries love to send up the river. He's an addict, he's accused of killing his widowed mother and, if he had gotten away with it, he would have become rich in the process. That's catnip for a prosecutor. The defense could show time-stamped security tapes with Kahn buying underwear at Macy's and the jury would still find a way to convict. Instead, we know Kahn was there, in his mother's house and now we even have witnesses… Holy hell."

"What?"

"The older kid. What's the name and address again?"

Liz looked at her notes. "Brian Snipes. Nine Blueberry Lane."

"Brian Snipes," Flynn said. "That's Tom Snipes' kid. There's only one house on Blueberry Lane and it belongs to Tom Snipes."

"You've lost me." Liz kept thinking, *Snipes? Who are the Snipes?*

"You obviously don't watch football. The New England Patriots. They have a quarterback. His name is Tom Snipes. He wears number nine on his jersey. He has twenty acres on the

Charles. The access road is called Blueberry Lane. Brian Snipes lives there. It was the first thing I was shown when I got to town. 'This is where Tom Snipes lives.'"

"I guess I'm more of a baseball fan."

"Well, we certainly just complicated things. I am required to produce all evidence, corroborating and exculpatory, to the Norfolk DA. He, in turn, has to make that evidence available to the defense – in this case, the Public Defender's office. Even a green attorney straight out of Suffolk Law is going to understand that this changes the case."

"Is that good or bad?" Liz asked.

"It means one thing," Flynn said. "I have to hand over a murderer. Not a suspect and not something someone can turn into 'reasonable doubt'. I have to find out who did this and get conclusive evidence. And I have to do it behind Harding's back, off the clock, and out of sight."

"You're welcome to this kitchen counter, but what's wrong with doing it from home? You do have a home, don't you?"

"Yes, but it's complicated. Leave it at that. Won't your husband wonder who the guy is in the kitchen?"

"David will be home tomorrow evening at six-thirty, assuming USAir is on time. My husband is an itinerant CEO. He fixes and sells broken companies. That's his business. Phillips Management LLC. At present, the broken company is in Pittsburgh, and he's in month six of what was supposed to be a five-month assignment. Right now, it looks like another two months. He leaves every Monday morning at six-thirty, he arrives home every Friday evening, weather permitting."

"I'm very sorry. It must be rough on you."

"Don't be sorry," Liz said. "When this assignment is over, we'll have about six weeks before he starts again and, if my schedule allows, we'll spend a good part of it in Italy or France, or somewhere with very nice weather and luxurious surroundings.

His services are in very high demand these days. Being an itinerant CEO pays very well. It's just that the hours are hell."

Flynn smiled. "Just like being a detective, except for the pay thing."

"By the way, as long as we're solving mysteries, what do you suppose those boys were doing inside that foundation?" Liz asked.

Flynn laughed. "That's no mystery. They were downloading porn."

"From a basement?" Liz looked confused.

"Liz, how many computers do you have in this house? Three? Four? And does each one have some dial-up line to go to AOL? No, you have ultra-high-speed broadband either from your cable company or the phone company. And they gave you a block box called a router that allows all of your computers to be on line without all those messy wires. Right?"

"Two computers plus the one David travels with, and yes, it's all wireless."

"And when you turn on the computer, what access code do you enter? What's your password?"

"There isn't one. I go straight to the Internet."

"Exactly," Flynn said. "That router is a little tiny transmitter and receiver that, as far as you're concerned, covers the house. Except that it actually covers about a hundred and fifty feet in all directions. And, I'll bet everyone on the street has exactly the same set up. Now, you're back about two hundred feet from the street, and so no one can tap into your router. But up on Pequot Court, all the houses are about fifty or sixty feet from the street. And they've all got routers, too. And, the McStupids, who really want a strong signal in the basement, take it all a step further and buy a booster to put on their router, so its broadcast range is more like five hundred feet. So the kids find a nice little place to plant themselves where they can choose between three or four networks. They log onto the one with the strongest signal and head straight for the web sites that offer porn."

"Don't those sites charge?" Liz asked.

"Sure, and the kids bill it straight to you. Do you buy stuff on line?"

"Yes."

"And when you fill out an order form on that 'safe and secure' site, do you let your computer save that information so you don't have to type in your complete name and address? Well, these kids are smart. You and I had to learn how to use computers as adults. They've been using them since they were toddlers. It's second nature, and grabbing your credit card information off your computer from your router is a piece of cake, because you store it there for your convenience."

"That's awful," Liz said.

"Exactly," Flynn said. "So on Tuesday evening, little Brian Snipes and little Kyle Wallace and three or four of their friends were busy eavesdropping on routers on Pequot Court in order to download 'Hot Teenage Tarts' or something like that, and I'll bet that next month, three families are going to find some unexplained charges from a company they never heard of with some innocuous name like, "Middlefield Marketing Corporation". And, because it's twenty bucks, they'll pay it and think their spouse charged something. Eavesdropping on home networks isn't against the law. It's just stupidity on the part of the homeowner. But swiping credit card information is a federal offense. And, if 'Teen Tarts' is on Brian's iPad – and I'll bet dollars to donuts that it is – and if there's also a record that he paid for it with the McStupid's Visa card, all of Tom Snipes' lawyers aren't going to be enough to get that charge dismissed."

Liz had an idea. "Could I eavesdrop? You said it's not illegal."

"On who?"

"Irina Burroughs. She was frightened that the police would want to know about her email or web site usage."

"Borrowing a router's signal is one thing, Liz. Using it to mirror someone's computer kind of pushes the envelope."

"But you were going to have to question her anyway, weren't you?"

"Yes, but that was back before the case got 'solved' for me by my boss. I don't have a reason to talk to Irina any more. And, if I rely on information that you obtained under questionable circumstances, that's 'tainted fruit' in the eyes of the law. Nothing's admissible. The case gets thrown out."

"I watch '*Law and Order*', too," Liz said. "Isn't there a thing called 'inevitable discovery' that gets around that?"

"It depends on the judge and on the competency of the attorneys," Flynn said. "If we were in Boston, I could tell you with about ninety-five percent accuracy if you told me who was handling the case and in what court. I don't know Norfolk County. But the first question is, why are you so interested in Irina as a suspect? In a world of motives to kill, being made a fool of at a club meeting doesn't exactly ring the bell."

Liz shook her head. "Call it woman's intuition. Or, maybe it's knowing the realities of small-town life. If Sally was really going to prove Irina was a thief right in front of thirty-five people, that's a big thing in a small town. Clubs are important and, for a lot of reasons, the garden club is one of the 'high status' organizations in Hardington."

Liz looked at Flynn's face to see if he was accepting her argument. "And people love to talk. By Wednesday night, those thirty-five people would have told a couple of hundred people. Irina Volnovich Burroughs, who not many people liked to begin with, would find herself utterly friendless in a town where people have a long memory for gossip. She's got a big house she's trying to sell and, while this sounds crude, she needs a husband. She's gone through two and needs number three or else she's going to be in big financial trouble. And believe me, getting a job selling clothes at Talbot's isn't going to cover the mortgage on a house in Shady Oak Estates. She got the equity in two houses from her second divorce, but not much else. She's probably tapping into that equity to live on."

"Why not just drop the price and sell the house?" Flynn asked.

"She would if it were that simple," Liz said. "You have to see that house of hers to understand why it isn't selling. The first realtor, who had the listing for three months, is someone in the garden club, and she said she had trouble getting people through the front door. The ones she did get to go in – and she said most of them were 'relos' from New Jersey – took one look at the decoration and said, 'get me out of this place.' Irina's got a white elephant and the only way it will sell is for her to accept a price that will wipe out all her equity."

"So, you think she would kill someone to keep her reputation intact?" Flynn asked.

Liz nodded. "If she thought she could get away with it – and I mean never be suspected and watch someone else go to prison for it – would she push Sally down the stairs and make certain she was dead? Yes. Yes, she would. Because for Irina, this is about whether she has a future. At the risk of sounding catty, I'll bet she's got someone – and by that, I mean some guy – hooked right now. But he isn't reeled in. And, until that guy is truly landed – and that means married, not engaged – she's at risk. Sally threatened all of that, all over a hundred dollars worth of flowers."

Flynn was silent. He said, "Hmmm," a couple of times. Then he said, "Even if I buy it, how do you prove it? It's a nice theory, and I admit that I'm starting to like it, but there's no evidence. We can put a woman who may or may not have been Irina at Mrs. Kahn's house around nine. But the woman left without ever going into the house. There's nothing in the physical evidence collected at the scene that would link her – unless we get lucky on fingerprints. She's an émigré, so her fingerprints are on file. And, by the way, we need to eliminate all of the prints we can. You need to provide a set, too."

"Mine are already on file," Liz smiled.

Flynn looked at her in surprise. "Are you an émigré, too? Or do you have a record?"

"I had a 'secret' clearance. For that, the government gets a set of your fingerprints."

"Do I get to ask why you had such a clearance, or is that a secret, too?"

"No. I spent five years at Brookhaven National Laboratory out on Long Island. I was a particle physicist, working on their big linear accelerator. Or at least I was trying to."

"You were 'trying to'," Flynn repeated. "What happened?"

"I discovered two things. First, that a Masters in physics, even if it's from MIT, entitles you to calibrate equipment. It doesn't qualify you to do research. No PhD, no research."

"What was the other thing?"

"That even if I spent two or three years getting a PhD, I would still be qualified only to calibrate equipment. And do you want to know why?"

Flynn nodded. "Because you were a woman, and someone in a skirt would distract all the geeky guys trying to do research. But that was, what, the early eighties. By then, things were changing, weren't they?"

"I got my MS in 1977. And things wouldn't change for at least another fifteen years."

Flynn quickly added five years to his estimate of Liz's age. *She's my age. My god.*

"So you gave it up to be a wife and mother?"

"No, I gave it up to sell lab equipment."

"Calling on the same geeky guys who wouldn't let you do research?"

She smiled. "Calling on lots of geeky guys. Who were only

too glad to buy lab equipment from me."

"One of whom asked you to marry him?"

"No, I met David on a flight from Boston to San Francisco. He was the rising executive. And to finish out the story, we were married in 1983, which is when we moved to Hardington the first time. Sarabeth was born in 1985. Except for three years in Hong Kong when he was running his company's Asian operations, we've been here ever since."

"For a scientist, you've approached this as more of an intuitive process," Flynn said.

"Scientific research is all about intuition," Liz said. "The best scientists get 'hunches' – feelings that become a theory. If it withstands initial scrutiny, then they put together a set of tests to prove or disprove the theory. No one just starts experimenting."

"Do you want to hear my theory?" Flynn asked.

Liz nodded.

"I like Landini Brothers. I don't have a motive for them – and getting tired of having someone in your face all of the time complaining about noisy trucks is not a motive – but something about that place isn't right. You have an operation that seems to go out of its way to avoid creating an auditable paper trail – I mean, no computers, and records kept on little scraps of paper. You have three guys out in a flatbed truck at six in the morning coming from the opposite direction from where their biggest job is. If I were taking bets, I'd say they're linked to Sally Kahn's death. I can smell something rotten going on."

"Maybe Sally saw something?" Liz asked.

"If there's a link, that's probably it. I have old buddies in Major Crimes. If the Landinis are crooked, there may be something in their files." Flynn looked at his watch. "You're a gracious host, but I've got a visit to pay on the Wallace and the Snipes families. I always wanted to see where a genuine sports legend lived."

Liz waited until Flynn's car was out of the driveway. Then she called a neighbor on Old Schoolhouse. "Monica, it's Liz. I'm having a serious computer problem. I know it's a school night, but do you think I could borrow Jason for about half an hour?"

Twenty minutes later, Jason Kincaid, swearing that he had never done such a thing before, and acknowledging only that he had heard such things discussed by other kids at Hardington Middle School, was providing Liz with step-by-step instructions on how to set up a peer-sharing network using an unprotected router and a shareware program found readily on the Internet.

* * * * *

Twelve-year-old Kyle Wallace's father was not, in fact, an attorney. He was a portfolio manager at Evergreen Asset Management and was astonished to find a detective on his doorstep on what had been, to that time, a rather quiet evening. The interrogation was gentle and designed not to alarm the parents, who had been under the impression that their son had been at a neighbor's home, playing video games on Tuesday evening.

Kyle confirmed that he had stayed until about nine o'clock, that 'Brian' was still there when he left, and that a woman dressed principally in black and with short, dark hair had approached the house, gone around to the side, and then re-appeared. The woman had entered and exited through the foot trail leading from Pequot Court down to the schools.

Kyle also confirmed that Sally Kahn had left the house shortly before eight and returned less than twenty minutes later with a man in her car. She did not come out of the house nor did the man leave. Flynn probed for descriptions of the dog walkers and the cars that came into the cul-de-sac, but could learn only that the dog being walked was a golden retriever. Flynn never asked what was transpiring in the foundation. He assumed an adolescent could concoct a parentally suitable lie given a few minutes to work on the subject.

Armed with that information, he drove the mile and half to Blueberry Lane. He was not surprised to find that the road was gated about a quarter mile down, and he patiently identified himself to a woman whom he surmised to be either a housekeeper or Felicity Snipes, who frequently appeared with her husband in commercials for Chevrolet and Honeydew Donuts that appeared on local stations.

Nine Blueberry Lane was an authentic-looking English country house built with Cotswold stone and a slate roof, but instead of deer or bear heads on the wall of the paneled room where they sat, the wall was adorned with football memorabilia and autographed photos. The impact was intended to be both impressive and intimidating.

"Your son may have unknowingly observed events that led up to a murder, Mrs. Snipes," Flynn said, using his best manners. "I can speak here with him, in the privacy of your home, which I'm certain is preferable to his coming to the police station. Assuming his statement is consistent with what I've already learned, it is quite likely that his presence there will never need to be disclosed, nor his reasons for being there."

Felicity Snipes was dressed in a cashmere sweater and jeans, her countenance radiant but her hands on her hips in an aggressive stance. "And why was he there?"

"That's a subject for discussion between you, your husband, and your son. I'll just say that what he was doing was illegal. I don't want it to be part of the record. I want to respect your family's privacy. If you can give me about two minutes alone with him – and because you won't be present it means that everything said is completely off the record – I think I can work it so that nothing we say *on* the record can be discoverable."

Felicity Snipes, who was widely regarded to be twice as bright as her husband, nodded. She paused for a few moments, and then said, "I'll get him. You have five minutes alone, then I'll join you.

And, if at any point I believe I don't like where the conversation is going, I'm going to shut it down."

"Which is your right, except that the next time we meet, it might well be under much more public circumstances," Flynn said.

She nodded. She understood.

Brian Snipes, age fourteen, had his mother's good looks and the budding musculature of his father. He did not look the least bit scared, or even concerned. Clearly, he had several hours to think through his story and was ready.

"Brian, what we're going to say for the next few minutes is strictly off the record. When your mother comes in, we're going to be on the record. Do you understand?"

"Yeah."

"Son, you've gotten your family into a world of trouble. You and your buddies broke about five federal laws down in that basement. Sitting on that computer in your room is a bunch of videos you downloaded, and you paid for them with other people's credit cards. Now, after this conversation, you can go in and erase them, but you know as well as I do that they're still going to be there."

Brian Snipes had been prepared for one conversation. It wasn't this one. "I want a lawyer," he said.

"No, you don't, son. In fact, a lawyer is the last thing you want because, right now, it's just you and me talking off the record. The minute your mother walks in, or some lawyer sits down, it all becomes official, and that's when ESPN is going to start reporting that the son of Tom Snipes is under investigation for federal anti-piracy and computer fraud. Do you understand that?"

Brian Snipes' mind was racing and his eyes were darting around the room. "I didn't do anything…"

"That's the wrong answer, son, because that's a lie. I know exactly what you were doing and, by tomorrow morning, I'll know the credit card numbers you used and I'll get a subpoena for your iPad. And even if you take a sledge hammer to it and toss it off the dock into the Charles River, we'll still be able to recover that information. Like I said, you've gotten your family into a world of trouble, and the only thing that will save them – and you – is the truth. Do you understand?"

Now Brian Snipes was pale. "Yes."

"The correct answer is, 'yes, sir.' Flynn paused.

"Yes, sir."

"Brian, what time did Kyle leave to go home?"

"Just at dusk, sir. He said he had to be home before dark."

"And did you see the woman in black go around the back of the house?"

Brian started to speak, then paused. "Yes, sir."

"And what time did you leave?"

"A few minutes after Kyle. Right at dark," Brian said quickly.

"Son, that's your first lie, and it's the only one you get. You lie again and I bring your mother in here. What time did you leave?"

"A little after ten." Brian's face was ashen.

"What time did your parents get home?"

"Ten-thirty, roughly. I beat them home by about ten minutes."

"You don't have a housekeeper?"

"Yes, but she watches television in her room at night."

"Did you see the man whom Mrs. Kahn drove come out of the house?"

"Yes, sir."

"What time was that?"

"Right at about ten. I was checking the clock on my iPad."

"Did you see Mrs. Kahn?"

"She was at the front door. She said she'd feel better driving him to the train station, or something like that."

"Did you observe anyone else in the vicinity between the time that man left and when you left?"

"There was someone in the bushes. I think it may have been

that same woman. It was dark, though, and I couldn't see. The guy who came out of the door was acting kind of strange. It was all kind of spooky."

"How was he acting spooky?"

"Like he was jumpy. He really wanted to get out of there."

"Thank you, Brian. Now, let's talk with your mother here."

Felicity Snipes had been on the phone in an adjacent study. She cut short her conversation when Flynn stood in the doorway. "We're ready," he said.

"Our lawyer doesn't think it would be wise to continue."

"I thought you'd have a better lawyer than that, Mrs. Snipes. Let's have the conversation and, if you don't like the direction, you can cut it off."

Felicity Snipes reluctantly agreed.

Flynn pulled the same small tape recorder he had used that morning with Tim Kahn from his jacket pocket and turned it on. "I am taking a voluntary statement from a minor whom I will identify only as Brian. Brian's mother is present and has assented to her son giving this statement. Brian's mother has further requested and I have assented, that this statement may be voluntarily withdrawn at any time. Are these statements correct?" He turned the tape recorder in the direction of Brian and Felicity. Both said, "Yes."

"Brian said he was in the vicinity of 11 Pequot Court on the evening of June thirteenth. At approximately 7:40 p.m., he observed a woman matching the description of Sally Kahn leave her home in a Toyota Prius. The woman left the house alone. Is that correct, Brian?"

"Yes, sir."

"And the woman returned approximately twenty minutes later with a man in the passenger seat of her car."

"Yes, sir."

"And, at approximately ten o'clock., what did you observe?"

"I saw the man leave by the front door of the house."

"And did you see the woman?"

"She was standing in the front door and asked if she could give him a ride to the train station."

"Brian, I believe that completes the statement insofar as we are prepared to accept it this evening. I understand that you may have additional information to volunteer at a later time but have elected to hold in abeyance for the present. Is that correct?" Flynn looked at Brian and nodded vigorously.

"Yes, sir."

"That completes the statement. Thank you."

Flynn snapped off the recorder. "Mrs. Snipes, as I told you earlier, my hope is that your family will never get involved with this beyond Brian's statement just now. I'll drop off a copy of the statement tomorrow for your attorney to review."

"That won't be necessary," she said, and showed him a digital recorder about the size of a pack of gum. "But I thank you for the offer."

Flynn got up to leave. "One last thing, and I need to say it to you in private."

"Go to your room," Felicity said to Brian. He left, wordlessly.

"Mrs. Snipes, this is a pivotal time for your son. What happens over the next few days is going to determine how Brian perceives the fairness of society and his place in it. I predict that tomorrow, your lawyer is going to suggest that you take an action that would have the result of ensuring that your son can never be held responsible for what he was doing Tuesday night, and it will be very tempting to do so. But, if you follow that advice, you will undermine the value of what Brian said in that statement. That's because, without the evidence that incriminates Brian, there is no rational explanation of why your son was able to observe activities spaced several hours apart. As you may have figured out, Brian saw Mrs. Kahn's son leave her house, with Mrs. Kahn very much alive, at a time before Mrs. Kahn was killed. Your son is his alibi. We can account for Tim Kahn's movements the rest of the evening. We know he didn't go back to the house."

"And if I ask my lawyer to take care of this?" Felicity Snipes asked.

"If you or your attorney takes care of this for Brian, then it sends him a signal that there are no consequences for his actions," Flynn said. "Mom and Dad will pay or do what it takes. And that vastly increases the chances that Brian will keep doing things that get him in trouble, which means he and I will become much better acquainted, which is not a good thing."

"Mrs. Snipes, I'm working to put together a case that proves who the murderer was. If I do that, I don't need Brian's statement because Tim Kahn's comings and goings are irrelevant. Brian's statement will come to light only if I fail. And so I'm asking you and your husband to do what it takes to make certain that Brian knows that what he did was very wrong. Is that clear?"

"It's perfectly clear."

"Then I'll say goodnight to both of you."

The time was nearly ten o'clock, the hour when drug dealers and customers connected. Flynn drove to Washington Gardens and set up an observation post near Dwayne Jones' door. He waited for a customer to show up, observed a man whom he assumed to be Jones make a sale and then go back inside. Flynn waited five minutes, then went to the door and imitated the knock the earlier customer had used.

Jones opened the door expecting the same customer. Flynn shouldered his way into the apartment, knocking Jones to the floor. Flynn showed his badge. Jones scrambled to get up and Flynn held his foot to Jones' chest. "This isn't about drugs, Dwayne. This is about your friend, Tim Kahn."

"I don't know Tim Kahn."

Flynn pressed harder on Jones' chest and the man cried out in pain. "Lies like that will get your friend sent to Concord for the next twenty years and get you a semi-private room in Walpole for about five, where I strongly suggest you do not bend over to pick up the soap in the shower. Do you want to reconsider?" Flynn kept the pressure steady on Jones' chest.

"I know Tim Kahn," Jones said cautiously.

"Good, then get up," Flynn said. "My predecessor more or less left you alone, for whatever reason. I'm willing to do the same, but the price of that is the truth. And when I say, 'the truth,' I mean a bullshit-free truth that leaves out nothing. Do you understand?"

Jones nodded.

"Then let's talk about what time he got here Tuesday night," Flynn said.

Jones got up, his eyes going to the kitchen. "Tim got here around eleven."

"What did he buy?"

"Coke. Poppers. Some bennies."

"How did he pay?"

"Cash, twenties."

"And how long was he here?"

"Five minutes."

"No longer?"

"People don't hang around."

"How did he look?"

"Like he was getting ready to celebrate. Said his mama had come through."

"Did he say where he was going?"

"Haskell's place. That's…"

"I know where he lives," Flynn said. "That's it. I don't think you'll ever have to testify to that in court, but you may want to write it down just in case. Mr. Jones, I'm glad we understand one another. You stay away from the school-aged crowd, I stay away from you. Otherwise, it will be my pleasure to station a patrol car outside of your apartment every evening for an indefinite period."

"You need anything?"

Flynn smiled. "Just the truth. Good night, Mr. Jones."

Driving back to Roslindale, Flynn allowed himself to say aloud what he had been thinking much of the day. *"God damn it, I miss you Vicky. Where the hell are you when I need you, Vicky Lee?"*

Annie, his wife, was sound asleep in their bedroom when he got home. Flynn silently retrieved clothes for the next day, stretched out on the family room sofa, and was soon sound asleep.

6.

Friday

Liz was awake before five. She allowed herself ten minutes to scratch and pet Abigail while she planned her day. Long before six, she had showered and had breakfast. Just before six, she was at Sally Kahn's wayside garden site, weeding tools at the ready – and prepared to watch and observe.

She called David a minute before six. "You'd better be packed," she said, brightly.

"Packed, fed, and ready to check out. Eight hours in the office, half an hour to the airport, an hour through security and in my seat at 3:35. I know the drill."

"Sally's memorial service starts at seven, it'd be nice if you could make it."

"Then I will make it."

"I'm told I'm speaking. Thoughts on what to say? I don't have a lot of experience in these things."

"Tell jokes. Tell the most amusing things you ever did with Sally. Tell about the time the two of you talked your way into that flower show as judges."

It was an amiable chat, fifteen minutes of normalcy after two days of tension. But as she talked and exchanged endearments, she scanned the area. Did the cars in the driveway opposite the site seem to belong there? Was there something about the way the driver of the Lexus looked at her as he paused for the 'yield' sign? She said goodbye, and then she saw the truck and remembered Detective Flynn's words. *"Three guys out in a flatbed truck at six in the morning coming from the opposite direction from where their biggest job is…"*

Three guys in a flatbed truck. The back of the truck contained dirt-encrusted black drums. No writing on the truck identified its ownership.

She dropped to her knees and began pulling at imaginary weeds. The truck paused at the yield sign, then stopped as it became apparent it could not ease into traffic on Main Street. The drums, strapped to the rails of the flatbed, sloshed loudly. Whatever was in them was liquid. Liz did not look up. The truck was still for what seemed like an inordinate time, then it lurched forward, gears grinding. As it did, a trickle of liquid from the flatbed sprayed onto the bark chips. Only then did Liz look up and memorize the license plate of the truck.

When the truck was out of sight, she gathered the bark chips onto which the truck had just sprayed the liquid. For good measure, she also pulled up two of the annuals that had died, the ones immediately adjacent to the bark chips. All these items went into plastic bags.

Liz worked steadily for another half an hour, then gathered her belongings and drove to Shady Oak Estates. She drove two or three houses beyond Irina's and waited. Less than ten minutes later, two garage doors went up simultaneously at the house next to Irina's. A man and woman in matching BMWs backed out and drove away. As soon as they were out of sight, Liz backed into their driveway.

She judged herself to be less than thirty feet from Irina's house, which was sufficiently close to capture a router signal if there was one. She opened her computer and followed Jason Kincaid's instructions. Right-click on the computer icon to VIEW AVAILABLE WIRELESS NETWORKS. A window popped up. CHOOSE A WIRELESS NETWORK. There were two: "MCCORMICK" and "LINKSYS-G". "McCormick" must be the house in whose driveway she was parked. Jason had told her "Linksys-G" was the default network name for a common brand of router. Liz doubled clicked on "Linksys-G" and held her breath.

Thirty seconds later, she was connected.

She launched the program Jason had downloaded and waited while it initiated. She then clicked, "SCAN FOR COMPUTERS."

Nothing.

Which meant Irina's computer was not turned on. Frustrated, Liz clicked repeatedly, each time getting "NONE FOUND".

Then, one of the three garage doors at Irina's house began to go up. Liz lay back in her seat, convinced Irina was about to walk over and demand to know what she was doing.

Instead, a mud-spattered Range Rover backed out of the garage. It was driven by a man in a brown windbreaker and plaid shirt. He was handsome in a rugged way and appeared to be in his early forties. He gave a little wave and a smile to someone in the garage, then completed the backing-out process and turned onto the street. The garage door went back down.

Irina's lover. Or one of her lovers. And he looked vaguely familiar.

Liz waited ten minutes, then clicked, "SCAN FOR COMPUTERS". This time, the message came back, "ONE COMPUTER FOUND." It asked "MIRROR? YES/NO".

Liz clicked "yes."

* * * * *

At six o'clock, Flynn and Billy Toole drove slowly past the Landini Brothers entrance. Flynn pointed out the squat main office by the road and the large concrete mixing facility a hundred yards into the complex. Billy wore jeans, a dark gray tee-shirt, construction boots and a yellow hard hat, attire identical to that of the dozen men Flynn had seen during his earlier visit.

"Blend in. Carry something," Flynn said. "Don't talk to people, just wait for my signal. He handed Billy a small walkie-talkie and a handkerchief. "When you hear this squawk, it means the truck passed me and is on its way into the complex. Tell me where it goes. If the drums get unloaded, keep an eye on them. If you can get close without drawing attention, wipe any liquid you see on any of the drums. But if you're in there fifteen minutes after that truck pulls in, you're in there too long. Walk out and try to stay out of sight of the office. I'll be at the boat ramp."

Flynn stopped the car. Billy gave him a 'thumbs up' and started walking back to the entrance. Flynn drove to the boat ramp. Ten minutes later, the unmarked truck passed him, carrying what appeared to be eight or nine black drums encrusted in dirt. He pushed the button on the walkie-talkie and prayed it worked.

Twenty minutes later, he saw Billy walking the shoulder of the road toward him. Even at a considerable distance, he could see a smile.

"Mission accomplished, sir." Billy saluted and then handed Flynn his handkerchief, now enclosed in a plastic bag.

"I walked in, saw a five gallon bucket and started carrying it like I belonged there," Billy said. "Nobody paid any attention to me. I saw the truck pull in – three guys like you said it probably would be. They had nine drums in the back. I started walking toward the concrete mixing building and kind of veered off when the truck went by so they couldn't see my face. The truck stopped at the mixing facility's loading platform. The three men got out of the cab, unlashed the drums, and wheeled them onto the dock. That took about five minutes. Then the men got back in the truck and drove it toward the gravel pit out back."

"Didn't they do something with the drums right away?" Flynn asked.

"The drums just sat there on the loading dock with no one paying any attention to them," Billy said, "but I was starting to hear machinery starting up inside the building, so I figured it was now or never. I just walked in an arc and ended up by the drums. Nobody was back there so I just got out the handkerchief, wiped my forehead, then turned and wiped down as many of the drums as I could reach. Then I picked up my bucket and started walking toward the road. Nobody stopped me. It was like I was invisible."

Flynn examined the handkerchief through the plastic bag. The caked dirt he had observed on the barrels made it clear they did not contain machine oil or any lubricant. He could make nothing of the greenish-black stains on the handkerchief. The evidence Billy had just gathered – if it was indeed evidence – had been garnered illegally. There was no warrant, no probable cause. Evidence gained through illegal trespass had no standing and certainly no admissibility in court. The rules of such things, at least in Massachusetts courts, were perfectly clear. But it was the only thread, however tenuous, that linked Landini Brothers to Sally Kahn's murder.

Had the drums contained machine oil, then Landini Brothers would have been a dead end, barring physical evidence from Sally Kahn's home. And, had they contained common lubricants, then the motive for the murder of Sally Kahn would have receded into an implausible retaliation for making a nuisance of herself.

But drums that were covered with dirt were drums that had had until recently been buried somewhere. Whatever was in the drums was now on this handkerchief, and whatever the substance was, it was apparently worth killing for. Now, it all made sense.

Testing the handkerchief, though, was problematic. There was no way to put it through the state testing laboratory because doing so raised the question of how it had been obtained. Flynn thought to himself, wryly, that his position was exactly that of young Brian Snipes. An illegal action had led to potentially important evidence. *I have friends, they have friends, and together we can find a way to get this tested without questions being asked.*

Flynn dropped off Billy Toole at the Hardington train station to ride back into the city with the morning commuters. By seven o'clock, he was at his desk in the police station, which was empty except for the dispatcher. The shift change did not come until eight, and Chief Harding seldom arrived before then. Flynn had an hour.

He first scanned the Department of Justice criminal database using phonetic variations on the names of the three drivers and found one hit. Michael Pastore of Quincy had three arrests for assault, including one in which a victim had been slapped repeatedly while being threatened. There were no convictions because key witnesses had failed to appear in court. Pastore's fingerprints were on record. LaRusse and Sypek were unknowns.

An email was also waiting for him, a report on fingerprints found in Sally Kahn's home. It showed:

Drip coffeemaker: SALLY KAHN, unidentified
Coffee pot: SALLY KAHN, unidentified
Sugar canister: SALLY KAHN, unidentified
Beer cans: SALLY KAHN, TIMOTHY KAHN, unidentified
Coffee vacuum pack: insufficient to identify
Cereal bowl: unidentified
Kitchen counter: SALLY KAHN, TIMOTHY KAHN
Refrigerator: SALLY KAHN, TIMOTHY KAHN
Cereal box: SALLY KAHN, unidentified

He had hoped – no, he had expected – for there to be fingerprint evidence, and for that evidence to provide the concrete lead he needed. Then he read the list again. *Coffee pot: S. Kahn, unidentified.*

Where were Liz Phillips' fingerprints? Her prints should have been all over the handle.

Flynn picked up the phone and called the BPD Crime Lab. His watch said 7:20 a.m., so his chances of getting someone were…

"Crime Lab."

The gods were smiling. Ten minutes later, Flynn had established that the search for matching fingerprints has been restricted to those supplied by the medical examiner and the "local interest" subset maintained by a consortium of Boston-area law enforcement agencies. Flynn asked for a wider search.

"Make sure it includes the FBI, whatever jurisdiction includes things like government laboratories, and also the Immigration and Naturalization Service."

"That'll add a day," Flynn was warned.

"Do it."

Next, Flynn walked out to the dispatcher's desk and asked who would have been on patrol duty Tuesday evening.

The dispatcher pointed to the locker room. "Eddie Frankel. He's in there right now."

Flynn found Eddie Frankel at his locker. They had met briefly when Flynn joined the department a month earlier. Frankel was in his early twenties and very earnest. He also stood out as the only African-American on the Hardington police force.

"You were the guy who walked in on the Boston PD crime scene guys?" Frankel acknowledged that he was, and the answer raised Flynn's estimation of the young officer. When something was out of place, he noted it and investigated. "Does your evening patrol include the school parking lot?"

"I'm through there usually three times before midnight, once after."

"Think about what kind of cars you might have seen Tuesday evening – the night Sally Kahn was killed."

Frankel did not answer for nearly a minute.

"White Ford Explorer parked overnight," Frankel said, finally. "Didn't move. Couple of kids in one of those cars that looks like it has a Port-a-Potty strapped to the back. It wasn't there at eight. They left as soon as I drove by. That was at ten. Black Mercedes SUV. No one inside. It wasn't there at eight but it was there at ten and it was gone at half past eleven."

"The Mercedes. Where was it parked, and did you get a plate?" Flynn asked.

"West end of the lot. Sorry, no plate. Nothing distinguishing about it."

Flynn attempted to orient himself to the geography. "That's

near the footpath that goes up to Pequot Court?"

"That's the closest point, yes."

"And the kids in the Port-a-Potty car?"

"Parking. At least I assume they were parking. I saw a transfer station sticker on the car and so I left it alone. I've seen the car around town."

"What's a transfer station sticker?" Flynn asked.

"For the dump, or what used to be the dump," Frankel said. "If you take your trash and recyclables to the transfer station, you need a sticker. It's a green 'H' on the back windshield. You don't see a lot of them because most people have curbside pickup from one of the private hauling firms. It's kind of a townie thing."

"Would the car likely be in the high school lot?"

"It's worth a look. Is this about the murder?"

"Yeah," Flynn said. "I'm trying to tie up all of the loose ends. Can we take a drive?"

Hardington High School's first classes were at 7:30, and the student parking lot was filled as they drove through in Frankel's patrol car. Flynn noted the preponderance of new, sporty cars and SUVs.

"Don't these kids' parents believe in handing down their old pieces of junk to their kids?" Flynn asked.

Frankel grinned. "That's Boston thinking. These kids... I pulled over one driving a brand new $35,000 Road Runner yesterday. He ran a red light. The kid pulls out the license and registration... the car's registered in his name. I asked, 'is this a graduation present?' and the kid says, 'naw, I'm only a junior.' These Hardington kids, they think they've got it rough because they've got a two-year-old SUV. I grew up in Brockton. We drove fifteen-year-old Toyotas and thought we had it made."

"Is that it?"

They pulled alongside an olive-colored Honda Element and Frankel looked it over. "That's the one. Sticker's in the right place and everything."

Frankel punched the license plate into the patrol car's computer. "William Esdale, 52 Pinnacle Road. One outstanding ticket for speeding. Got tagged out on the Pike. Eighty in a 65 zone."

"How do you speak to students during school?"

"Unless it's an emergency, they ask us to wait until lunch," Frankel said. "The dean gets them from their last class and brings them to the office. They don't like police in the hallways."

"How very civilized," Flynn said, sardonically. "OK, let's go back to the station."

For the next hour, Flynn busied himself typing up reports and witness interviews. He carefully constructed a timeline that showed Tim Kahn's arrival in Hardington, his presence at the house, his drug buy at around eleven o'clock, and his spending the night and into the next day with Joe Haskell. He noted the fingerprint evidence and the discrepancies in Tim Kahn's earlier statements. Left out of the narrative were the statements by the two boys and any alternate theory of the crime. These, he would prepare separately.

At nine o'clock, he knocked on Chief Harding's door.

"There are more details, but this is the basic report," Flynn said. "I'll flesh it out so that it's all complete on Monday."

Chief Harding read through the three pages carefully, his face showing suspicion. "I don't see anything about the confession in here."

"I didn't take the confession so I can't write it up. I assume you're appearing at the arraignment and will respond to any questions about it."

"I had planned to go." Chief Harding was again in his dress blues. Flynn noted the six ribbons and wondered if they were for perfect attendance. "The arraignment is scheduled for eleven, I'll ask the Norfolk DA to call you for copies of all of the interviews."

Flynn turned to leave. "John..." Flynn turned back. *What now?*

"I was rough on you yesterday," Chief Harding said. "I shouldn't have been. You've been used to doing things a certain way for a long time. We do things differently here. You can't be expected to learn everything about how this department works overnight. Just remember, this isn't Boston. It's a small town and things are much less complicated."

"I appreciate that, Chief."

Flynn went back to his desk and called the high school to arrange for an interview with William Esdale. He was told to be at the guidance office at 11:45. Then he pulled the bagged handkerchief from out of his desk drawer and stared at it.

How do I get this into evidence?

* * * * *

Liz sat at her desk and looked at the plastic bags holding the bark chips and dead annuals.

Where is a mass spectrometer when you need one?

She drummed her fingers. She thought about people she knew. Abigail rubbed her legs and purred.

In for a dime, in for a dollar.

She reached for her address book and thumbed through entries. Alvin and Linda Duclos. *It's been a long time, Alvin.* She dialed the number.

Two secretaries later, she was on the phone with the chairman of MIT's Chemistry Department.

"Alvin, I need a huge favor...."

The conventional wisdom among the residents of Hardington was that driving into Boston or Cambridge is only for those who don't care about their cars, or who had a fatal disease and expected to die anyway. Those who worked in the financial district or Back Bay rode the train and walked a well-worn path from the train station to their office. The idea of driving in for pleasure, to go shopping, or to go to a museum was simply unthinkable. Fenway Park was an exception, especially if it was a day game. But even then, the act of paying an extortionate thirty-five or forty dollars for parking reinforced the belief that driving into the city was foolhardy, if not dangerous.

Liz found a metered spot in front of the Dreyfus Building, which housed MIT's Chemistry Department. The sleek, I.M. Pei structure came long after her student days and was only an artist's concept during her days selling lab equipment. The building seemed quiet and she realized it was June and the bulk of students had departed weeks earlier. A security guard said that Alvin Duclos would meet her in the sub-basement, two floors down.

"Liz, you look wonderful." Duclos said, kissing her cheek. He was short, more rotund than she remembered from their last meeting, two years earlier at a Christmas party. He also now sported a full, gray beard. He bore more than a passing resemblance to Santa Claus in khaki pants and she hoped it was a good omen. "I love a good mystery. So tell me what it's all about."

Liz pulled the baggies from her purse. "Tuesday evening, a friend of mine was killed out in Hardington…"

"That was in the *Globe* this morning. Her son pushed her down the stairs to get the inheritance, or something like that. That sounds awful."

"I'm the one who found her.

"I'm terribly sorry for you…"

"The problem is that the son almost certainly didn't kill her. I've been working with the detective investigating the case…"

"You've become a policeman in your spare time?"

"I'm starting to feel like one. Anyway, he's convinced that, well, that a local industry is involved. The day my friend died, she had a run-in with the owner of the business. She and I are members of a garden club, and we all take care of wayside gardens.

A truck from the company ran over her site that morning and spilled something from one of the drums in back of the truck. It fell on these plants." She held up the baggie. "Then, this morning, I was watering her site when what I believe is the same truck went by and dripped something at the stop sign. It fell on the bark chips, and I collected a few."

Liz collected her thoughts for a moment. "Maybe it's connected, maybe it isn't. Maybe all we're doing is ruling out a suspect. When I saw the truck this morning, I decided to take a chance. Then I thought of you."

"So this is police evidence?"

"Well, yes, but no," Liz said. "I don't think it would be admissible because no one can prove conclusively that it came from their truck or that it was never tampered with. But *I* know where it came from and *I* know it hasn't been out of my sight. And, if there's something in it that's worth killing over, then I'll tell the detective. If it's just something ordinary, then you're the only person who'll know that I did something really stupid."

Duclos smiled. "If my arithmetic is still sound, it's been thirty-five years since we were starving graduate students together. You had one of the best intuitive minds of anyone I know. You used to run circles around all of us. Your thesis paper was so good I wanted to drop out of school and go to work for the telephone company. If your intuition is that this material needs examining, then I'll run the analysis myself. And God knows I need the brushing up."

"Alvin, thank you. But before you start, I actually have a better suspect in mind, but for that one I'm tapping into the twelve-year-old computer genius next door."

"Liz, you never cease to amaze me. Well, our lab currently houses thirteen mass spectrometers, including six NMR spectrometers, one EPR spectrometer, one Mössbauer, one high-rez fourier transform mass spectrometer, a GC-MS, a polarimeter, and two that are so specialized that even I don't understand how they're used. But I know the FT system and I know it's very fast and highly accurate. You're also here at a good time. Demand is low, the grad students are all dispersed. Let's go see what's in these samples."

The process took an hour. Duclos extracted two small chunks of the bark mulch. One mulch nugget looked to be saturated and he placed it on one tube. A second chunk appeared to be unstained. He took a wilted flower petal and put it in a third tube. The tubes went into separate chambers.

"Now we go to the work station," he said. "No more strip charts, no more matching plates. The age of the computer has freed the researcher. Matrix-assisted laser desorption replaces all those hours of... but you were in particle physics. You missed all of the grunt work."

"Not all of it. You don't want to know how many hours I spent staring at cloud chambers."

He initialized a screen and worked the keyboard. Ten minutes later, he showed the results. "There's a ton of stuff in these samples, but here's what I think we're looking for. Polycyclic aromatic hydrocarbons, specifically, Benzapyrene. It's in the bark chip and it was absorbed into the flower. What exactly does this company do?"

"They make concrete. Alvin, please remember I majored in physics, not chemistry. Polycyclic whatever is a new one on me."

"Polycyclic aromatic hydrocarbons, or just PAH," Duclos said. "You get PAHs from fairly normal activities, like grilling a steak. Benzapyrene, though, is a different issue. It's a super-saturated PAH, industrially made, and used in things like insecticide. It is a known carcinogen, there are strict guidelines on its disposal. And I assure you that adding it to concrete is not one of them."

"Then why would a company that makes concrete have drums of the stuff?" Liz asked. "Why would it be on the back of flatbed trucks?"

"Were they taking the drums out of the plant or into them?"

"The truck was driving toward the plant at six in the morning. I only saw the drums for a moment, but they looked like they were caked in dirt."

Duclos stroked his beard. "If you're willing to accept a guess – and it's a wild guess at that – I'd say that the fine people who run the concrete company think they've found a great way to dispose of a toxic chemical cheaply. You can't burn PAH's because they can be inhaled – that's the 'aromatic' part of the name. You bury them at controlled facilities and it's horribly expensive. I've heard figures of ten thousand dollars a drum."

"That's incredible!" Liz said.

"That's the cost of environmental protection," Duclos said. "Conversely, you could disperse a forty-two gallon drum of the stuff in, say, ninety cubic yards of concrete – ten truckloads – and have no effect on the concrete's ability to set. The problem, of course, is that the Benzapyrene leaches out over time. It will go into suspension with water, but it won't combine. Five years down the road, you've just transferred the problem from one site to another."

"Unless it was going into a river…"

"Beg your pardon?"

"The detective said the company had a contract to supply concrete for a big new sewage treatment plant being built in Milford."

"In which case the Benzapyrene leaches out into the outflow of the plant," Duclos said. "It's a cute trick. Except that it eventually works its way into the food chain because it doesn't break down."

"Who would try to dispose of something like that illegally?"

"Not the manufacturer, that's for sure. Today, they have to account for every gallon they produce. But, thirty or forty years ago, companies just dumped barrels. The more unscrupulous ones went out in fields, dug pits, buried a few hundred barrels at a time, covered over the pit, and then repeated the process somewhere else."

"And if I bought that field and found the barrels?" Liz asked.

"You couldn't build and you couldn't sell. Oh, you could sue whomever you bought the land from, but it wouldn't make any difference. You own it and you're responsible for the remediation. And if remediation is ten thousand dollars a barrel for seven hundred barrels, your cost of development just went up by seven million dollars, plus paying for the removal of every cubic yard of contaminated dirt. Call that another three million."

"Versus paying a crooked concrete company to take away the whole thing in the middle of the night." Liz said.

"Except that it sounds like the barrels are being taken away a few at a time," Duclos said. "You don't want to store this stuff at your site. The question is, how long has it been going on, and how much longer will it continue?"

Liz shook her head. "That's anyone's guess. It sounds like someone has to move very quickly. Do you think the EPA does raids?"

"Liz, I have some very highly placed friends in the EPA. The head of the EPA's Boston office is someone I've known for years. And, to answer your question, yes, they do raids. And in this case, they'd better do one very quickly because it sounds like every day, eight or nine drums of this stuff is getting disposed of illegally. And, if it's going into concrete for a sewage treatment plant, it's got to be stopped immediately. And, I don't pretend to know government politics very well, but catching someone red-handed like this is the sort of thing that can make someone's career. Usually the EPA finds the stuff a couple of decades after the fact."

"But Alvin, it's also likely that someone from Landini Brothers murdered my friend. Is there a way to catch them at one thing without losing the chance to convict them of the other?"

"Is Landini Brothers the concrete company you're talking about?" Duclos asked.

Liz nodded.

"Well, we'll just have to ask them that question. Do you have time to talk to my friend at the EPA?"

Liz looked at her watch. Almost noon, exactly. "Alvin, I'm supposed to deliver the principal eulogy for my friend in seven hours, and I haven't written a word. I'm also going to see David for the first time since Monday morning, and I had this grand idea of welcoming him back with a home-cooked meal. It's kind of a ritual because for the past couple of years, I haven't seen a lot of him. And I had another suspect and was going to go through her emails. But Benzapyrene pretty well nails down the motive for the murder. So, sure, let's go talk to your old pal at the EPA. But you have to let me buy a sandwich first. I'm starved."

7.

Flynn sat in the guidance office of Hardington High School. His watch showed ten minutes of noon. The clock on the wall showed 11:45. Time for him had always run slowly in school. Now, he finally had his first tangible proof.

The guidance counselor entered with a kid whom Flynn assumed was William Esdale. The counselor said, "I'll give you some privacy," and left.

The boy, tall and gangling, sat, fidgeting.

"Do you go by William or Bill?" Flynn asked, trying to put the kid at ease.

"Willy. What's this all about?" the boy asked.

"Relax, Willy. You're fine. You own a 2005 Honda Element?" Willy nodded. "And Tuesday evening, you were parked in the west end of the high school parking lot?"

Willy looked confused, then paled. "Did Darlene's parents get you to come here? Because…"

"No, Willy. Darlene's parents have no idea that I'm here. I need to know what time you pulled into the parking lot."

Willy looked relieved, though still apprehensive. He thought for a moment. "We got there a little before nine. It wasn't quite dark. More like kind of twilight."

"Were there any other cars in the lot when you got there?"

"I don't remember. There could have been one or two."

"And what time did you leave?"

"About ten. We were only there about an hour."

"Now, Willy, this is the important part. What car or cars came into the parking lot while you were there?"

Willy let out a little 'whoo' of relief. "Well, we left because a police car came through the lot…"

"I know about that one. I'm interested in any other cars."

Willy thought for a second. "It was kind of weird. This black SUV pulls into the lot, right at the corner…"

"By the path that goes up the hill?"

"Yeah, right by it."

"And what time was it?"

"About ten minutes after we got there. Anyway, neither Darlene nor I recognized the car, so we figured it wasn't anyone we knew. About two minutes later, a woman gets out of the car. We only saw that it was a woman because the car's interior lights came on."

"Can you describe her?"

"Uh, short dark hair. And she was kind of short. She was dressed all in black. Anyway, she got out of the car and walked up the hill. She came back down the path about ten minutes later. She got back by the car and made a cell phone call."

How did you know she made a call?" Flynn asked.

"It was dark when she got back. When she made the call, there was a kind of green glow from the phone. She only talked for about a minute. Then she sat in the car, which kind of freaked out Darlene. About ten minutes before the police car came through the lot, she made another call – real quick – and then got out of the car and went up the path again. Like I said, ten minutes later the patrol car came through the lot and we decided it was too crowded."

"What's Darlene's last name if I need to speak to her?"

"Giberson. She's a junior."

Flynn left Willy Esdale to contemplate alternate lovers' lanes for the future. He drove back to the police station and looked in the DMV database for a car for Irina Burroughs.

2009 Mercedes SUV. Black. *Time to go pay a visit on the much-married Ms. Volnovich* he thought.

And then the phone rang.

"Detective Flynn, this is Felicity Snipes."

Now what? he thought.

"My husband and I had a long talk with Brian last evening. I want to thank you for your advice which, I might add, was exactly the opposite of what our attorney suggested. Tom and I have talked it over. If Brian needs to testify, he will. And, if he needs to say what he was doing with his computer down in that basement, he'll admit to that, too. I don't think he realized how much trouble he put himself in. I think there's very little chance that, as you put it, you and he are going to get better acquainted. Tom came down pretty hard on him."

"I appreciate that very much, Mrs. Snipes. Like I said, my goal is to build a case that doesn't require your son's testimony. That's still my goal, though I can't promise anything."

"I do have one question, Detective. Brian said there was a woman who talked to him yesterday afternoon. She said she was a lawyer and her husband was a judge. Do you know who that was?"

Flynn laughed. "I think she was engaging in a little one-upsmanship. Brian's friend claimed his father was a lawyer and would sue her for every dime she had, or something like that. There were no lawyers, or children of lawyers present, if that's what had you worried."

"But who was it?"

"Her name is Liz Phillips. She was a good friend of Mrs. Kahn. She's president of the Garden Club. Does that help?"

Flynn heard Felicity laugh. "Yes, it sets my mind at ease. And it will make our lawyer very, very happy to hear that."

* * * * *

Fifteen minutes later, Flynn drove up Shady Oak Road. The first thing he noted was that there were no oaks and that what trees were in evidence were about five years away from providing any meaningful shade. He turned onto Apple Valley Lane, which the DMV database said was the home of Irina Burroughs. He noted the "For Sale" sign and the fountain with urinating cherubs. "Good God," he muttered to himself.

He rang the doorbell several times, long enough to establish that Irina was not home or that, if she was home, she wasn't answering the door. Using his cell phone, he left a message on her answering machine. On his way back to the station, he called the number listed at the bottom of the realtor's sign, spoke to the listing agent, and ascertained that yes, Irina Burroughs had a cell phone and of course, the number was available to the police.

Back at the station, he did not call the cell number immediately. Instead, he contacted Verizon Wireless and asked for a set of incoming and outgoing numbers for the preceding two weeks. It could take a day, he was told, but the records would be emailed to him.

Then he dialed Irina's cell phone. She did not answer. He left a polite message indicating that it was important that they speak as soon as possible.

As he hung up, Flynn wondered, for the first time, whether Irina Burroughs might be a flight risk.

* * * * *

The first conversation with the Environmental Protection Agency, among Alvin Duclos, Liz, and Loryn Wolff, the head of the EPA's Boston office, was a model of efficiency and urgency. Wolff listened to the story, asked half a dozen questions, and almost immediately had an explanation for the source of the drums.

"Puritan State Chemical created more than two dozen of these secret Benzapyrene dump sites in the '40s and '50s," Wolff explained. "The ones we've found typically contained about two hundred barrels. The largest had more than five hundred. That was just before the company declared bankruptcy in 1957. The smallest we've found was a hundred and forty barrels in a patch of land less than a hundred feet on a side. They knew what they were doing was illegal, even then. They just didn't care."

She cleared her throat and continued. "Our problem is, we don't have a map, and the last of the Puritan people who knew where the sites were died more than a decade ago. We've found twenty of them and we know there are least five more within a fifty mile radius of Boston. If I were making an educated guess, I'd say that a developer bought what he thought was a pristine piece of property somewhere south or west of Boston, started laying drains or water pipes, and hit one of these barrels. The developer took one look and made an economic, but highly unethical decision."

"I think you're going to get a gold star for this, Liz," Duclos said, quietly.

Wolff continued. "The problem for everyone is that, after fifty years, the barrels are starting to disintegrate. They've been buried in soil that is naturally acidic, and they're holding a toxic chemical. We have no way of knowing how they're being removed, but there's a good chance that some of them are either leaking or will rupture when moved. That's probably how Ms. Phillips was able to get her sample. One or more of the barrels have developed weep holes."

"What are your options?" asked Duclos.

"We can go at it two ways," Wolff said. "We can look at who has filed with the state Department of Environmental Protection for development permits of say, at least ten acres within the past six months and should be at the infrastructure stage and do site visits. Or, we can intercept the truck, either on the road or at Landini Brothers. In the meantime, we can take concrete samples at locations where their concrete is being used and verify that the Benzapyrene is present, starting with that treatment plant in Milford. What's critical is that you tell your story to the EPA counsel and investigation staff. I'll put together the conference call right now."

The second call with the EPA, held fifteen minutes later, was not going as planned. The EPA counsel reminded Wolff that he was scheduled to be at a training seminar all of the following week. The principal staff investigator had three agents out on scheduled vacation plus a two-month backlog of cases still under investigation.

"And you don't think this rises to the level of 'urgent' and perhaps some re-prioritization?" Wolff asked.

"This seminar has been on my schedule for six months," the attorney said. "And besides, getting a subpoena to intercept a truck is about as tricky as it gets. You can't just go to a judge and say, 'I want to stop a truck...'."

"Jesus Christ," Alvin Duclos said to Liz, listening to the six-way call. "How does anything get done by the federal government?"

The one thing both the EPA administrator and attorney had agreed upon, however, was that no approach should be made by any local law enforcement agency either to Landini Brothers or to the three truck drivers.

"This is a federal matter now, the local LEOs have to step back," the attorney said. "Tell your guy, don't take them in for questioning, don't pull them over for speeding, don't do anything that would cause them to change their behavior. We can't have this screwed up by local law enforcement."

"They're perfectly capable of screwing it up all by themselves," Duclos muttered.

At two o'clock, having successfully brought the matter to the attention of the highest-ranking EPA administrator in the northeast, but having learned that the EPA would first have to resolve the vacation and training requirements of its staff, Liz got back in her car and headed back for Hardington.

Her first call was to Roland Evans-Jones.

"Roland, I have never asked a favor like this of anyone, but I promised David a home-cooked meal, and I have no time to cook it. You're the only person I can trust."

"It was a slow afternoon here anyway," Roland said. "I shall dirty up many pots and pans and leave them around your kitchen to make it look authentic. You will be proud of the meal and I will leave you a complete list of ingredients, not that anyone would care."

"I'm in your debt," Liz said.

"And speaking of being proud," Roland said, "I was at the church at noon and you will be thrilled at what your committee is doing. It's so good that not even Sally could have found fault with it. Those ladies are terrific."

Her second call was to the Hardington Police Station.

"I'm afraid I've been playing Nancy Drew," Liz said. "This morning, that truck from Landini Brothers went by the wayside garden at the Post Road turnoff. I was there, watering. The truck had the same barrels on it that Sally described. Anyway, one of the barrels leaked onto the bark chips, and I took it to a friend at MIT."

"You had the stuff analyzed?" Flynn asked, incredulous.

"The chairman of the Chemistry Department and I were starving graduate students together about a million years ago. He has an entire floor full of mass spectrometers. I think he collects them as a hobby. He did the test himself."

"Tell me the material was never out of your sight," Flynn said.

"It was never out of my sight, and I have an official report on MIT letterhead, plus the original samples. Do you want to know what's in those barrels?"

"I'm suspecting that it's not hot fudge sauce."

"A rather nasty toxic chemical called Benzapyrene," Liz said. "It was probably buried in an illegal landfill about fifty years ago by a company called Puritan Chemical."

"You learned that from the analysis?"

"No, I got that from the EPA, which says you'd better stay as far away from Landini Brothers as possible."

"Liz, you better start from the beginning…"

* * * * *

At three o'clock, Flynn had drawn a neat line down the center of a sheet of paper. On the left side of the sheet he had written:

LANDINI BROTHERS

*SK SAW UNMARKED TRUCK WITH CHEMICALS

*SK FOLLOWED TRUCK TO LB AND COMPLAINED

*LB KNEW SK KNEW ABOUT TRUCK

*SK COULD BLOW THEIR OPERATION

*SK MURDERED SAME DAY AS SHE SHOWED UP AT LB

*LB HAS THUG WITH RIGHT MO ON PAYROLL

*NO EVIDENCE ANYONE FROM LB WAS AT SK HOUSE

*ALL THE MOTIVE IN THE WORLD – HOW TO PROVE?

On the right side of the sheet he wrote:

IRINA VOLNOVICH

*SK WAS GOING TO 'UNMASK' HER

*IRINA WOULD LOSE CHANCE TO LAND HUBBY #3

*IRINA SEEN OUTSIDE SK HOUSE 10 P.M.

*CSI: "A FEMALE KIND OF CRIME"

*WHO DID SHE CALL AT 9:30?

*SHE WAS THERE BUT THE MOTIVE STINKS

He stared at the paper, wondering what to add. A column for Tim Kahn? The Snipes kid had seen him come out of the house and heard Sally Kahn's offer to drive him to the train station. In theory – and only in theory – Tim could have come back to the house a few minutes later, having decided to make one more plea for a check. Instead, he got into a struggle that ended with Sally Kahn dead at the bottom of her stairs. That would explain the time gap between his leaving the house and not showing up at Joe

Haskell's until sometime after eleven o'clock. Otherwise, either Jones had poor appreciation for time or else Tim Kahn had taken a highly circuitous route to get from his mother's house to his drug buy – nearly an hour to go a mile and a half. Tim Kahn could even have gone back to his mother's house after buying the drugs, disappointed that Sally Kahn's largesse had barely covered an evening's entertainment. But that theory required that Tim have the presence of mind to try to throw off the time of death, something everyone who knew him said he lacked. And it required that he have no remorse. Haskell said Kahn had shown no tension during the night. He partied as usual, took drugs, had sex, and then slept into the afternoon.

At the bottom of the page he wrote:

TIM KAHN

*WHO WERE THE GIRLS?

A new thought occurred to him. What if Tim had an unwitting accomplice? What if Tim did return to his house and struggle with his mother but, terrified at what he had done, run from the house. Irina, who had gone to the house either to confront Sally or to kill her, sees Tim flee the scene. Irina goes in and finds Sally, and decides to give herself an alibi by throwing off the time of death. That way, everyone sees Irina at the gym the next morning. She couldn't have been at Sally's at the same time.

It all kept coming back to motive.

Tim did not get the check he expected from his mother. He had a motive – anger – that added up to a charge of manslaughter.

Landini Brothers faced the very real probability that their scheme to dispose of other people's toxic waste could be unraveled by a meddlesome old lady. *Oh, yeah, they had all the motive in the world, namely lots of money… versus going to jail as a criminal polluter.*

Irina had a motive, sort of. The more he thought about it, the harder time he had accepting that a woman's reputation would be ruined because someone stood up in front of a garden club and accused them of stealing a hundred dollars' worth of plants.   It might drive her out of the club, and it might be embarrassing for a day, but ruin a reputation? Liz had spoken of it vehemently, but it made less sense every time he probed it. Could the woman in front of Sally Kahn's home have been someone working for Landini Brothers, and the black SUV just a coincidence?

And, where was the evidence that Sally Kahn 'had the goods'? When he had gone upstairs to find the daughter's address and telephone number, he had made a point of leafing through the items on the desktop. There were no photographs, and no receipts for plants or flowers. Of course, if Irina had been in the house, she could have taken those items. He closed his eyes and mentally reconstructed the desk top. There had been the day's mail and some bills to be paid. A stack of charitable appeals on top of a lined pad of paper with notes on how much money to give to each one. A file folder labeled, '9 Pequot Court' in which were copies of correspondence between a Hardington attorney and Mahoney Construction. This was the lawsuit the daughter had spoken of. Sally Kahn's attempt to buy the property next door or stop construction of the large house. Another folder had been labeled, "Wayside Gardens" and he had seen in it only watering schedules, lists of plants to buy, and a budget.

And the desk, like the rest of the house, was neat – though Tim Kahn had apparently taken several checks from the back of his mother's checkbook, which could have been either upstairs on in her purse.

Was it on her computer? To the best of his knowledge, the computer was still in place on her desk.

Landini Brothers' motives were as close to perfect as he ever had seen. But Liz had also made clear that the EPA demanded that he keep away from the company. Until they moved at their federal pace, all he could do was rule out other suspects.

Which is when the phone rang with the Norfolk County DA

demanding to know why he had been handed a "piece of crap" case, and why the hell were Boston police investigating crime scenes in Norfolk County?

Flynn sighed, and then began explaining. Not the whole story. Just enough to buy some time. What he needed was time.

* * * * *

Liz stared at the mantle clock and then back at the lined pad of paper. It was five thirty and she had generated four paragraphs of useful material. This was shaping up to be the shortest principal eulogy in history. From the kitchen, Roland sang Italian opera and insisted he needed no help. David had not yet called, but if he had made the flight by minutes, as was his usual practice, he might not call until he landed.

I have called Sally Kahn a friend for more than twenty-five years, but she has been more than a friend. Most of what I know about gardening I learned from her. Much of what I know about sharing I learned from her...

It just wasn't coming. Not awful, but not sincere. This was going to be a disaster. She wadded up the paper and threw it into the basket, adding to a dozen other failed starts. With a fresh sheet, she drew a line down the middle of the page. On the left side, she wrote:

IRINA

-   She knew Sally was going to prove her a thief – publicly

-   Word would quickly get around, Irina's reputation would be ruined

-   Move, sell at a loss, get out of town. *Dasvidanya* Hardington

-   She was at Sally's house the night she was killed and she went to great lengths not to be seen

-   She also went to great lengths to establish an alibi for Wednesday morning, it would make sense that she set up the kitchen to throw off the time of death

-   What evidence links her to the crime, other than her presence in front of the house?

- Who was the guy in the Range Rover?

On the right side of the page she wrote:

LANDINI BROS.

- They're dumping toxic chemicals!
- If they're caught, they go to jail and they're out of business
- Sally saw their unmarked truck and followed them to Overfield – then complained
- Sally was a threat who had to be eliminated
- Make it look like an accident and there's no investigation
- Why try to throw off the time? Who cares what time she died?
- Why didn't anyone see them? (but Sally could have been killed up to midnight)
- Much, much stronger motive – but is there any evidence to link them to the crime?

Liz read what she had written. It was the first satisfying words she had put to paper in an hour and a half of effort. But she re-read the page and then added a third column:

OTHER POSSIBLITIES:

- Tim came back after Brian left and argued with Sally
- Tim is more resourceful than anyone thinks
- Tim had help
- There are people and motives we don't know about.

She put this sheet to the side.

We cannot lay Sally to rest without knowing who killed her, she thought.

Officially, Tim Kahn was the suspect. He was in the Norfolk County lockup having been arraigned for second-degree murder. Liz had heard the news on the drive home, the story now relegated to a brief mention. By tomorrow, it would be forgotten.

She put down her pen and walked into the kitchen. "I think I'm going to be ad-libbing things tonight," she said to Roland.

"I think you're going to be fine," Roland said. "And so is your dinner."

"Roland, I want you to think back very carefully and tell me about your lunch with Sally. I mean, word for word. What did she say? Was there anything in her body language?"

Roland signed. "All right. We went to Zenith. Tuesdays are a good day for me, and I didn't want to be away from the shop. If you tell Henrietta when you get there that you're in a hurry, you can actually get out of there in forty-five minutes. Right from the start, Sally was talking about Tim. She was very nervous because she was going to tell him, 'nothing more until you get yourself straight.'"

"Had she said that to Tim before?"

"Yes. And then he would start crying and making promises, and she'd give him a hug and a two thousand dollar check. This time, it really looked like she had the courage to say it and make it stick."

"What was different?" Liz asked.

"It was getting pretty clear – at least to me – that Tim's addiction was getting worse. My own guess is that what used to be a hundred-dollar-a-day habit had doubled. What he's hooked on, I have no idea, and I never discussed that with Sally because it would have hurt her too much. Instead, we just talked about his 'needs' and let it go at that."

"Did Sally talk about any of his friends?"

Roland paused. "You mean, on Tuesday or in general?"

"Either, but especially on Tuesday," Liz said.

"She considered them all bad influences. She didn't mention anyone on Tuesday."

"Had Tim brought by any of his friends on previous visits?" Liz asked.

"Oh, yes. Last month. One that Sally said was like a 'mother's worst dream'. It was one of his friends from high school, someone who still lives in Hardington. Oh, she told Tim not to bring that one back."

"Anything else?"

"Just that she had decided, 'This is it. I'm going to do what Charlie and I should have done twelve years ago'," Roland said.

"Would it surprise you if Sally gave him three hundred dollars?"

Roland looked surprised. "Yes. We had agreed that it had to be cold turkey. Not a dime. She'd pay the rent and the utilities. He had to do the rest himself."

Liz mulled that. *If she didn't give him the money, how did he get it?* Let's talk about Landini Brothers. Tell me again what she said about what she did after the truck ran up over the curb."

"Well, she said she was just about finished working her site when the truck hit the curb. She said there were three men in the truck but that it didn't say 'Landini Brothers' or anything on the side. It had some kind of barrels or something on the back and, when the truck went over the curb, it sloshed some kind of liquid onto some of her annuals. She started yelling at the truck. It pulled away but the man sitting by the passenger side door looked out and gave her the finger. Well, she said she ran to her car and started following them. Right through town, over the bridge, and into the Landini Brothers property. She said she went into the office and demanded to speak to whoever was in charge. She wanted an apology from the driver and from the person who gave her the finger. The owner came out, listened to her for a minute, and then ordered her off the property and said they'd have her arrested if she ever came in again."

"Did she give any other details about what happened?" Liz asked.

"Oh, it was just the latest in a line of indignities. She hates that company and the company hates her."

So Sally had no idea of what she had uncovered. If Landini Brothers was responsible, she was killed only because she had put together the unmarked truck with its owner.

"And Irina? What specifically did she say about Irina?" Liz asked.

"She said…. 'I've finally got the goods on Irina.' Those are the exact words she used. So I asked what she had, and she smiled and said, 'You'll see, and you'll be surprised. All I can say is, after Wednesday, Irina isn't going to be stealing from this club anymore. This time, I've got concrete evidence.'"

"Was that the end of it?"

"Oh, you know me. I kept pushing her for details. You know, 'Oh, come on, Sally, if you can't trust me, who can you trust.' And she was starting to loosen up. She says, 'Irina's a thief, and in more ways than anyone in this club imagined.' And I said, 'How?' And then… she got very quiet. Some people sat down at the table next to ours. She looked over at them, and then she said, 'Never mind, I'll tell you later.' Five minutes later, she had finished the rest of her lunch, gave me the money for her half of the bill, and said she had to run. She looked upset."

"Do you think she knew the people who sat down at the next table?" Liz asked.

"I know I didn't know them. Two men, neither of them exactly the Zenith type. Both of them looked like they eat their lunch at the Dunkin' Donuts drive-thru. Plaid shirts and jeans, that sort of thing. One very muscular, good tan, but mean-looking, if you can picture it. The other was putting on the pounds around the middle and a definite candidate for Rogaine."

Landini Brothers? Liz thought. "Did it seem like they were paying attention to the two of you?"

"Not really. They were still looking at menus when I left. I just went back to the shop and polished silver. Some woman from Sherborn came in and looked at a credenza for the three hundredth time. I swear, if she had bought it the first time, she'd have paid for it in saved gas. There, done!" He lifted a lid and invited Liz to smell. "Let's plate it and put it in the oven. David will be very impressed."

Which was when the phone rang.

"Reports of my death are only slightly exaggerated," she heard David say.

"Don't tell me you missed your flight," Liz said.

"No, my flight is still right here. I'm looking at it out the window. Unfortunately so is every other flight going out of Pittsburgh. There's a squall line that got to the Alleghenies and decided to stall. Nothing has gone out of here in nearly three hours. I've been waiting for some word from the airline before calling you, but they apparently don't know anything, either. We're all watching the Weather Channel. So, here I am."

"Oh, David."

"Presumably, we'll get off the ground in the next hour or so. I'm sorry I'll miss Sally's service. I'll either call or text message you as soon as I know something. I'm really sorry."

"It's OK. You couldn't do anything," Liz said.

Liz hung up a few moments later.

She turned to Roland. "I assume, Mr. Evans-Jones, you will be staying for dinner."

* * * * *

Who were the two girls? The question gnawed at Flynn's consciousness. "Damn it," he muttered to himself and got up from his desk.

Ten minutes later, he was at Joe Haskell's back door, pounding on the peeling frame. Perhaps because it was nearing five o'clock and he had been awake longer, the door opened more quickly this time, but Haskell's reflexes were also somewhat faster. As soon as he saw Flynn, he instinctively tried to slam the door shut. Flynn had his shoe in the door and pushed it back open.

"I remember you, and you ain't no goddam priest," Haskell yelled. "Get out of my house or I'll call the cops."

"I *am* a cop, Joe. I have a couple more questions, then I'll leave you alone."

"Well I ain't answering questions. You put Tim in jail. I heard about that."

"Joe, we can do this two ways. You can answer my questions, and I will leave here in peace. Or, you can try my patience, in which case I will use the time constructively to find all of the drugs you have in this house. And, to save you from yourself, I will flush those drugs down the toilet, assuming your toilet works, keeping just enough to run you in for felony possession. The choice is yours. Will you answer my questions?"

Haskell's eyes darted to a kitchen cabinet. "What do you want to know?"

"Tell me about the two girls on Tuesday night."

"I don't know anything about any girls."

Flynn went to the kitchen cabinet Haskell had eyed and opened it. He took down a Quaker Oats box and took off the lid. "Let's see what we have in here..." He shook out a baggie filled with pills.

"Laurie and Janice."

"Laurie and Janice who?"

"Laurie... I don't know their last names. Goodie. Something like that."

Flynn shook the contents of the baggie onto the filthy kitchen counter. "Are they sisters?"

"No, they just live together. Over on Depot Street. The apartments."

"And who was with whom?" Flynn took the clip off of a second baggie and six red pills spilled onto the counter. Flynn moved to begin breaking the pills apart.

"Tim was with Janice. Well, with Janice at the end." Haskell's eyes were on the pills.

"And would you describe these sweet young things?"

Flynn got a description.

Hardington was not all five-bedroom Colonials on two-acre wooded settings. As it evolved from farming community to manufacturing town to suburb, it acquired a town center. Along North Street and Main Street, the buildings housed boutiques and restaurants, banks and realtors, with Taylor's Department Store occupying the prime corner of North and Main. But off of these two thoroughfares were other streets filled with older houses on small lots. Most were like houses in many small New England towns. Pleasant Capes and saltboxes with modest lawns and climbing roses. These were the houses that passed from parents to children, with each generation adding a porch or raising the roof. But for a block on either side of the rail line that ran through the center of Hardington, there was a different town, comprised of old frame houses broken up into apartments and distressed-looking red-brick apartment houses. When Chief Harding had first driven him through town, he had slowed down on these streets. "This is where the riff-raff lives. These are the people that give us trouble."

The two-story brick apartment building on Depot Street had neither trees nor lawn to speak of. There were only desultory tufts of grass, mostly parked on by the tenants. By the mailbox count, there were eight apartments, with the embankment of the rail line directly behind the structure.

"Laurie and Janice" lived on the first floor, he had been told. One of the mailboxes said "Good/Mills" and he figured it was a close enough approximation to "Goodie". He knocked at the door.

It was answered by a woman in her mid-twenties, her platinum blonde hair gelled and pulled into spikes setting off an exaggerated amount of eye liner. She opened the door just far enough to see who was knocking. She wore a 'New England Patriots 2007-2008 AFC Champions' tee-shirt.

"Is this the residence of Laurie Good and Janice Mills?"

"I'm Laurie Good," the woman said. "There's a Janice Hervey

here."

"The mailbox says 'Mills'."

"Oh, that was Connie. She moved out about two months ago. I guess I haven't gotten around to doing anything with the mailbox. You know."

Flynn introduced himself. "I need to speak with both of you about Tuesday evening. It's important."

The woman started to open the door, then there was a flash of recollection of where she had been. She shook her head vigorously. "We don't have anything to say to you."

Flynn kept the door from closing with his hand. "I know you were at Joe Haskell's house. I know there were drugs. This isn't about the drugs. It's about what may have been said. Please let me come in."

The woman paused and looked at him, a helpless look on her face. "OK."

The interior of the apartment was dark and musty. A sliding glass door opened onto weeds and the steep slope of the train track. Laurie Good disappeared into what was presumably the bedroom and was gone for about a minute.

"Janice is, like, just getting out of the shower. We just got home from work."

"Where do you work?"

"Stitches. We both do order fulfillment." Stitches was a mail order catalog company, and was virtually Hardington's only industry.

"Like it there?"

"It's a job," she shrugged. She rummaged in her purse and extracted a package of cigarettes. "You mind?"

"It's your apartment," Flynn said.

Janice Hervey came into the living room, her hair in a towel. She was short and thick-waisted, her size exaggerated by a knee-length beach cover-up that said "Cancun" in faded pink. Like

Laurie Good, she appeared to be in her mid-twenties. They arranged themselves on an aged, flower-print sofa.

Flynn found a chair and leaned forward so that he was at their level. "Like I told Laurie, I know both of you were at Joe Haskell's Tuesday evening. I don't especially care about what happened there including what pills you might have taken or what you may have put up your nose. That's not why I'm here. I need to know everything else about that evening. Tell me what you saw, what you heard."

The two women looked at one another and were quiet for several seconds.

"Laurie, why don't you go first?" Flynn prompted. "Janice, you chime in with anything Laurie leaves out. Let's start with when Joe contacted you and invited you over. When was that?"

"Ummm, Tuesday afternoon. There was, like, a message on the answering machine," Laurie said.

"Did he say who was going to be there?"

"He just said it was a party and that, like, an old high school friend was going to be there."

"What time did you show up?"

"A little after eleven. We watched, like, *Dancing with the Stars* and then some other show. Some lawyer show. We went over after that."

"Who was there?"

"Just Joe. Tim showed up, like, about fifteen minutes later," Laurie said.

So Tim got there about eleven-thirty, Flynn thought. He also thought, *what in the hell is with kinds and 'like'?* He began mentally screening out the word from their responses.

"How did Tim look?"

Laurie looked at Janice. "Kind of out of breath. But happy. You know?"

"Happy how?"

"Happy like… like something good had happened. He said he had scored some good shit – pardon my French – and he was happy to see two girls."

"Do you think he had already started the party?"

"Oh, yeah. He said he had popped a bennie and it was dynamite," Laurie said. "He was definitely starting to fly."

"So what happened?"

Laurie shrugged. "Joe got us some iced Stoli and we all popped one. He put on some music and a video."

"Some lame porno thing," Janice added.

"We did some lines. You know."

"What did Tim talk about?" Flynn asked.

"What did he talk about?" Laurie laughed. "Mostly he was trying to, you know." She motioned circles with her hands, not wanting to complete the sentence.

"Well, he did talk," Janice said. "He was going to be rich… he was going to move to Florida and buy a boat…All that crap. He was high."

"Janice, what do mean, he said he was going to be rich?" Flynn asked.

"He said, you know, 'hey, I'm going to come into a lot of money real soon,' and I said 'you're going to win the lottery?' and he said 'no, my old lady is gonna give me what's coming to me and I figure that's a couple of million dollars.'"

"Janice, this is important. I know you were probably pretty high by then…"

"Zonked, you mean," Laurie interjected. "Smashed and down to her Victoria's Secrets."

"Janice, think very hard, and try to remember the words he used," Flynn said.

Janice sat still for several moments, her eyes closed. "'I'm going to move to Florida and I'm going to buy the biggest damn boat I can find and live on it, right on the ocean.' And I asked him, 'how are you going to swing that?' And he said, 'baby, I'm going to come into a lot of money and it's going to be real soon.' I mean, he was bragging. So I asked him if he had some kind of winning lottery ticket and could I go through his pants and look for it. We were kind of messing around. And he said, 'I know what's coming to me. It's a couple of million dollars. My old lady owes me. She owes me big time.'"

Flynn breathed in deeply. *It all depends on what your definition of 'real soon' is.* "Laurie, did you hear any of this?"

Laurie nodded. "I mean, we were all right there in the room. I think I was a little farther gone than Janice but I heard it all." Her mouth opened, a recollection. "Joe said something like, 'bullshit, man, you've been saying that for five years.' And Tim said, 'Not after tonight, man, not after tonight.'"

"He did say that," Janice nodded. "Yeah, 'not after tonight.' I thought it was all crap. I mean, he's trying to get in my pants... he's going to say anything. This guy, he's like way past thirty and he's still hanging out with his high school buddy. What else am I going to think? Anyway, we did one more line and there wasn't much talking after that."

"Nuh uh," Laurie agreed. "No more talking."

"When did you leave?"

"About four," Laurie said. "We have to be to work at eight. And until that Navy pilot comes in with that new white uniform and sweeps me off my feet, I got to punch that clock."

"You ladies are going to have to give me a formal statement," Flynn said. "Just tell me what you told me here. There are no repercussions for you. You are simply witnesses."

"Witnesses to what?" Janice asked.

"To Tim Kahn's actions that evening."

"Is that his last name? Why do you need witnesses?"

Jesus Christ. They have no idea.

"Tim Kahn has been accused of killing his mother. I take it

you don't look at the news."

"Killed her? Oh, God, and I let that guy…" Janice said, a look of revulsion on her face.

"I said he is accused. It doesn't mean he's guilty. In fact, there's considerable evidence that someone else did it."

"What do you mean?" Laurie asked.

"It just means that you need to collect your thoughts and tell me, in a formal setting, what happened. I'll record it. I don't see this going to trial, but it will be part of the evidence pool."

"You mean we're going to stand up in court and say we partied with this guy?" Janice asked.

"You just have to tell the truth. What you said just now is extremely important. Like I said, it's very unlikely this will ever go to trial. But I need to have your statements. I can do it this evening if you like, and it will be all over and done with."

The two women looked at one another.

"Could we, like, sell our story to a newspaper?" Laurie asked.

"Why don't we go take the statement now," Flynn suggested. "Afterwards, I'll tell you how it works with the newspaper."

* * * * *

The parking area of the Congregational Church was filled, as was the neighboring Bank of America lot. "This can't all be for Sally," Liz said.

"Believe in the power of the Internet," Roland replied. "You have a powerful bunch of ladies at your disposal, and they have a worthy cause." They found a space two blocks away.

Inside the church, an organist played a very passable rendition of "Adelaide's Lament" from *Guys and Dolls*. Eight enormous bouquets, each more than three feet in diameter, were displayed in a semicircle around the front of the church. Smaller bouquets were at the entry. The room was brilliantly lighted and already filled to overflowing. Liz gasped.

Linda Tenzer, one of the women Liz had worked with at the

church a day earlier, spotted her by the door and took her by the arm. "We saved you a seat up front. You, too, Roland."

"Linda, where did these people come from?"

"The garden club, the school, her golfing buddies. Sally had a lot of friends. A lot of her old students are back home from college. There was some kind of a Twitter or Facebook feed. Word got around pretty quickly. I hope we have enough food. We thought two hundred people would be max. I think we may have underestimated."

Fifteen minutes later, the rector of the church stepped to the pulpit. The organ paused. People looked ahead.

"We are here to celebrate the life of Sally Kahn..."

And then her name was being called.

Liz got to her feet. Roland squeezed her hand.

She stood at the pulpit. *It's a very large garden club meeting,* she thought. Two hundred fifty faces looked at her, expecting wisdom and enlightenment.

"Three weeks ago," Liz began, "Sally and I were at a garden tour in Wellesley. Sally utterly fell in love with a flower, an *iris reticulata bucharia* if I recall correctly. It was a beautiful yellow and white iris. The owner of the house was conducting the tour, and Sally asked the homeowner where she had bought the kernels. The homeowner replied, rather haughtily, that these are very *special* iris and they're *very* hard to get. Which to any gardener listening means that the woman had no idea where they came from because some landscape designer had put them in for her. This didn't faze Sally at all. She just said, 'That's all right. I have a flashlight and a trowel, and I know where you live.'"

"That was my friend Sally."

"Two years ago, Sally called me at eight o'clock at night and said, 'let's go to the Philadelphia Flower Show tomorrow. We can fly there for forty-nine dollars on Southwest.' And I thought about it for a minute and said, 'sure, why not?' So the next day we fly to

Philadelphia. It was a great idea, a real lark. Except that Sally's research left a little to be desired. We were there a day early. The flower show hadn't opened yet. It was judging day and no one was allowed on the floor except the two hundred or so invited horticultural and landscape judges. Of course, we were welcome to hang around until later in the day when, for a mere three hundred dollars per person, we could sip wine and mingle with the society bluebloods at the preview party. I said, 'Sally, let's go back to the airport,' and she says, 'you took German in college. Start speaking German.' So I start speaking college German and Sally walks up in a huff to one of these women with a huge corsage and she points to me and says, 'Zees ees Frau Doktor Gruber of Heidelberg. She ees ze premier floral judge in all of Germany and one of ze top three judges in all of Europe. And she hass ben invited by your American society to be an honorary judge during her American tour, and zees is how you treat her?'"

The audience laughed.

"So, while I'm spouting Spinoza and Goethe, Sally is freely translating for me about the shameful hospitality of Philadelphia. And the next thing you know, we're not only inside, but we've attracted a crowd as we go through all of the floral exhibits, with Sally providing a wonderful running commentary of what I'm supposed to be saying about the European theory of flower arranging and how Americans have different ideas of spatial relationships. We kept this up for nearly three hours, including fielding questions, and ended up as guests of the flower show committee at a luncheon at the Ritz-Carlton. On the cab ride back to the airport, I'm utterly exhausted. Sally is just grinning from ear to ear. And so I turn to her and I say, 'Sally, if you ever do anything like that again… you darn well better tell me to speak French.'"

Liz spoke for another ten minutes, telling tales of her friend. Everyone in attendance was laughing at every punch line.

Ninety minutes later, seven people had offered tributes or told tales from every facet of Sally's life. The speakers included several student reminisces, an aspect of Sally's life little known to Liz.

Liz paid attention to one vignette offered by a man now somewhere near thirty.

"Mrs. Kahn's sense of moral indignity about cheating was something everyone in school knew about," the man said. "You could expect that, in the first few homework assignments, Mrs. Kahn would look for students who had either copied one another's homework or copied out of a source. You'd come into class one morning and, on everyone's desk, she'd have placed a Xerox of the plagiarist's homework and its source, with a big 'F' through it. If it was one student copying from another, everyone would get both homework assignments with that 'F'. She would black out the names, but it was obvious to everyone who had cheated. Up until the time I took her class, I had sometimes given into the temptation to take shortcuts. The first morning I found one of those Xeroxes on my chair, I got the message. It wasn't my homework, but not only did I never think of cheating on anything in her class, it cured me for all time. I can honestly say that, because of Mrs. Kahn, I never cheated again in high school, I never cheated in college. I was never even *tempted* to cheat. And the fact that, a dozen years later, that silent, but incontrovertible evidence on everyone's desk is still vivid in my mind, speaks to the power of her moral outrage and the effectiveness of her method."

In the church's reception hall following the service, Liz was listening to a garden club member's memories of Sally, when she caught a glimpse of a man, standing against one wall, drinking a cup of coffee and nodding intently as someone near him spoke. *I know him*, she thought. Liz broke free of her conversation and drifted toward the man, who was engaged in a four-way conversation. Standing beside him was Jane Mahoney, another garden club member. The other two participants were unknown to her.

"Liz!" Jane Mahoney said, taking Liz's hand. "Everybody, this is Liz Phillips, who not only gave the funniest eulogy I've ever heard, but who organized this whole thing. Liz, this is Ray and Megan Sullivan." She then turned to the man next to her. "And I think you've met my husband, Chuck."

Liz smiled and nodded. "From the Garden Party, back in March. Of course."

And from backing out of Irina's garage in a mud-spattered Range Rover, she thought.

"You're a… lawyer, aren't you?" Liz asked. "I think I also keep seeing you around town."

He smiled easily. "You may see me around town, but I'm certainly not a lawyer. I'm a contractor. In fact, one of the houses I'm building right now is for the Sullivans." He nodded in their direction. "I think you'll know the location. It's the property next door to Sally Kahn."

Liz felt the floor sinking beneath her feet.

* * * * *

Apart from the dispatcher, who passed the time by reading a book, Flynn was alone in the Hardington police station. He had prepared his notes and listened twice to the taped statement by what he had come to think of as, 'the good time girls.' Underlying their narrative was a truth that a defense attorney would be quick to divine and use to advantage. *Ladies and gentlemen of the jury, believe what these two women say at your peril because they will trade sex for drugs, anytime, anywhere.* In the taped statement, the more unpalatable parts of the story had been sanitized. It now omitted any mention of drugs and the sexual nature of the encounter was downplayed.

It would not fool a defense attorney, however, and it would take a sympathetic judge to keep that defense attorney from eliciting the exact circumstances of the conversation of which they had been part. The key words, *'not after tonight,'* though, rang true.

Both women had heard it.   Joe Haskell could, presumably, corroborate the statement though no prosecutor would ever put him on the stand.

And it also confirmed the gaping hole in the time line after Tim Kahn left his mother's home. The girls placed his arrival at 11:30. Tim Kahn had spent only a few minutes buying drugs. Depending upon the speed at which he had walked, Tim Kahn was doing something else for up to an hour on Tuesday night. It was more than enough time to have gone back to the house, argued with his mother, and then pushed her down the stairs.

But what was Irina doing in the yard Tuesday evening? He wrote the question on a pad of paper and circled it repeatedly. And, were the Landini Brothers just some incredibly unfortunate timing coincidence? Or did they figure into this?

Sally Kahn, who killed you?

Flynn's cell phone rang, startling him.

"Detective Flynn, it's Liz Phillips."

"I'm 'Detective Flynn' again? I thought we were on a first-name basis."

"Sorry, John. I just got back from Sally Kahn's memorial service. There's something else you need to know about this morning. After I got the samples from the wayside garden, I went to Irina's house. You wouldn't approve of the reason why I went there, so I won't go into the reason, but I had occasion to… ummm, park near Irina's house. And I observed a car – a Range Rover – coming out of her garage this morning at about half past seven. I got a good look at the driver.

"Tonight, I saw that same man. His name is Chuck Mahoney. He's a local contractor. His wife is a member of the garden club. And here's the interesting part. He's the builder putting up the new house next to Sally's. He's the developer she was suing to stop construction of the house. And Irina is apparently his girlfriend."

"Jesus Christ," Flynn said.

"If I were you, I would want to know who Irina called, and maybe who she's corresponding with on email. I guess you need a warrant for that sort of thing."

At least now I know what you were doing there this morning, he thought.

"You may be sure that is going to be high on my list of things to do tomorrow," Flynn said. In the meantime, though, Liz, please don't write off young Mr. Kahn. There's now an hour and a half gap between when he left his mother's house and when he showed up at a friend's, with less than half of that time accounted for. When he got to his friend's house, he also made some very incriminating statements, though they fall short of being conclusive. He said that his mother was going to give him a lot of money 'real soon' and when one of his friends said you've been saying that for years, he said, 'not after tonight'. Like I said, not conclusive but this isn't a slam-dunk anymore."

"Good night, John."

"Good night, Liz."

8.

Saturday

The phone rang promptly at six. David was at once apologetic, angry, and sheepish.

"They formally cancelled the flight about ten-thirty," he said. The problem is that, now, everything is stacked up from yesterday. Useless Air is telling me they can get me out on a flight at five o'clock tonight."

'Useless Air' was David's sobriquet for US Air.

"Why do I think there's more?" Liz said, cautiously.

"Because you know me. While I was at the airport, I got a call from the bankruptcy court trustee. He wants an 'all hands' meeting Monday morning. Even if I get out of here this afternoon, I'm going to have to fly back Sunday afternoon."

"Oh, David." And then she wondered if this meant something else was going wrong. "What happened to 'just three more months'? Is that what this meeting is about?"

"No. The troops will be home for Christmas," David said. "I've found the buyers. Give it two months for due diligence and a month to close. Call it September fifteenth to be safe."

"I remember when you said it would be over with by now."

"I didn't count on an insane CEO. But he's in a box, now."

The company David was now running had, for many years, held a lucrative contract to supply the Department of Defense with a particular piece of equipment. A year earlier, the government had awarded the contract to a new supplier. Instead of taking the contract termination compensation and using it to find new customers, the CEO had instead elected to sue the Department of Defense. Six months later, the company was at the edge of bankruptcy, with the CEO seeing a vast conspiracy among its bankers, lawyers, and government procurement officers. "Proprietor of an unholy mess," was David's description of his job.

"While I was waiting for the airline to decide whether or not to cancel the flight, I did some thinking about your friend, Irina, and her email," David said. "I learned more than I care to on the subject when we went through Carrollton's computer." Pat Carrollton had been the former CEO of the company David had spent the prior six months nursing back to solvency. "It turns out that the problem with computers is that Microsoft thinks all people are prone to second thoughts – and that their computers have unlimited storage. The problem with people is that they're basically technologically incompetent. Put those two elements together, and it is a recipe for perpetual storage."

"What do you mean?" Liz asked.

"Let me explain," David said. "For instance, the default setting for Outlook is that a copy of all outgoing messages are saved. Unless you tell Outlook *not* to save a copy of a message, it saves one, regardless of the file size. Second, when you push that 'x', the 'delete' button, on an incoming message, it isn't really deleted. It just goes into a 'trash' file where it stays until you manually delete it."

"Should I be writing all of this down?" Liz asked.

"I'll talk you through the mechanics after you've had some time to wake up," David said. "Just remember that, with Carrollton, all of the bizarre emails he denied he was sending to the board and to the Department of Defense were right there in his 'sent' file. He had deleted anything in his 'inbox' from board members or managers that said he was sending the company over the edge, but left those messages sitting in the trash for us to find. My suspicion is that Irina is no brighter than was Carrollton. Depending upon how many of Irina's incoming and outgoing emails you copied, you may well have all of the link you need between Irina and Chuck Mahoney. Your detective friend will likely do the same thing once he has a search warrant."

"And I've been thinking, too," Liz said. "I know this ought to wait until Monday, but Diane Terwilliger was Sally's attorney. I saw her at the service last night, and I wanted to say something to her. I don't even know if she can talk to me, or if she has to talk to the police, but if there's one person who can help establish Irina's motive, it's her. Sally was suing Chuck Mahoney. That suit presumably is now moot. Was it just a delaying tactic while Sally got her act together on some better means of stopping construction, or was this real? Anyway, we're having coffee in a little while."

David laughed. "'Detective Liz Phillips'. It has a nice ring to it."

* * * * *

Flynn was at the wayside garden well before six. Landini Brothers was receding as a prime suspect, but he could not rule them out. Further, he had no way of knowing whether the transportation of Benzapyrene was a Monday-to-Friday affair or, in order to suit the requirement of contractors trying to take maximum advantage of the summer construction season, Landini Brothers transported toxic chemicals every day. The EPA had said not to confront the company, but they didn't say not to gather evidence. Flynn's goal was to replace his illegally-obtained sample with a legitimate one in the event that Liz Phillips found that hers failed a chain of custody test.

He wasn't disappointed. At ten minutes before six, a black, unmarked flat-bed truck bearing nine barrels came down Post Road. Flynn, dressed as a jogger, bent down to do stretching exercises as the truck approached, then straightened as the truck approached the 'yield' sign. Flynn took a fresh handkerchief out of his pocket preparing to wipe the deck of the truck.

The truck zoomed through the intersection without stopping. Flynn jumped back, cursing.

If nothing else, I got the bastards for failing to yield to a pedestrian, he thought.

At eight o'clock, Flynn was at the Norfolk County Courthouse in Dedham, clad in a sports jacket and tie. He was standing at a 'parade rest', a standard police tactic to show deference to authority.

Judge J. Penrod Toles, clad in considerably more leisurely attire, read through the application for a search warrant a second time. "I have a nine o'clock tee time, Detective Flynn. If you make me late for that tee time, you will rue this day, and any good deeds you may or may not ever have performed in the past will not count for squat. I'm here as a favor, and because I know from asking around that you're good at what you do. Do we understand one another?"

"Yes, Your Honor."

"Mrs. Burroughs does not respond to phone calls nor to her doorbell?" Toles asked.

"I've tried both her home and her cell phone, your honor. I've been to her home twice."

"And is there a reason in this first statement why you do not identify the juvenile that claims he saw Mrs. Burroughs?" the judge asked.

"The identification is tenuous, Your Honor. The juvenile saw a woman fitting the general description of Mrs. Burroughs on Mrs. Kahn's lawn at ten o'clock. The second statement, corroborated in large part by the police officer's supporting statement, provides a much better description. It also indicates that she went back up the path at a time consistent with the murder."

The judge nodded. "And why do you want her computer?"

"Mrs. Burroughs placed a call between the first and second trip, your honor. It seems logical that she may well have either emailed or text messaged the same individual. If there is a conspiracy, an email trail would be strong evidence."

"And you are, of course, going to share this with our prosecuting attorney before he makes an ass of himself on television?"

"He will have a copy of all relevant documents, Your Honor."

"And do you intend to execute this warrant personally, or are you farming it out to some other jurisdiction?" Judge Toles grinned. "Detective Flynn, you have managed to royally honk off the state police something fierce. I would suggest that you steer clear of them for a while. If you don't, they will do everything in their power to both make your life miserable, and imperil your cushy pension."

"I will serve it myself and use one uniformed officer to observe and corroborate."

Judge Toles nodded. "All the right answers. And you had damned well better be right. Your captain vouched for that pitiful 'confession' yesterday morning in court. You've got to wrap this one up tight, or else you're leaving him swaying in the breeze. I wouldn't care to be in your shoes."

Flynn thanked the judge. He then went upstairs and left a copy of the application, minus the Brian Snipes affidavit, under the door of the county prosecutor.

An hour later, Flynn and Officer Eddie Frankel were letting themselves into the home of Irina Burroughs. Mrs. Burroughs was not at home.

A Mercedes SUV was in the garage. Gaps in her extensive closet indicated that a substantial body of clothing was missing. No large suitcases were found and, while the absence of suitcases did not conclusively indicate that they ever existed, it was strong coincident factor, especially in a large and well-appointed home. A jewelry case containing only a few pieces of costume jewelry and with many indentations indicating pieces that had been removed was found. No substantial pieces of jewelry were found, though this too was inconclusive. They found no purse, car keys, passport or travel folders. The bed had been made. There were no dishes in the dishwasher.

In her breakfast room, they found a desktop computer. When booted up, it connected to the Internet without a password. Opening Internet Explorer and going to "History", they found no activity since Friday at noon, but extensive activity during the morning, including visits to several travel sites, including Orbitz and Expedia. Clicking through the history, they saw pages requested on flights from Boston to Moscow.

"She's probably halfway there," Flynn said in frustration.

Opening Outlook, they found an Inbox message from Expedia. CONFIRMING YOUR TRAVEL ARRANGEMENTS. Irina Burroughs had been confirmed on a 5 p.m. British Airways flight to London, connecting to a second British Airways flight to Moscow landing at 3:45 p.m. local time. Her return was a month hence. The ticket had been paid for with an American Express card.

"Do you want to take a guess at how far ahead Moscow time is from here?" Flynn asked.

"Something like seven hours," Frankel said. "It's five to England and Ireland. I know that because my cousin went there for her class trip. She called us and it was five hours ahead. I figure Moscow is probably another two hours."

"In which case, Irina Burroughs is on the ground in Moscow and well beyond any jurisdiction. Damn!"

"Look at this, Detective," Frankel said.

Flynn focused his attention on the screen. Frankel scrolled through the inbox. "Six or seven messages from 'robert.portman'. They're all asking pretty much the same thing, 'where are you?'"

"Who the hell is Robert Portman?"

"Maybe we ought to go listen to her phone messages."

"Maybe we need to just take all this stuff to the station and start printing it out," Flynn said. "Start taking photos, and then let's grab this stuff."

*   *   *   *   *

A few minutes after eight, David and Liz were on the phone again. Liz had opened the folder with the contents of Irina's computer. "Fifteen minutes at six megabytes per second," she mused. "It's amazing how fast you can download someone's life."

The contents included Irina's Outlook folders. "Let's start with what she's sent," David prompted. As he had predicted, a copy of every email Irina had ever sent was included. "You can choose whether to start with the most recent messages or the people she emails most frequently."

"Oh, let's go with the most recent," Liz said.

The scroll of emails was prolific. Irina was someone who forwarded jokes and cartoons, a practice Liz had always found annoying. Ignoring the emails sent to lists, there were a dozen recent ones that merited attention.

The most recent was to 'chuck.mahoney46@tmo.blackberry .net'. "What kind of an address is that?" she asked.

"Ah, the Blackberry," David said. "What did we do before it? Oh, that's right, we called people."

Darling Chuck,

Tickets bought, the flight is at 5. Can you come by at noon? We can have an hour of love before we go to the airport. I will miss you so much!

Your ballerina

"She left town?" Liz said. "When I saw her Thursday morning, she made up some stupid excuse about having to go see a sick relative to explain why she wouldn't be at the memorial service."

"It's under an hour to Logan, which means she was checking in more than two hours early. My guess is, she took an international flight."

The message before that was to 'robert.portman@comcast. net'.

"Does the name ring a bell?"

Liz shook her head. "Not really."

She began reading:

My darling Robert,

My sister has called. Mother has taken a turn for the worse. I fear that if I do not go now, I may never see her again alive, and that is a tragedy that I could not bear. I must go, even if it is just to say goodbye.

I will carry your love with me across the miles, and I pray I will return very soon and that we can be together as before. I know you must stand by Millie and I…"

"Oh, my God! That's Bob Portman! Millie is his wife. She hasn't been to a meeting in nearly a year. I think she's in a nursing home."

"Were they at the Garden Party back in March?"

Liz thought. "He was. She was too frail. I called her afterward and she said she had asked Bob to go in her place. She said to tell everyone she was thinking about them. That sort of thing."

"Looks like Irina was really making the rounds that night," David said. "Two fish in one outing. Pretty good haul."

"She looked you over pretty well, too, as I recall," Liz said.

"I wasn't biting."

Liz continued reading:

"I know you must stand by Millie, and I respect you for your devotion. But you must also think of your own happiness. You deserve so much happiness, and I long to provide it for you. So, you are on your own for the next few weeks. I will think of you as I care for my mother, as you think of me while you see Millie through her final days.

Love always,

Irina.

"Oh, my God. I think I finally understand it," Liz said excitedly. "Two men – two fish on the line. Both from the garden club. The Portmans aren't wealthy, but Bob was a – what –

stockbroker? – for more than forty years. They live modestly but I'll bet he's salted away a couple of million dollars. He's the one she wants to marry. She'll kill him off in two or three years. Chuck Mahoney is the ace in the hole. He's a long shot, but he's principally there for fun."

"So this hasn't been about missing plants?" David asked.

"That may have been how it started," Liz said, "but Sally raised the stakes. Sally said, 'Irina's a thief, and in more ways than anyone in this club imagined.' Now I know what she was talking about. It wasn't about plants, it was about husbands. Sally had evidence that Irina was having an affair with at least one and possibly two of the husbands of club members."

"And she was going to go public," David said.

"If I heard correctly last night, she wasn't just going to announce this at the meeting and let it go at that," Liz said. "She was going to put evidence on everyone's chair. There was a eulogy from a man who has been one of Sally's students ten or twelve years ago. He said Sally would make copies of homework assignments where there was obvious cheating and hand them out to everyone in the class."

"To publicly shame the person who cheated," David said.

"Exactly," Liz said. "I think Roland quoted Sally as saying, 'Irina's never going to steal from this club again'. I don't think that's the half of it. Had Sally passed out photos or whatever, Irina could never walk down the street again. And that would be the end of Bob Portman and Chuck Mahoney."

"David, she killed Sally. She had no choice."

* * * * *

The printouts continued at a prodigious rate with Flynn and Frankel categorizing them into stacks. One such stack contained Cyrillic alphabet characters and, from these, Flynn hoped to glean a name and address in Russia where Irina had taken refuge. A second stack was love notes to men, including many from computer dating services. He discarded any over three months old and set aside those that had elicited positive responses. One stack documented the flowering relationship with Robert Portman, another, the affair with Chuck Mahoney.

"Snagging a husband was a full-time occupation for this woman," Officer Frankel observed. "It's downright creepy. She was really obsessed."

"But being obsessed about finding a husband is hardly a motive for murder," Flynn said. "Granted, one of her prospects was also the husband of a garden club member, but that's a…"

"Look at this one," Flynn said.

A one line note from Irina to Chuck Mahoney:

Chuck,

Call me when you get this. I think Sally has pictures of us.

"Did you see any pictures in her files?" Frankel asked.

"If there had been pictures, I would have seen them," Flynn said.

"Unless they were in her computer," they said, more or less in unison.

Ten minutes later, they were at Sally Kahn's house. No one had been in the house since Wednesday afternoon and it smelled musty.

"I didn't ask to have the computer or desktop dusted for prints," Flynn said. "Don't touch anything if you can avoid it. I'll get Norfolk Sheriff's in here this afternoon, assuming they work weekends."

Sally Kahn's computer was also a desktop model, but very new and with many peripherals, including an impressive looking scanner-printer combination. Using pencil erasers, they booted up the computer.

It asked for a password.

The blinking cursor confronted them.

"We need to call Liz Phillips. She'll know the password."

Liz answered the phone.

"Irina's gone to Russia," she said.

"Tell me something I don't know."

"Chuck Mahoney took her to the airport."

"I know that, too. I'm going to track him down this afternoon. What's the password on Sally's computer?"

"I didn't know it had a password. What kind of passwords do people use?"

"Pet names, children names."

"Try CHIPPER."

Flynn tried CHIPPER. No response.

"Try CHARLIE. That was what she called her husband."

Flynn tried CHARLIE. No response.

"Liz, did Sally have a pet before Chipper?"

"Yes, a Labrador. She had to put it down just a few months before Charlie died. What as its name? A flower. Dahlia? Periwinkle? Petunia! Try PETUNIA."

At PETUNIA, the computer displayed the contents of the desktop.

"Liz, it looks as though Sally may have had photos of Irina with Chuck Mahoney. We suspect they may be in Sally's computer. There weren't any photos in the house when I cleared the scene Wednesday afternoon."

"Look for a folder," Liz said. If it isn't called 'Irina' it may be something like 'Homework'.

There was indeed an innocuous folder called, 'Homework Examples'. In it were six photos. There were three each of Irina with Chuck Mahoney and Bob Portman. Irina and Bob Portman in a garden setting, kissing. Chuck Mahoney backing out of Irina's driveway, Irina in a nightgown. Irina and Chuck Mahoney in what appeared to be a hotel elevator.

"You get the clowns from Norfolk Sheriff's in to dust for prints. Try not to let them touch too many things," Flynn said.

"It's time that I got to know Chuck Mahoney."

* * * * *

Liz dialed Diane Terwilliger's home phone with some trepidation. Terwilliger had handled the purchase of their home six years earlier upon their return to Hardington and, at the time, there had been talk of a need for a general attorney for other work. But David had insisted in using 'downtown' attorneys for his work and so their association had dwindled to the occasional, quick 'hello' at the supermarket.

But Terwilliger was warm and cordial and suggested that they meet for coffee at the Silver Spoon, Hardington's answer to a Starbucks.

"Diane, I'm in uncharted waters," Liz began. "I'm helping the Hardington Police with some aspects of Sally's death, but I have no official standing in any of this. I found her body and it just seems that, ever since, things keep coming my way."

"What you're trying to say is that jackass Amos Harding arrested the wrong person," Terwilliger said, bluntly. Terwilliger was a woman past sixty, her gray hair accented by glasses with large black rims. "I've been on the phone with that sorry excuse for a public defender three times since yesterday morning."

"Let's say there are a lot of things that don't add up," Liz said.

"Liz, I've known the Kahn family for thirty years," Terwilliger said. "I'm no criminal defense attorney, but I've helped clean up after her idiot son since his first shoplifting arrest. And I know people, and I get a pretty good sense of what they're capable of, and Tim Kahn isn't a murderer. He's a lot of unpleasant things and we spent a lot of time constructing a trust that took in those realities…"

"You mean Tim has a trust fund?"

Terwilliger shook her head. "After Charlie died, Sally had to face up to the fact that Tim was never going to live a 'normal' life. And believe me, Carol is no poster child for stability, either, though at least she's trying and it all looks pretty normal on the surface. But Sally knew she needed to provide for Tim, and that money wasn't the answer. What she set up is something that helps him to help himself. That's as much as I can say about it."

"Any idea why Tim would have concluded that he was going to come into a lot of money from his mother and that Tuesday evening somehow changed things?" Liz asked.

Terwilliger nodded slowly. "She had never explained it to him or sat him down and showed him the paperwork. It was too emotional. But turning sixty-five changed her. It made her acutely aware of her own mortality. The amounts of money she had been giving him had pretty much gotten out of hand, and I think you know she had been talking 'tough love' for a couple of months."

Terwilliger paused to take a sip of coffee and a bite of croissant. "If Tim came to the conclusion that Sally was going to drop some large amount of money on him, he was mistaken. That wasn't going to happen. In fact, everything about Sally's will is to ensure that Tim *doesn't* get some huge windfall that will likely destroy him. Maybe Sally explained it wrong, though that's not likely. I'd say the likely answer is that Tim heard what he wanted to hear. Nothing less. You understand that I can't go into specifics."

"You were also handling her suit against Mahoney, the builder," Liz asked.

Terwilliger nodded. "That one I can talk about. Chuck Mahoney is a real piece of work. When the house next to hers went on the market, Sally tried to buy it. Made a full-price, all cash offer. What Sally had in mind was to control the sale so that whoever ended up with the house didn't do what Mahoney is doing – tearing it down and putting up a McMansion. Sally loves the neighborhood. She saw what's going on all over Hardington and said, 'it stops here.' How Mahoney got the house is anyone's guess, but you can be sure that it involved money under the table."

"Why would Mahoney care about getting this particular

house?" Liz asked.

"It's about getting an acre and a half," Terwilliger said. "Some of the houses on Pequot Court have very deep lots. The house next door to Sally's had an acre and a half of land, and that much land supports five thousand square feet of house. That's the new zoning rule, which was put into place after those monstrosities over in Shady Oak Estates went up. The town got to see what those kinds of houses look like when they're built cheek by jowl with one another, and it turned into one of the more enlightened decisions our little town has made in quite a while."

Terwilliger took another bite of her croissant. "You see, right now, it's all about size. When you get right down to it, a house is mostly air. A builder can put up a five thousand square foot house for about five percent more than a four thousand square foot house, but charge twenty-five percent more. That's two million dollars instead of a million five. So the scramble is on for older houses – meaning houses built in the sixties and seventies – that have that magic acre and a half."

"Like the house next door to Sally's," Liz said.

"Exactly," Terwilliger said. "So a builder does the math. Let's say a house on an acre goes on the market for $400,000. The builder buys it and spends $20,000 to tear it down. Then the builder spends $875,000 to put up a four thousand square foot house. In round numbers, that's a total development cost of $1.3 million. The house sells for a million five. The builder has a profit of $200,000."

"So what's wrong with that?" Liz asked.

"You forgot about greed. The Robinsons – they were the people who lived next door – listed their house for $500,000 because it has that extra half-acre that gives a builder bonus square footage. Let's say Mahoney bought it for the listing price and also gave them cash or a check for another $50,000, something the IRS will never see."

Terwilliger continued. "Let's assume he also spent $20,000 to tear down the house and he's going to put $900,000 of labor and materials into that five-thousand-square-foot mega-house. The house is pre-sold for two million to someone who wants a big house with a Hardington address. Now what's his profit?"

Liz did the math in her head. "$530,000."

"And that includes paying a fifty thou kickback," Terwilliger said. "More than double the profit on the same amount of work, and he'll put up three houses this season."

"So how did Sally figure out how to stop him? Or is the lawsuit just a delaying tactic?"

"Vernal pools, and it's a killer," Terwilliger said. "When those houses were built, no one cared about wetlands – in fact, filling them was a public service because it kept down mosquitoes. Thirty years later, we care about ecology, salamanders and frog habitats. You can't build within fifty feet of any place that is wet in the spring – which is the definition of a vernal pool."

"Did Sally have evidence?" Liz asked.

Terwilliger nodded. "Sally took hundreds of photos of the property between February and May, and it shows fairly conclusively that the new footprint of the house encroaches way into the vernal pool zone. Now, Mahoney has filed twenty affidavits saying he has had a certified biologist check the buffer zone around the house and there's no encroachment, but now it's June and those pools have long since dried up."

"No pools, no proof," Liz said.

"I think you understand," Terwilliger said. "The basis of the suit is simplicity itself. 'Here are the photos. If you don't trust the photos, put the construction in abeyance until next spring and see for yourself. Or, scale back the size of the footprint to conform to the vernal pools."

"Which would be expensive?"

"Which would be ruinous," Terwilliger said. "Mahoney has

more than half a million dollars tied up at, probably, ten percent. He has subcontractors lined up, he has materials ordered. And if you don't finish the house by, let's say, mid-September, he's into penalties, plus the buyer can back out and buy someone else's mega-house."

"But Sally's dead. Doesn't that mean the suit doesn't go forward?" Liz asked.

Terwilliger shrugged. "Anyone can file it. Anyone who cares. I've brought her daughter, Carol, up to speed on the suit and she said she might carry it forward. I might even do it myself in Sally's memory. We've certainly got Mahoney running scared."

"How do you know?" Liz asked.

Terwilliger motioned to the waitress for another cup of coffee. "You ever see how a house gets torn down these days? You start with a backhoe. It pulls out all the shrubbery and puts it in a pile. Then the backhoe starts tearing off the 'skin' of the house – bricks, siding, whatever. Then the backhoe pushes everything into the foundation, chopping everything into pieces as it goes. All that takes one day. Then, one of two things happens. If you're not in a hurry, you have a front-loader take away the debris a dump truck-load at a time, and it takes about a week. If you *are* in a hurry, you hire what's called an 'excavator'. It's a monster machine that crunches up everything, foundation and all, into little pieces and you just line up ten trucks. Reducing the house to rubble takes an hour, and hauling it away to some landfill in Rhode Island is done the same day. Instant vacant lot. Well, yesterday, Mr. Mahoney got on the phone, called in some favors, and hired himself an excavator for his second house, which he wasn't going to start on until July."

"How did you hear this?" Liz asked.

"Oh, there's a network of people who care about Hardington and housing affordability. It's a sort of townie grapevine. Excavators are usually spoken for weeks in advance but, for a price, you can bump someone's place in line. He's probably going to put up the Pequot Court house on the other site. He'll just divert the materials and subcontractors. I'll bet there's a foundation poured by this time next week."

Liz pressed for an answer. "But how do people know?"

Terwilliger looked exasperated. "Let's just say that when Chuck Mahoney hires someone for office help, he ought to make certain that they're as gung-ho about tearing down houses and pricing people out of a community as he is."

"So he just builds the other house first and finances an empty lot for a season," Liz said. "Sounds like he can afford it."

"You're friends with Jane Mahoney, aren't you?" Terwilliger asked. "Nice lady, unassuming."

"She's in the garden club," Liz said. "I don't know her well. She's very quiet; meek, almost. I've met her husband once or twice."

"Well, don't judge the husband by the wife. While Jane is clipping coupons and making Rice-a-Roni for the kids, Chuckie is living very, very well. Lots of 'contractors conventions' in Las Vegas and weekends at Foxwoods. My source…" Terwilliger smiled, "My source tells me that Chuck also considers himself something of a ladies' man and that wedding ring comes off often enough that there's no tell-tale tan line. In short, Mr. Mahoney may be clearing a million a year by building three luxury houses, but that's also what he's spending. So, carrying a half-million-dollar lot at ten percent plus some under-the-table payment means he's out roughly a hundred thousand with zero return on investment. When you live as close to the edge as he does, you're always one bad deal away from bankruptcy."

Liz nodded. It was starting to become clearer.

9.

Flynn slammed down the phone in frustration. *Doesn't anyone in this damn county work weekends?* Eight calls to eight agencies produced eight voice mail prompts. If anyone associated with Norfolk County spoke or read Russian, they were taking this Saturday off. In Boston, it would be easy. One call to the Department of Russian Studies at BU would produce at least two graduate students eager for the practice, or for the glamour of being peripherally associated with a criminal investigation. Flynn had gone through this procedure a dozen times, finding speakers of languages as diverse as Croatian, Urdu, Flemish and Tagalog.

Chief Harding had been adamant. Stay within the system, no going back to old pals, no calling in favors. Stay local.

Now Flynn looked through the suburban directory. Boston University had a Dedham campus. Dedham was in Norfolk County. In theory, if anyone had answered at the special services desk of Norfolk Sheriff's, they might have directed him to call BU's Russian Studies department, and there was even a slim chance that, when he called, he might be speaking to someone in Dedham. It was all theoretically possible.

He placed the call.

Fifteen minutes later, he was faxing pages to a graduate student who was enamored of the opportunity to assist in a murder investigation. The translation would not only provide relief from the boredom of a Saturday afternoon at the departmental help desk, but be fodder for several evenings of gossip as the saga of the would-be Russian home wrecker made its way through the graduate student population.

Another call went to British Airways. Passengers were required to provide next-of-kin notification and residency-while-abroad information on international flights. Irina might well have used the name of whomever she planned to stay within Russia. At least it was worth a shot. Getting a human being at the airline took ten minutes in voice-prompt hell. Getting someone who knew what they were talking about took another fifteen minutes. Flynn explained the problem and was promised a call back with the information, "...if we determine that the airline had the responsibility to provide it."

I can't wait till we get to the extradition part of this farce, he thought.

Twenty minutes later, he was at the home of Jane and Charles 'Chuck' Mahoney. It was hardly the home of a prosperous builder. Powissett Road dated to at least the days of the King Philip Wars, and it had built up slowly over the intervening centuries as farms were broken up and subdivided into home sites. The Mahoney home looked to be about 25 years old and set back nearly 300 feet from the street. It appeared soundly built and was clearly from a custom design, but it did not fit the 'McMansion builder's home' image that Flynn had formed in his mind. Nice flower beds, though.

He knocked at the front door.

He heard footsteps inside, then saw a woman's face peer at him suspiciously from a window. The door opened slightly.

"We don't accept solicitations," the woman said, and began to close the door.

"Mrs. Mahoney, I'm with the Hardington police," Flynn said. That stopped the door from closing. He introduced himself and asked if he could come inside. Reluctantly, Jane Mahoney opened the door enough for him to enter.

The interior of the house matched the exterior. The furniture in the room he could see was old and unmatched and the drapes seemed as old as the home. *This is not the home of a guy who builds multi-million-dollar houses*, Flynn thought.

"Mrs. Mahoney, is your husband at home today? I need to

speak to him about an investigation." He instinctively knew the answer would be 'no.'

She shook her head. "He's on a site today. You may be able to find him up on Lake Drive." Jane Mahoney was a small woman in her mid-40s, her hair streaked with wisps of grey. She was not unattractive, but Flynn sensed an inattention to personal appearance. It was at odds with what he had seen in the other women he had encountered in Hardington, where age was disguised by creams, lotions and personal trainers; grey hair was colored away professionally in a salon; and where clothing was important even when company was not expected.

But then, this was a woman who may have been well aware that her husband was having an affair, perhaps one is a series of affairs that stretched back over more than a decade. Such knowledge might well induce a sense that there was nothing to gain by investing in clothing or hair style. The realization made Flynn slightly embarrassed for his knowledge.

"Can you give me the address?"

"What do you need him for?" she countered.

"It's probably nothing," he lied. "He's working on a house over on Pequot Court and there was some trouble there with kids. I'd do it by phone but I'm still getting to know Hardington and I want to get out as much as possible."

She nodded. "You're the detective investigating Sally Kahn's murder."

"Well, that's one of the things I'm working on," he said. "That's pretty well wrapping up now with Mrs. Kahn's son in custody."

"Then why do you need to talk to Chuck?"

"Like I said. I just need to check a couple of things about one of the houses he's building. And it's a nice day to be out of the office."

He added, "Listen, Mrs. Mahoney, if I'm not able to find him this afternoon, would you give him my card and ask him to call me? I'll be on duty tomorrow as well." He smiled and handed her the card. *And if it so happens that you use the card, that's OK, too*, he thought.

He left the house and parked by a bridge over a stream. He called Liz Phillips.

"What can you tell me about Jane Mahoney?"

"Funny you should ask," Liz said. "I just got an earful from Sally's attorney. In addition to being a first-class louse, Chuck Mahoney is also apparently a gambler with a big appetite. Diane Terwilliger – that's the attorney – said that the Mahoneys live one bad deal away from the edge. He gambles away what they make."

"What about Jane Mahoney?"

"Quiet," Liz said. "Very quiet. She doesn't speak up at club meetings and sometimes you'd hardly know she's there. But she always volunteers for projects. I always thought her husband was a carpenter or something. Jane drives around in a fifteen-year-old station wagon that's held together by baling wire. It turns out her husband probably makes a million a year building three houses. I guess I never put together 'Mahoney Construction' with Chuck and Jane."

"You've had a busy morning," Flynn said.

"Oh, there's more," Liz said. "I also learned that Sally's death really freaked out Chuck because of the lawsuit. Diane says it's practically an open-and-shut case that the foundation he poured over on Pequot Court is encroaching on vernal pools…"

"What's a vernal pool?"

"Think frogs in the spring. Anyway, he's shifting the Pequot Court house plans onto another tear-down that he wasn't going to start work on until later in the summer. Diane says he's lined up one of these big house-crunching machines to come in tomorrow to tear out the existing foundation, and he's busy tearing down the house today."

"Jesus Christ! Where does your friend get information like this?"

"Townie grapevine. Chuck Mahoney is apparently oblivious to it. You ought to get out more."

"I just got out to the Mahoney's house on Powissett," Flynn said. "That's why I asked about Jane Mahoney. I had this sense that she's both trapped and afraid."

"Gosh," Liz said, "if you were married to a guy with a Russian mistress on the side and a million-dollar-a-year gambling habit, maybe you'd feel trapped, too. I guess my conversation with Diane really made a lot of things fall into place about Jane. She and Chuck both grew up in town and they married young. I guess Chuck has been pretty good at keeping Jane in her place while he goes out and has a great time. Come to think of it, the garden club is just about Jane's only activity outside of her home. I know her son graduated from high school last year but I don't know where he is now. Like I said, Jane doesn't talk much."

"Well, that's a good start," Flynn said. "Just so you know, I've got someone from BU reading Irina's Russian-language emails to see where she's staying. I also called the airline to get whatever name she put down on her contact form when she checked in."

"One last thing," Liz said.

"Yes?"

"If you're still in Hardington later today, I have a pair of pound-and-a-half lobsters that are going to die one way or another, and I'd rather that it be in boiling water. Can I interest you in an early dinner?"

"Uh, sure. Just say when." A few minutes later, Flynn found himself humming as he drove across Hardington. The tune fragment, from deep in his subconscious, was from his youth. "...*Last night I met a new girl in the neighborhood, oh yeah. Something tells me I'm into something good...*"

It was not hard to spot the demolition site on Lake Drive. It had once been an older house, probably from the thirties. It was frame construction with shingles. A pile of shrubbery was already in place. There were yews, junipers, and rhododendron all in a tangle. One end of the house was gone. What remained was the side of the house containing the kitchen, a second floor bedroom, and an adjoining one-car garage.

The backhoe was operated by a well-tanned man and, even from the back, Flynn could recognize him from the photos Sally Kahn had taken. Flynn watched for a moment as Mahoney worked the claw of the backhoe. It raked across the kitchen, tearing out a sink and dishwasher. The backhoe banged several times on the kitchen floor and it broke through, sending the contents of the kitchen into the basement.

Flynn beeped his horn several times and Mahoney's head turned to find the source. Flynn waved and the backhoe stopped. Mahoney hopped down from the backhoe's cabin.

"Sorry to bother you, but I'm John Flynn with the Hardington police. I need to talk to you about your property over on Pequot Court." *Ease into it. Make it casual. Don't set off alarms.*

"Is there a problem with it?" Mahoney asked. Flynn felt himself being eyed and assessed. Mahoney probably knew every cop in town, and so he would know this was the new guy – the detective. Flynn relaxed his body language, leaning up against Mahoney's Range Rover, and simultaneously taking the opportunity to peer inside of it.

"We caught a couple of kids playing down in the foundation," Flynn said. "One of the neighbors is convinced someone's going to get hurt. You know kids."

Mahoney smiled. "Yeah, little boys and construction projects. You can't keep them away. I can probably throw a tarp over it if that would help."

"You're not starting work there anytime soon?"

Mahoney threw his thumb over his shoulder at the house

behind him. "I've got a buyer for this house who can't wait to move in. The people buying the Pequot house still have to sell theirs. So this one comes first. I'll get back to Pequot after this one is framed up. And I'll make certain that the foundation is secured. That'll keep the kids out."

"Thanks," Flynn said. He shook Mahoney's hand and started to leave, then turned around. "Look, Mr. Mahoney, we're also going to have to talk about one other thing before long, so it may as well be now." Flynn paused to look for any reaction. He saw Mahoney unconsciously clench his fists. "I've also got to wrap up my investigation of the death of Sally Kahn, and the foundation you poured is right next to her house. Chief Harding is going to grill me left and right on this, so I've got to cover every base. You knew Sally Kahn, right?"

"Of course I knew her," Mahoney said. The fists remained clenched. "I think everybody in town knew her. I had her for history my junior year."

"Were you at your job site at all on Tuesday? The one on Pequot Court?"

The hands unclenched slightly. "I was there with the people who are buying this lot. Ray and Megan Sullivan. I never saw Mrs. Kahn's son there, if that's what you're asking."

"You've met her son?"

"I grew up here, Detective Flynn. Tim was a couple of years behind me in school, but we crossed paths occasionally. Carol – his sister – was a year behind me. That's one screwed-up family, especially Tim. You know Tim used to steal cars, do drugs – the whole nine yards."

"I've heard." Flynn noted that Mahoney's fists had relaxed.

"Are you still looking for witnesses? I heard you had a confession."

"Oh, you can expect his lawyer is going to try some funny business," Flynn said. "They always do. You know, 'the confession was coerced, my client needed a fix and would have said anything'. That's why the chief has me tying up loose ends. For instance, one of the neighbors said they saw a woman in Mrs. Kahn's front yard just after dark on Tuesday night."

"A woman?" The fists, so recently relaxed, clenched tightly.

"Yeah. I've got a line on who it might have been. I'm not worried. I'll find her and then all the loose ends will be tied up. How much do these houses you build go for?"

Mahoney was hooked. "More money than you or me will ever have. Tell me about the woman. Nobody in town has told me about that."

"Aw, there's not much to say. A neighbor says he saw a short woman kind of lurking around. She came up the path from the school. A couple of kids necking in the parking lot saw her, but they were kind of occupied. One of our policemen out on patrol remembers seeing a couple of cars in the lot. Like I said, we've got something to go on. And, if she saw Tim Kahn leaving the house, that's good. Hey, I'd love to stay and chat, but I've got a mountain of paperwork to finish up. Please put a tarp over the foundation and make the neighbors happy."

"Is that the same neighbor who told you about the woman in the yard?" Mahoney asked.

"No. Different neighbors." *What an interesting question.* "Nice meeting you. Good luck with the house."

Flynn backed his car out, watching Mahoney carefully memorize him and his car. *You and Miss Russia deserve one another*, he thought.

There was one more stop to be made, and it would not be a pleasant one. Fourteen Hillcrest Road was a nice house, the kind of home that, in the 1980s, before McMansions came along, symbolized prosperity in suburbia. A fine colonial with what appeared to be fresh coat of paint. Large, beautiful and fully mature trees providing cool shade. A large white Cadillac in the circular driveway.

Flynn rang the doorbell. A few moments later, an elderly man, nearly six feet tall and bald except for a white fringe, answered the door. There was the sound of a football game from inside the house. Flynn thought to himself, "*football in June?*"

"Robert Portman?"

"Yes?"

"My name is John Flynn and I'm a detective with the Hardington Police. We need to speak. Is your wife at home?"

Portman shook his head. "Millie is in a nursing home. I saw her this morning. And I suspect I know what this is about." Portman led Flynn into a living room. A push of a button on a remote and the television went mute.

"You don't need to turn off the game," Flynn said, apologetically. "We could talk another time."

"I already know how it's going to come out. That's ESPN Classic, Notre Dame vs. Navy, 1965. I don't really recognize the game anymore the way it's played today. The uniforms are the same, but the players are just steroid cases. I just watch the old ones."

Flynn smiled, grainy images of a game seen on television decades earlier and written about for weeks thereafter. "That's the one where Navy learned to beware of kicking the ball to Nick Rassas. You played?"

"Tight end. Brown. Class of 1959," Portman said. "And you?"

"Running back. Holy Cross," Flynn replied.

Portman regarded him. "Yes. What did you weigh?"

"One-eighty-five in a towel."

"I'll bet you were good."

"I started for two years. Then I discovered I wasn't college material, as they used to say."

Portman continued to regard him. "What years?"

"Seventy-five and seventy-six."

Portman shook his head. "Not much of a team behind you."

"It was a rebuilding year. A whole bunch of rebuilding years."

"I'm having a gin and tonic. I hope you'll join me."

Flynn started to decline, then thought better of it. "It sounds perfect," he said.

Portman went into the kitchen, Flynn remained behind. A grand piano in the living room was filled with photographs, chronicling a life. A young Robert Portman and wife smiling in black and white. The Portmans in fading color with small, towheaded children. Then, the children, three of them, apparently, growing up, graduating, and getting married. The most recent photos were of a new generation, growing toward adulthood.

Portman returned with the drinks.

"You said you suspected that you knew what this is about," Flynn said.

Portman nodded slowly. "It is about a lonely man being a damned fool."

"I'm here about Irina Burroughs," Flynn said.

"I suspected so."

"Mrs. Burroughs appears to have left the country," Flynn said. "I need to talk to her about the death of Sally Kahn. In reviewing her computer files, you and she appear to have emailed one another frequently. I was hoping you could help me locate her."

"You are a diplomat, Detective Flynn, but there is no need for diplomacy. I met Irina at a wine and cheese party a few months ago. She was charming as someone of her native land is wont to be. I had recently placed my wife in a nursing home and was very, very depressed. She brightened my life. I called her my 'pretty ballerina' and I was her 'brave warrior.' Oh, I know exactly what she was after. I'm no fool. But she made me believe that I could... She made me believe that there was a life after Millie. That there could be a life after Millie."

"Did she ever talk about Sally Kahn?"

Portman nodded. "She hated the woman. At first, I thought it was just some silly business over garden plants. But it was deeper that than. I did not know Sally Kahn well, but what I did know was admirable. A woman of strong beliefs. Both of our families were at the Congregational Church, and she was the one who spoke up at Parish meetings. Anyway, Irina was convinced Sally was following her. Sally drove one of those funny little hybrid cars which was very noticeable. And, over the past several weeks, Irina was convinced she would see Sally's car parked outside of her house. She may have been right."

"What do you mean?" Flynn asked.

"Friday morning, I received a message from her," Portman said. "An email, actually. You probably saw it if you've looked at her computer. She said her mother was dying and she had to return to Russia to say goodbye. The thing is, she told me on at least two occasions that her mother had died when she was young. I called her as soon as I got it – you probably know that, too – but she was gone."

"Do you know with whom she might be staying in Russia?"

"She told me she has a brother in St. Petersburg. He's a software engineer of some kind. She once mentioned Gazprom. I don't have an address or telephone number. I can't say I've ever met any of her friends. For Irina, Russia was in her past. Until she left, she had never said anything that indicated she wanted to return, even for a visit."

Flynn nodded. "Did you speak to her Wednesday or Thursday?"

"No. We had no specific plans to meet until tomorrow. We were going into the city for brunch. Irina has her own life, I have mine."

"Did you know where she had planned to be on Tuesday evening?" Flynn asked.

"I have no idea."

"How about her friends?"

Portman paused. "In the past few weeks, I became aware that I was not the only man in her life. There is another person here in Hardington…"

"Chuck Mahoney."

Portman nodded. "Then you know. I never confronted Irina with my knowledge. There was really no point to it. I have no basis for anger or jealousy…"

"Mr. Portman, do you have reason to believe that Irina Burroughs may have been connected to Sally Kahn's death?"

There was a long silence. "Do you mean conjecture or do you mean facts?"

"If you had facts, I assume you would already have told me," Flynn said.

Portman nodded again and drained his glass. When he spoke, he looked at the ice cubes in his glass rather than at Flynn. "There was a visceral dislike that long predated me. I believe that it was initially over some business about whether or not Irina could account for all of the flowers that she planted on behalf of the garden club. But it grew into something much stronger. Certainly on Irina's part and, if Irina is to be believed, on Sally Kahn's part as well. When I probed, I got a very harsh reaction, almost as though I was somehow involved."

"Go on," Flynn said.

"Well, as I said earlier, about two weeks ago, Irina became convinced that Sally was following her," Portman said, now looking into Flynn's eyes. "I do not know if there was any hard evidence but, in Irina's mind, it was certainly real. And, the last time we saw one another, which was on Monday, Irina said that she intended to – let me make certain that I get the words as she spoke them – that she intended to 'stop' Sally in order to 'protect' me. She did not spell out any course of action, but the way she said it, I had no doubt but that it was not talking that she had in mind. I have seen Irina's temper on two occasions. She is quite capable of harming someone physically."

Portman seemed to tire visibly as he spoke. "When I got the message from her on Friday saying that she was going to Russia, I put two and two together. Irina felt a need to lie low, to get out of town and let the heat die down, if you will. And, Russia makes perfect sense in that regard. She presumably knows people there and language is no barrier. And I suspect that extradition would be rather problematic."

Portman seemed to have said all he was going to say. Flynn let the silence hang in the air, then said, "You should know that Sally Kahn was in fact following Irina, or was having someone follow her. She had taken photos of the two of you together, as well as of Irina with Chuck Mahoney. The photos of the two of you show you kissing in some kind of a nature walk setting..."

Portman nodded. "Garden in the Wood. Last week. It may be the only time I ever kissed her in public." He smiled. "I thought we were alone."

"The photos of Irina with Chuck Mahoney are more risqué. Chuck is leaving her home. She's waving goodbye to him wearing a fairly suggestive nightgown. There's also one of the two of them getting into an elevator at what appears to be a hotel and she has an overnight bag."

"And what will become of the photos?" Portman asked.

"My hope is that nothing will become of them," Flynn said, gently. "Sally Kahn apparently intended to show them at the garden club meeting on Wednesday. She had apparently not thought through what their impact would be on your wife or Chuck Mahoney's wife. If I understand it correctly, her motives were to expose Irina as a cheat much as she did students in the high school classes she taught over the years. There was certainly no animosity toward you or your wife that I can see."

"What are you going to do now?" Portman asked.

"My hope is that I can find Irina in Russia and persuade law enforcement authorities there to put her on a plane back to the United States," Flynn said. "If I can do that, then it's likely that I, or the district attorney, can reach an agreement with her that avoids any trial, and any discussion of the two of you."

"Millie will eventually find out, of course," Portman said. "Once one person knows, eventually everyone will, and they will tell her."

"Mr. Portman, I have seen the photos – which by the way exist only on the hard drive of a computer, as far as I know – and a young policeman who has been working with me saw them. I intend to tell him to forget about them until and unless they're needed as evidence. You can be absolutely certain that I will mention them to no one."

Portman nodded slowly. "Detective Flynn, I am seventy-four years old. I am retired now and my health is frankly not what it was six months ago. Those of my friends who are not dropping dead of heart attacks or cancer are moving away. Even before you came to the door, I already knew that I had learned a painful lesson about the folly of an old man and a younger woman."

Portman turned slowly, his gaze resting on the family photos on the piano "What you've done is to ensure the finality of that lesson. This morning, Millie asked me what was wrong and I lied and said 'nothing, except that I miss having you at home.' I can't tell her about this. I know what it would do to her. But it's proof, as if I needed it, that Millie knows me better than I know myself. Detective Flynn, I hope you won't need to use those photos. They've already done their damage. All they can do now is shorten two people's lives."

Flynn rose and they shook hands. As he left the house, he heard the football game's sound come back on. Navy had punted. Nick Rassas was making another long return.

* * * * *

Liz hung up the telephone and immediately started regretting the impromptu dinner invitation. *What on earth did you do that for? What are you going to talk about for two hours?* She put the thoughts out of her head.

The phone rang almost immediately.

"Liz? Alvin. Got a minute?"

What now? "Sure. What's up?"

"Liz, you have stirred up a hornet's nest but I haven't had this much fun in I don't know when. I've had half a dozen calls up the chain of command with the EPA, and every time someone new gets involved, they see headlines."

"Am I supposed to be happy or frightened by this?" Liz asked.

"Let me tell you what's happened," Duclos said. "They've compared the Benzapyrene sample you brought in with what they have in their Puritan Chemical database, and the signature is an exact match. This is definitely a new cache. I also know that this morning, the EPA put about a dozen cars out at various entrance ramps to Route 128 and they spotted your friends getting on at Route 24 with ten barrels. They followed the truck to Landini Brothers and got enough trace samples at stop signs and traffic lights to independently verify that it is, in fact, PAH. Those barrels are definitely fragile, and the big concern is that one will give way between the dump site and the concrete plant. Anyway, it's all recorded, all official. On Monday, they'll stake out the entrance ramps on Route 24 and, if all goes as planned, on Tuesday they'll use a plane to make the final site identification based on building permits accessible from that exit."

"That sounds like they're moving very quickly," Liz said.

"You don't know the half of it," Duclos said. "At the same time, the EPA followed outgoing concrete trucks and will be taking samples at the locations where Landini made deliveries, starting with that treatment plant. I swear, I have never seen the EPA move like this. It usually takes weeks – you heard that conversation yesterday."

"That's wonderful, Alvin. It sounds like we've done everything we can do."

"Well, not exactly. That's the other reason I'm calling. Would you be willing to make a trip out to Landini Brothers?"

Liz paused and gulped. "Why?"

"They want a non-threatening presence to see if anything is amiss. You know, if there's any activity at the facility that indicates they're concerned."

"Wow."

"You've already done a world of good – and, by the way, there's a monetary reward somewhere down the line – but they're nervous and they're flying by the seat of their pants. You're the right person in the right place. They just want you to go into the main office, strike up a conversation on some plausible pretext, and see if anything seems amiss."

"I can do that," Liz said, warily. "I don't want to do that, but I'll do it. I have this vision of myself going out at the bottom of the next load of cement."

"I have faith in you," Duclos said.

"I don't see you volunteering."

"They've got me – and three graduate students I dragooned – preparing expert testimony to get subpoenas for bright and early Monday morning," Duclos said. "I had promised Linda we'd spend the weekend in Little Compton. Well, scratch that. Linda is not only not amused, she's livid. On the whole, you've got the better assignment."

"I'll call you when I get back," Liz said.

Liz sighed. *Just what I needed.*

Half an hour later, Liz pulled into the dusty parking lot of Landini Brothers. It all looked very quiet. She opened the door of the small main office building. A receptionist who appeared to be college-age, with a fuchsia streak in her hair and wearing a Joan Jett tee, removed a set of ear buds.

"We're not really open on Saturday," she said, only somewhat apologetically.

"Then that makes two of us," Liz said, smiling. "I'm hoping, though, that Mr. Landini is here today. I'm going to hit him up for a donation and I figure that Saturday is my best shot."

"Are you, like, with the Salvation Army?"

"Sweetie, it's worse than that. The garden club. Is he around?"

The girl looked down at her switchboard. "He's on his phone. I don't know how long he'll be."

"I'll wait," Liz said. "It's not like it's a beautiful day or anything. No, wait. It is beautiful day! Why do you have to work if you're 'not really open'?" Liz held up fingers to put quotes around the last few words.

"The girl rolled her eyes. "Tell me about it. He's my uncle. He's got this, like, thing to make certain nobody goes in or out without him knowing it. So I get to sit here and watch every car go in and out, and yell if I don't know who it is."

"Am I the first interloper? Did you have to yell?"

"Naw," the girl said. "You pulled right up in front of the building. I had, like two people this morning looking for directions."

"Which beach would you rather be at?"

The girl shook her head. "It's still way too cold for the beach. Which garden club?"

"Hardington."

"Cool. Do you know Sandra Rollert?"

"On Hillcrest?"

"I think so."

"I know Ginny Rollert and I've met her daughter," Liz said. "She's at Framingham State. Is that where you go to school?"

The girl nodded. "He's off the phone."

"Do I go back?"

"Uncle Frank?" the girl shouted.

"That answered my question," Liz said. "By the way, what's your name?"

"Karen. Karen Lungarella."

Frank Landini shouted back, "What?"

"Lady here to see you."

"Jesus Christ," came audibly from the rear of the building.

"When you see Sandra, tell her Mrs. Phillips says 'hi'."

"I will."

"We're closed, for crying out loud," Landini said as he lumbered toward the reception desk. "Come back on Monday."

"Hi, I'm Liz Phillips with the Hardington Garden Club," Liz said, ignoring Landini's words and offering her hand. "You've probably seen our roadside gardens around town."

"Jesus Christ." Landini pointedly did not accept Liz's proffered hand.

"Well, up to now, we've always paid for and maintained those sites on our own, but as we start to expand several of the more prominent ones, we're looking for business sponsors. For a three hundred dollar donation, we could give you a sign on one of our most prominent locations, like the one at Main and Post, or North and Main, or even the western gateway on the Charles. We're upgrading each of those gardens this year and…"

"Can't we do this Monday?"

"I suspect Monday is probably your busiest day. It certainly is for me. So, why not today?" Liz could not believe her own cheerfulness, especially since she was making up everything.

The phone rang. Karen answered it. She put her hand over the phone and said to Landini, "It's Uncle Phil again."

Landini looked at Liz and then at the phone. Exasperated, he said, "Karen, write her a check. I can't deal with this. I'll take it in my office." He quickly retreated to his office.

As Karen got out a check register, Liz asked, "What was that all about?"

Karen shrugged. "They've got, like, this huge contract to supply concrete for some treatment plant, but the contractor is saying there's a work stoppage or something." She shrugged again. "I mean, it's like, three days that they won't need deliveries and Uncle Phil and Uncle Frank are treating it like it's the end of the world." She rolled her eyes for effect. "So they're trying to work with the union to fix the problem. Who do you want the check made out to?"

"Hardington Garden Club, please. Is there always this much commotion around here on a Saturday?"

"This is, like, my fourth week," the girl said. "I didn't even know I was going to have to come in on Saturday until last week. It's this treatment plant thing. They've never had a contract this big, and they only use certain trucks for it. And, like, if the contractor says he needs a hundred and twenty yards today and he only pours a hundred and he sends back the trucks, my uncle goes ballistic and gets on the phone."

"You could always get another job."

"As if. This is a family business," Karen said in a sing-song voice as she made a face. "Spare me."

"I hope it works out," Liz said.

"Thanks. Here's your check. Boy, he must be distracted. I don't think I've written a check this big since I've been here. Maybe I ought to ask him for a raise."

Liz left and drove across the Charles. She stopped alongside the road and called Alvin Duclos. "Your spy is reporting on her reconnaissance mission," she said. "Unless you've got a labor negotiator up your sleeve, you may have a problem on Monday. The contractor at the water treatment plant is shutting down work for several days because of some labor dispute. There won't be any deliveries for a couple of days, so I suspect the Benzapyrene Express isn't going to be running, either."

"I'll pass the information along," Duclos said. "I don't know if there's anything they can do about it."

"Also," Liz said, "if push comes to shove and you need someone inside Landini Brothers who will answer questions truthfully, the receptionist is the owners' niece, and she has an intense dislike for her uncle. She doesn't know what's going on – I mean, she had no idea about what's in the drums – but she knows all the pieces. She knows when the truck with the canisters goes in and out and she knows who's driving it. I'm sure she knows which concrete trucks are earmarked for Milford – she also told me that some trucks are sent back if the contractor can't use all of the loads, and that Landini uses certain trucks for that job."

"How long were you there?"

"About fifteen minutes. She's very talkative."

"You got all that in fifteen minutes?" Duclos said. "The EPA has been having people stop in looking for directions, and they're thrown out in about thirty seconds. As to the niece, I'll ask. What's her name?"

"Karen Lungarella. She goes to college with the daughter of a family I know here in town."

Duclos thanked her again. Liz started thinking about lobsters.

* * * * *

The little envelope on the Outlook box on Flynn's computer was illuminated when he got back to his desk. Two messages.

The first was his request for an expanded search for fingerprints:

Drip coffeemaker: SALLY KAHN, IRINA VOLNOVICH

Coffee pot: SALLY KAHN, IRINA VOLNOVICH, ELIZABETH PHILLIPS

Sugar canister: SALLY KAHN, IRINA VOLNOVICH

Beer cans: SALLY KAHN, TIMOTHY KAHN, IRINA

VOLNOVICH
> *Coffee vacuum pack: insufficient to identify*
> *Cereal bowl: IRINA VOLNOVICH*
> *Kitchen counter: SALLY KAHN, TIMOTHY KAHN, unidentified*
> *Refrigerator: SALLY KAHN, TIMOTHY KAHN*
> *Cereal box: SALLY KAHN, IRINA VOLNOVICH*

Flynn read the list. "I guess that pretty well nails it," he said to himself. "We have a winner." He noted the third set of fingerprints on the kitchen counter. *Unidentified.* It could mean something. It could mean one of the technicians wasn't wearing gloves. He let it pass.

The second message was a cell phone usage summary for Irina Burroughs. He scanned it for Tuesday evening and found three calls to the same number in the 508 area code. All three calls were shown as one minute in duration.

He dialed the number from his own cell phone, aware that "Hardington PD" would show up on Caller ID if he used the phone on his desk. His cell phone was programmed to send no identifying number.

"This is Chuck," the voice at the other end of the line said. The sound of machinery was in the background. The same noise he had heard when he drove out to meet Chuck Mahoney at the house being demolished on Lake Drive.

He hung up.

Irina had called Chuck Mahoney when she first went to Sally Kahn's house and found that Tim Kahn was still there. And then she had called him again, presumably when she determined Tim had left.

The first call tied to the time the two teenagers had seen Irina make a call from the parking lot. What could Irina say in a minute? The second call, fifteen minutes later, was similarly brief. Was she seeking advice? Was he giving instructions?

Chuck Mahoney was more than a lover and more than

transportation to the airport. Chuck Mahoney was, quite possibly, an accomplice.

This is where you need a partner, he thought to himself. *This is where you need backup.* Flynn grimaced. The he dialed a number he had avoided calling for three months.

"Victoria Lee," said a voice on the other end of the line. It was said as a statement.

"Vicky? Flynn. I need your help."

In twenty-four years as a detective with the Boston PD, Flynn had three partners. His first was Bobby O'Hara. Bobby O'Hara, who knew everyone and everything. He was an encyclopedia of perps and hangouts, of MO's and alibis. Bobby had gotten his detective's shield after serving in Patton's army as it rolled across North Africa and into Sicily and Italy and, within a few years, Flynn had heard O'Hara recount every day of his military service. Bobby O'Hara had been the perfect tutor. He was a detective of the old school.

After thirty years as a detective, the final seven with Flynn, Bobby O'Hara had retired with full honors. Two months later, he was incapacitated by a massive stroke and had died a year later. The cause was laid to a lifetime of smoking two packs of unfiltered Camels a day and drinking a fifth Jameson's whisky every weekend.

His second partner was Ray Missoni, a man of his own age and background. In twelve years, they had broken thousands of cases and put an equal number of miscreants behind bars. They had functioned as if joined at the hip, able to quickly decide how to proceed and parcel out the mundane responsibilities of any investigation.

They would have stayed partners another twelve years but an auto accident – speeding from home en route to a shooting in the South End – had put a premature end to Missoni's career. Ray had lost a leg and the resulting prosthesis was deemed inadequate to the requirements of an on-the-street detective. Missoni now manned a desk that parceled out scarce resources to detectives. He was, effectively, the keeper of an enormous 'goody-jar'.

It was Ray who had authorized a special CSI squad that had swept Sally Kahn's house. It was Ray who had commandeered a city medical examiner to venture to the western suburbs. It was far less an owed favor redeemed than a recognition that, if John Flynn asked for something, it was not for a frivolous reason. Fast-tracking fingerprints was not done as a quid-pro-quo for a dozen years of partnership but, rather, as an understanding that John Flynn did not ask for what he did not need.

At the time of Ray's accident, Flynn had nearly thirty years on the force, nineteen of them as a detective. In a perfect world, Ray Missoni would have recovered and the two of them would have continued together, creating a legend within the department. When it became apparent that Ray would be deskbound, Flynn briefly considered asking for early retirement. An hour's reconsideration and he asked when a new partner would be available.

His third partner was Victoria Lee. Vicky Lee. The new face of the BPD. Born in Hong Kong but an emigrant at the age of four. Twenty-five years old at the time she was assigned to him, with a BS in Criminology from BU and five years on the force during which she had also earned an MS in Public Policy from Suffolk University. A woman destined for leadership, for which a stint in the Detectives Bureau was, like her three years on the street and two years in Community Relations, a necessary notch in her belt.

On the day he had first been told of his new partner, he had been discreetly informed in confidence that half a dozen pair of eyes in senior command positions were on her. In three years – no more than four – she would be taking the lieutenant's exam. If she was not available 24/7 as detectives were ordinarily expected to be, it was because she had embarked on earning a JD from Suffolk

Law.

He had once asked her whether her multiple degrees were a source of pride to her parents. Vicky Lee has replied, "They said, 'Which part of 'medical school' didn't you understand?'."

Flynn was to be her mentor, filling the role Bobby O'Hara had played for him nearly two decades earlier. A circle completed.

If he expected kid-glove treatment or special assignments because of his rising-star partner, he was mistaken. From the start the two of them had been thrown those cases that required skill and tact, and Vicky Lee had shown herself to be a quick study. Not a natural detective, but one who seldom repeated a mistake and who had an instinctive eye for detail. In a year, Lee had the skill it had taken Flynn three to achieve. In two years, she was matching him, observation for observation and completing his sentences. Her internship was over.

They had cemented their relationship as equals over the following three years, longer than Flynn expected, and a result of Lee's refusing the first several promotions offered her. Their bond was one of mutual respect. When the inevitable call had come, Flynn again considered his options. This time, it was made known that a place would be made available on the Major Cases squad. In fact, he could transfer to any special unit of his choosing. He had properly groomed one of the department's next generation of leaders, and his services would be rewarded appropriately.

Instead, he had chosen retirement. At 56, he was not ready to start over. Except that, after two months of being idle, he had found starting over preferable to ending his career. Which had brought him to Hardington.

"Whatever help you need, you'll get," Vicky Lee said.

It was like her. No catching up. No reminiscing. Not even a 'how are you.' *Whatever help you need, you'll get.*

"What I need is your feel for a case. Here's the set-up. Two women, one man. There are also a couple of left-fielders. The first woman is Sally Kahn, age 65. A strong sense of morality and the will to act on it. She comes to resent the second woman, Irina Volnovich Burroughs, roughly age 45. Irina had been stealing from a club of which they were both members. Small things, stupid things. Cheating on the number of flowers ordered. Sally's resentment grows. She learns that Irina, who is twice- divorced and hunting for husband number three, has been carrying on affairs with the husbands of two members of the club. Sally is going to publicly humiliate Irina by distributing copies of photos she had taken of her with the two men. Irina learns that the humiliation will take place Wednesday morning."

"Go on," Lee said.

"On Tuesday evening, Irina goes to Sally's home to confront her. She's parked out of sight of the house. As soon as she gets there, she calls her lover, Chuck Mahoney, who is also guy number one. The call is about a minute. She goes up to the house and discovers that Sally has company, her son. Irina goes back to her car and calls Mahoney again. They talk for just a minute. Ten minutes later, Irina goes back to the house and presumably finds that Sally's son has departed. She calls Mahoney a third time, again for just a minute. Irina goes inside, Sally Kahn is slapped around and then killed by being pushed down a flight of stairs. Afterwards, Irina tries to disguise the time of death by setting up the makings of breakfast."

Flynn composed his thoughts for a moment. "Then, the body is discovered too soon, around noon on Wednesday. So, setting up breakfast becomes the giveaway that it wasn't an accident. I start investigating. Yesterday afternoon, Irina hopped on a plane back to Mother Russia, with Mahoney giving her a ride to the airport."

"An hour ago, I only knew Mahoney had taken Irina to the airport and that the two were lovers. I also just learned that Sally Kahn was getting ready to file a lawsuit against Mahoney to stop construction on a house next to hers. On that basis, I paid him a friendly call. Then I get two emails. One confirms that Irina's fingerprints are all over the crime scene, and the other that Irina talked to Mahoney three times before the crime."

"What else?" she said.

"I've got two suspects out of left field. The son is a 35-year-old druggie with an hour-plus-long hole in his alibi. He's got a couple of million dollars' worth of motive and, if it weren't for Irina's fingerprints all over the crime scene, he'd still be high on my list. The other one is a local concrete company owner. Without knowing what she had found, Sally Kahn stumbled into some major league environmental mischief that could send about half a dozen people to prison for a very long time. If they think she understood what she had uncovered, it would definitely be worth killing over. Once again, with Irina on the scene, they're a low-probability target."

"My problem is that I've got zero internal support," Flynn continued. "The chief of police thinks he solved the case on Thursday when he got a cryptic 'confession' from Sally's coke-head son, and he can't abide the idea of a killer being on the loose in peaceful, bucolic, Hardington. I'm only able to investigate because he hasn't come in on a weekend since the Carter administration and, if I let on to anyone that I'm investigating, the staties will descend in force and screw it all up. I've got a twenty-four-year-old rookie patrolman for a back-up. I'm getting my best information from the president of the garden club."

"Let's go back to the phone records. Do you have access to those right now?" Lee asked.

"They're on my screen."

"What calls did she make after she killed the woman?"

Flynn peered at the screen. "Nothing until noon the next day."

"What does that tell you?"

Flynn grimaced. *Stupid.* "Mahoney was there. The first call was to say, 'I'm here, what do I do?' The second was to say, 'not yet, she has company.' The final call was to say, 'the coast is clear, meet me.' But there's no fingerprint evidence on him."

"Why should there be?" Lee said. "He's smart. The breakfast arrangement was to ensure each would have an alibi for Wednesday morning, but who needed it more? Whether it's Tuesday evening or Wednesday morning, she's home alone. He's the one who needs witnesses. If I were a betting person, I'd say he did the slapping around. It's a man thing."

"The ME said the opposite," Flynn said.

"And the ME was a man," Lee said. "And, think about the slapping. Why? The only reason is that you're trying to hurt someone so they'll give you information. What did Sally Kahn have to give?"

"Photos she had taken. Lawsuit stuff. Divorce stuff."

"As motives go, this shaming thing with photos is pretty weak, and, plot points of romance novels aside, most wives have a very good idea of whether or not their spouses are running around on them," Lee said. "Tell me more about the lawsuit."

"Mahoney tears down little houses and builds big ones. They do that out here in the boonies. He paid a ton of money for the little house next door to Sally Kahn and poured a foundation for a big, new house. Sally, though, had documented that the larger foundation encroached on seasonal wetlands…"

"Vernal pools?"

"Yeah, vernal pools. Why am I the only person in Massachusetts who doesn't know anything about them? She was going to file suit to stop the construction. He's a small builder with a big gambling habit. If he doesn't put up his three houses this summer, he's toast."

"Now you're talking motive," Lee said.

"The lawsuit papers were still in her office," Flynn said. "The photos weren't, though they were in her computer."

"If the person filing the lawsuit isn't around anymore, you can have all the paperwork in the world, Lee said. "It doesn't matter. He wanted the password to her computer. She wouldn't give it to him. My guess is that Irina egged Mahoney on. It doesn't make any difference which one pushed her down the stairs. They're both culpable. Make sure you dust and sweep that office thoroughly."

"I have Norfolk County's finest working on it."

"I thought Ray sent you out a full team?"

Oops, Flynn thought. *Now how did she know about that?*

"They did the crime scene," Flynn said. "There was no reason to dust upstairs. The computer just came into the picture this morning. And my boss said there was to be no more 'outside interference.' That means Boston PD. He's got a Massachusetts map in his office and everything inside Route 128 is blank. It just says 'Here Be Dragons.' He's kind of touchy on the subject."

"Especially after he went on Channel 5 in full parade dress to say he had solved the crime," she said.

"You saw that? I didn't know you were a fan of the six o'clock news," Flynn said.

"A chief makes that big a fool of himself in front of a camera, it gets around. They're going to be showing that one in command training class for the next few years. Have you decided how you're going to approach Mahoney?"

"That's why I was calling, though it looks like we're upping the charge from accessory to homicide. I lured the cokehead son in with nothing more than a box of donuts and the promise of family riches. I don't think Mahoney will fall for the same deal."

"You remember the Hollingsworth murder?" Lee said.

"Of course."

"Do you remember how you got a confession out of Frank Sitta?"

"And you think that would work here."

"If I were working the case with you – and I wish I were – it's what I'd do," Lee said.

"Do you miss being on the street?"

"I think you know the answer to that question."

"I'll let you know how it comes out."

Flynn hung up the phone and immediately called his contact at the BU Russian Studies department.

"I have three leads," the student said.

"After you give them to me, I want you to do something else," Flynn interjected. "I need about twenty pages of something typewritten in Russian. It doesn't make any difference what it is. But on the first page, it has to say, in Russian and in English, 'Transcript of Interview with Irina Volnovich Burroughs' and today's date."

"Do you mean like a question and answer session?" the student asked.

"Exactly."

"I can give you that with her name in every answer field. I just have to do a global replace…"

"You don't need to tell me how you do it. I just need it this afternoon to show someone who doesn't read Russian but who will be impressed. Can you email it?"

"In about ten minutes. I just need to locate a St. Petersburg Police letterhead. I'll drop it onto the cover."

"Is that where she is?"

"Yes," the student said. "She asked three people if they could put her up for a month on short notice. They're all in or near St. Petersburg. Two said 'yes', although one said she could only stay a few days."

"Did she finalize arrangements with any of them?" Flynn asked.

"That's the funny part. She accepted the offer from all three. Kind of like double booking a hotel room. Would you like me to call to see which one she went to?"

"No, I'll let the St. Petersburg police do that. What are the odds that the police over there speak English?"

"In St. Petersburg, someone there will. I'll send the names and addresses in English." The student sounded disappointed.

Flynn started making notes. When he had finished, he placed his call to Mahoney. To his surprise, Mahoney agreed to come in and give a statement that afternoon.

At five o'clock, Chuck Mahoney sat by Flynn's desk. A twenty-page document in Russian was on one side of the desk, in plain sight, as was the tape recorder.

"I'm going to ask that you give me a statement," Flynn said. "You have the right to be represented by counsel."

"I'll stop the statement if I think it goes too far," Mahoney said.

"Mr. Mahoney, you were acquainted with Sally Kahn."

"I had her as a teacher in high school. I've known her from around town for many years."

"Was Mrs. Kahn threatening to sue you?"

Mahoney nodded, an unconscious affirmation to himself that he knew how to answer this question. "I received several letters from an attorney representing Mrs. Kahn. The letters made a series of allegations about a house I am building. I informed the attorney – Diane Terwilliger, I believe – that the allegations were without merit, and that I have all proper documentation allowing me to go forward with the house."

"Did you ever discuss the issue directly with Mrs. Kahn?"

"No. It was all done through her attorney," Mahoney said.

"Do you know Irina Burroughs?"

This time, there was a hesitation. "I know Irina Burroughs." The answer was cautious.

"How would you characterize your relationship with Mrs. Burroughs?"

Another hesitation. "We see each other socially."

Flynn kept the pace of questions smooth. "When did you last see Mrs. Burroughs?"

The answer came quickly. "She asked for, and I gave her, a ride to Logan on Friday afternoon."

"Did Mrs. Burroughs indicate to you where she was going?"

"She told me she was flying to Russia to be with her mother."

"Did you speak with Irina Burroughs Tuesday evening?"

"I don't remember," Mahoney said.

"Do you own a cell phone with the number 508-613-7004?"

There was a long hesitation. "Yes."

Flynn pushed a printout of Irina's cell phone calls across the table. "Here is a list of calls made by Mrs. Burroughs on Tuesday evening. You will see that all three of those calls were to your cell phone. Can you describe the nature of the three calls?"

Mahoney only glanced at the printout. "I don't remember receiving any calls from her. I see that all of them are for one minute. She may have gone to voice mail. She may have just let the phone ring long enough that the cell phone company charged her for a call. I think they do that if you let a phone ring more than a few times."

Flynn thought to himself, *that's nice, but I've got confirmation of Irina talking to you in two out of three of those calls.* "May I ask where you were on Tuesday evening between ten o'clock and midnight?"

The answer came promptly, another nod of the head. Mahoney was back to his well-rehearsed alibi. "I was at my office on North Street, reviewing construction schedules."

"Can anyone corroborate your whereabouts?"

"Not that I can think of."

"Did you see Mrs. Burroughs on Tuesday evening?"

"No."

"Did you see Mrs. Burroughs on Wednesday or Thursday?"

"I don't recall. If so, it would have been for a brief period."

Flynn pulled the Russian-language document into view. "Mr.

Mahoney, we have developed certain evidence that links Mrs. Burroughs to the death of Sally Kahn. We believe Mrs. Burroughs fled the country in order to avoid answering questions on the subject.   However, Mrs. Burroughs has been located in St. Petersburg, Russia. She has been interviewed by the police there and has responded to a set of questions I developed."

For the first time in the interview, Mahoney looked momentarily surprised. Then, his face relaxed into a smile that was only partially suppressed.

Flynn patted the document with his hand. "Mr. Mahoney, I have been given the gist of Mrs. Burroughs answers orally by a Russian translator with an imperfect command of English. It's likely to be a couple of days before I can obtain a translation of the transcript of the interview. What I can say is this." At this point, Flynn pulled out his handwritten notes.   "Mrs. Burroughs categorically denies any participation in Mrs. Kahn's death and says that the fingerprints we found on certain items in the house are attributable to her having been in the house previously. She says that her being sighted in front of Mrs. Kahn's house that evening is a case of mistaken identity.   She has, however, told the St. Petersburg police that she believes that *you* had a strong motive to kill Mrs. Kahn because of the pending lawsuit between the two of you. She says she called you from her home, although on her cell phone, to make certain you weren't going near Mrs. Kahn's home, and she says the second and third time she called you were, in fact, in or near her home."

Flynn turned off the tape recorder. "Let me lay my cards on the table, Mr. Mahoney. I think Irina Burroughs killed Sally Kahn. I think she is trying to build an alibi for herself at your expense. Why she's doing that, I don't know. There is absolutely nothing to link you to the crime scene. I've also gone through the lawsuit paperwork. It's a crock. Sally Kahn was an environmental nut case. Her suit would be thrown out in five minutes."

Flynn waited for a change in Mahoney's expression. There was none. "What Irina Burroughs has going for herself is that getting an extradition from Russia is a three- to five-year process and that, even if the process were expedited, she could just as easily disappear a second time. In short, she's beyond our reach unless we can find a way to lure her back on her own. I'm going to turn the tape recorder back on and we'll proceed."

Flynn touched the 'record' button again. "Mr. Mahoney, do you have any knowledge of Irina Burroughs' whereabouts on Tuesday evening?"

"None at all," Mahoney said.

Flynn turned the tape recorder off again. "Mr. Mahoney, I'm sorry if I did not make myself clear. I need to make it evident to Irina Burroughs that we've bought her story. She needs to believe that she's no longer a suspect, and that there's no reason for her not to come home."

He paused. So *much for the carrot. Let's try the stick.* "Now let me tell you what else I know. I've gone through Mrs. Burroughs' emails and I know about your relationship with her. That's not at issue, although, if need be, I would make it one. I also know that Irina believed that Sally Kahn had taken photos of the two of you and that Mrs. Kahn intended to distribute those photos. However, there were no photos in Sally Kahn's house and no other record in the digital camera we found in her home. I presume Mrs. Burroughs took the photos and the jpegs. I believe that was the motive for killing Mrs. Kahn. I'm going to turn the tape recorder back on now."

Flynn touched the 'record' button.

"Mr. Mahoney, I'll ask you again if you have any knowledge of Mrs. Burroughs whereabouts on Tuesday evening."

"I have no knowledge of her whereabouts," Mahoney said. "I wish you the best of luck in extraditing her. I have nothing else to say."

With that, Mahoney rose from the chair and, without looking back, left the police station.

He didn't bite, Flynn thought. *He had every opportunity and every motive, and he didn't take the bait. Why the hell not?*

10.

Flynn had run out of options. Flowers were out of the question. His visit to Hardington Wine and Spirits reinforced his belief that he knew nothing about wine. Moreover, whatever he brought could or would be misconstrued as a sexual overture. Chocolates? Even more potential for a misunderstanding. Now, he walked the aisles of Taylor's Department Store, looking at the display of Yankee Candles. Why would people buy these things as presents? Were they ever used? Or, was there a perpetual chain of Yankee Candles gifted and then re-gifted as the need arose?

He paused in front of a display of plants. On impulse, and perhaps with a sense of desperation, he seized one and paid for it before he could second-guess himself into putting it back. Even as the clerk placed it in a decorative bag that was half the price of the plant, Flynn began to regret the purchase.

Liz, too, was out of options. Her invitation to Flynn had been completely impulsive. She didn't even have the lobsters when she asked Flynn to dinner. But she wanted to talk about progress in the investigation with the one person who knew more than she did. Sometime that day, Liz had discovered finding Sally's murderer had become all-consuming. Finding the solution, she also realized, was the most important event in her life in months; perhaps even years. Moreover, Liz believed she alone understood all of the intricacies of the puzzle.

This realization had quickly been followed by an afternoon of second-guessing herself and then by a round of calls to everyone connected to the case in an effort to find a third, and preferably a fourth, for dinner. But Roland was in Ogunquit for the weekend and Diane Terwilliger had a house full of grandchildren. Everyone else had left for the Cape or other weekend destinations. More than at any time in recent months, Liz felt anger that David was always away.

How did this all start? David didn't have to start his own company. He had feelers. Hell, he had downright offers. Real CEO jobs within twenty miles of Hardington that would bring him home every evening and at least allow them to have breakfast together in the morning. Instead, he had to create Phillips Management, the original one-man show. A corporate savior for short-term hire. Except that every job was out of town. Atlanta twice, Syracuse, Greensboro, Alexandria, and now Pittsburgh. Didn't companies in New England ever get into trouble? And when the assignment in Pittsburgh was done, how much time would David really take off? Would it be three months as promised, or would another opportunity come along in two weeks, just like Pittsburgh?

You left me here alone with this too-large house. You left me with no one to talk to and too much time on my hands. Just once I'd like to...

The doorbell rang.

Liz looked at herself in a mirror and was dissatisfied. She smoothed an errant bang and said to herself, *it's lobsters with a cop, for God's sake.*

Flynn, from the vantage point of the front door, tried without success to make sense of the ebb and flow of the landscaping around him. He could not name a single plant or flower of the dozens – and perhaps hundreds that were within sight. He knew daisies and roses, and there were none of either specimen to be seen. One bed seemed to be planted entirely in shades of yellow, another featured no flowers but rather, only plants of different leaf textures. It was all too complicated for him.

"Your garden just goes on forever," Flynn said when the door opened.

"I hate to mow grass," Liz said. "This is the somewhat more expensive alternative."

"I suspect it's a considerably more expensive alternative," Flynn said, looking across the expanse of beds.

Liz smiled. "I was at the Chelsea Flower Show last year and I was standing in line to get a drink. Two British gentlemen in front of me were talking, and one said to the other – very matter of factly – 'Penelope has a hundred pound a week perennial habit.' That's all I heard of the conversation, that there's a woman somewhere in England who routinely buys about a hundred and eighty dollars' worth of plants every week. I figure, as long as Penelope is out there, I'm always going to be in the minor leagues."

"That man was right in one way, though – plants are addictive. You get hooked on hostas –" she gestured at an area on a shaded side of the house, "– and the next thing you know, you're looking for varieties with names like '*Fujibotan*', a very tiny one of which will set you back an unimaginable amount of money."

"Your husband apparently encourages you."

"My husband promised me he would put in at least five hours a week during the season and do all of the heavy lifting. Unfortunately, David holds up less of his end of the bargain every year. He calls the garden a 'canvas' where I can express creativity, except that this canvas needs to be weeded every week. Come on in and tell me how the case is going."

They went inside.

"I brought you this," Flynn said, proffering the bag.

"I was wondering if that was a purse," Liz said, smiling. She opened the bag and extracted a four-inch high cactus. "Cactaceae! I have a weakness for these. *Echinocereus* if I'm not mistaken – that's an orchid cactus. That's very thoughtful. Thank you."

Flynn relaxed slightly. He had only known it was a cactus with a flower on it.

"You were going to tell me about the case. And in return, I think I can bring you up to speed on Landini Brothers." She pointed him toward a rattan chair in a large screened porch. He could see more gardens in the back of the house.

"At this point, I'd bet the house that it's your friend Irina, aided and abetted by Chuck Mahoney," Flynn said. "Irina called Chuck twice from the school parking lot, and then a third time about ten minutes later, just after Tim Kahn left his mother's house. They didn't speak afterward, which tells me that she was probably calling that third time to say that the coast was clear." Flynn noted to himself that he was not giving credit for this last deduction to Vicky Lee. "Mahoney came in to give a statement a little while ago. He says he was at his office on North Street going over construction schedules, and he doesn't remember any calls from Irina. Of course, he has no witnesses to say he was in his office, and we have none that put him in Sally Kahn's home. We can, however, put Irina there. Her fingerprints are all over the items laid out for breakfast."

"Chuck Mahoney gave a statement?"

"Yeah, I've got to find a way to lure Irina back from Russia of her own accord. Russia's rules regarding extradition are essentially unenforceable unless the government has a compelling reason to do so, and Irina isn't exactly something the United States values. She is, by the way, almost certainly in St. Petersburg. The damn thing is that I gave him every opportunity to 'help bring her to justice' and he just walked away from it."

"As long as she's five thousand miles away, she isn't going to be testifying against him," Liz offered. "Here, she might decide to trade his complicity for a shorter sentence."

"Spoken like a good defense attorney," Flynn said. "I tried that. I read from a 'transcript' that I had some kids at BU cook up that Irina denied everything and said she was certain it was Mahoney who had done it, and that she had called him to tell him not to harm Sally Kahn. The damn thing is, he seemed to know it was a con job. He could barely suppress a smile during the whole thing."

"Maybe he knows that the Russian police could never move that quickly," Liz offered. "I mean, she only landed about eighteen hours ago. And how did she get from Moscow to St. Petersburg? My knowledge of Russian geography is a little sketchy, but it's got to be five or six hours by train, unless she flew. And, in that case, why didn't she fly straight to St. Petersburg from London? Either way, the St. Petersburg police are going to have to track her down and get that statement, and that takes time."

"By which time the trail will be cold," Flynn said quickly. "Liz, time is the enemy of solving cases. The first twenty-four hours are critical. Every day after that, memories fade and clues get covered up. And I spent the first day trying to prove that Tim Kahn was the perp, by which time Irina had time to get on a plane out of the country. Now, all I've got left to go on is a very smooth operator who has an answer for everything."

"How do you mean?" Liz asked.

"Did he know Sally Kahn? Of course, he had her as a teacher," Flynn said. "Was there a lawsuit pending? Of course, but all his paperwork was in place. Did he ever speak with Sally Kahn about the lawsuit? No, it was all handled though the lawyers. Then why did he pour a foundation and then shift the work to the site on Lake Drive? Because some people named Sullivan were all signed up to buy it. Did he know Irina Burroughs? Sure, he even tacitly acknowledges he was having an affair with her. Did he drive her to the airport when she fled the country? Sure, but he didn't know she was suspected of anything. Did he…"

"Wait a second," Liz said. "Did he say the Sullivans were all lined up to buy the house he was building on Lake Drive?"

Flynn reached into his jacket pocket for his notes and flipped through pages. "That's what I wrote down. He was at the site on Pequot on Tuesday afternoon, and it was with people who are buying the house he's building on Lake Drive. Name of Sullivan."

Liz's brow furrowed. "Then maybe I'm remembering it wrong, but I met them at the service last night. They were with Chuck and Jane. And I would swear Chuck said they were buying the property on Pequot."

"That's a strange thing to lie about," Flynn said. "But, even if he did – and he'd swear I misunderstood him – all it proves is that he took the lawsuit more seriously than he's letting on. It still doesn't put him at Sally Kahn's on Tuesday night."

As she prepared the lobsters, Liz related her discussion with Alvin Duclos and her reconnaissance trip to Landini Brothers. "It all comes down to when work resumes on the waste treatment plant," she said. "Presumably, the Landinis won't take any more barrels unless they know they can dispose of them."

"I would presume the EPA would have the weight to 'ask' a contractor or a union to set aside their differences for a day," Flynn said.

"Remember, this was news to Alvin as of about two hours ago," Liz said. "I think you're confusing the EPA with an efficient organization."

"They certainly seem to have moved with lightning speed in the past two days. You may be selling them short," Flynn said.

Wine was poured. Lobsters were served.

"A cactus is an interesting plant," Liz said. "It kind of warns you off with its exterior – 'don't get too close to me'. But it has magnificent flowers that manage to stay in bloom for a very long time. They need very little attention. In fact, they thrive on neglect."

"I just thought it was a nice plant."

"I'm beginning to think you brought me John Flynn in microcosm, Detective. Do you realize that in three days, you've heard virtually my entire life story but everything I know about you could be written on a three-by-five card, with room left over for care and feeding instructions?"

Flynn laughed. "I guess I'm not a very interesting person."

"You're married. Is that what your wife thinks?"

"That's a long story." Flynn took a drink of his wine.

"I like long stories."

"Well, this one isn't worth telling. Let's just say that my wife and I have been married a very long time but that we lead lives that cross only occasionally."

"Do you have children?"

Flynn was quiet for a moment. Then he said softly, "I don't really like to talk about myself. I'm sorry."

Do you have children? Yes, I have a son. His name is Matthew. And he is the reason why Annie and I barely speak. But I'm not here to talk about Matthew. I'm here to solve a murder.

He looked across the table, where Liz had an expression on her face that showed hurt. "That wasn't very kind of me, Liz. I'm not used to opening up with people. I was on the Boston PD for more than thirty-five years. I was a beat cop for nearly twelve years and I was a detective for twenty-four. I was – I am – a very good detective. I follow facts. I worked those years with a partner. I had three partners in twenty-four years. In Hardington, I'm working solo for the first time."

"Do I qualify as a partner?"

"Actually, you've done an incredible job for someone without formal training. I'll be honest. If you weren't helping, I would have called in the Mass state police on my own. Instead, we've got the case – and by 'we', I mean the two of us – at a place that is very satisfying – if you set aside the little matter that one perp has made her way to another continent and the other has this Cheshire Cat grin on his face when you talk to him."

"What do you still need to do?" Liz asked.

"Well, let's make a list. The first thing is to locate your buddy Irina. That means a call to the St. Petersburg police. I called British Airways to try to get the name on her 'next of kin' advisory form, and I'm waiting for them to get back to me... if they decide they're required to cooperate. There's a crew from the Norfolk County Sheriff's Department going over Sally Kahn's computer and her bedroom for fingerprints, and that may be our best hope, God help us. If we have Mahoney's prints on the computer, we have a case. If not, there's nothing that ties him to the scene except circumstantial evidence – which, in Massachusetts, is tantamount to no evidence."

Flynn took out his notes again. "The case against Irina is pretty solid. I'm going to go through the whole email trail tomorrow and see if there is anything from Mahoney that implicates him. In the world of business, you'd be surprised how often people put smoking guns into emails. Unfortunately, in the world of just-plain people, we just don't tend to email our co-conspirators and say, 'meet me at seven to go murder Fred.'"

"Actually," Liz said, "I'm fairly well acquainted with how incriminating business emails can be. My husband brings home the ones he finds in the companies he runs. I think he thinks they'll amuse me. But from what I know of Irina, and what I've seen of her emails, I wouldn't rule out her having sent out details of what she planned to do."

Flynn put down his notebook. "Which reminds me... I don't want to know if you have any electronic files from anyone, because those files are what the law calls 'tainted fruit', and they could make the case against Irina go south in a big hurry. Were I you, I would lose those files – if they exist. Is that clear?"

Liz said it was clear. And made a note to go through the complete files in case there were any smoking guns imbedded in them.

"Don't you have an obligation to tell the district attorney that you've cleared Tim? Why is he still in jail?"

Flynn's face showed a pained expression. "Tim hasn't really been cleared. I just have a much better suspect. And, Tim 'confessed' to our illustrious chief of police, who personally went on television to say that the streets were safe again. Chief Harding got himself into that one. Unfortunately, I've got to get him out of it. Also, the minute I ask the DA to release Tim, the staties are going to descend on the case like the Keystone Cops. The only reason they're not banging on the door now is because, officially at least, the investigation is marked 'solved'."

Liz tilted her head, thinking aloud. "Is there a chance that Tim saw someone? The kids said Irina was hanging around the house around the time Tim left. And, he walked to Washington Street."

"No one ever asked him." *Why didn't I think of that?*

"And, has Irina used her cell phone to call anyone since she got to Russia?"

"Would one of our cell phones work over there?"

"It depends," Liz said. "There's some sort of a chip that some phones have that allows you to call when you're not in the U.S. David's phone has one. I know mine doesn't because I couldn't call here from England. Could her cell phone company tell you?"

"I guess I need to ask. And it also means I ought to go if I'm going to finish this homework assignment."

Liz started to speak. *Don't be in such a hurry. It's still early. No. It will come out the wrong way.* She finally said, "If I'm your partner, what can I do to help?"

Flynn considered things. "Unfortunately, most of the questions have to be asked officially, meaning they have to come from a policeman, and I don't want 'impersonating an officer' added to whatever else is on your rap sheet. But you seem to have a knack for knowing people who add to the information list, so just keep asking questions."

* * * * *

Stupid jerk. Coward. Fool. Flynn called himself all these names on the drive into Dedham. *And you brought her a damn cactus.* He slammed his hand on the dashboard. *It's not your place. Don't get too close. You don't need that kind of trouble…*

Tim Kahn sat across from him in the interview room. The orange jump suit highlighted Tim's jaundiced appearance. Beside him, a woman who couldn't have been two years out of law school sat in jeans and a URI sweatshirt. The meeting had been brokered over his cell phone with the promise that there was a potential for good news.

"Tim, I need you to think back to Tuesday evening," Flynn said. "We know you left your mother's house at ten. We know you went to see Dwayne Jones over on the Washington Street projects. Then, you went to Joe Haskell's and partied with the two girls. I need to know what route you took to get to each of these places and what you saw along the way."

"What does he get in return?" asked the woman from the public defender's staff. Her name was Tiffany. *There are now lawyers with names like Tiffany*, he thought.

"Your client may get a ticket out of here." Then he said to Tim, "Let's start with the moment you said goodbye to your mother."

"Are you acknowledging that Tim's mother was still alive when he left the house?"

Flynn turned to the lawyer and glared. "There are times when the best thing that a lawyer can do is listen and pay attention. This is one of those times."

Tim glanced at the lawyer, whose face was red from Flynn's comment. A moment later, she nodded at Tim.

"I told Mom I was going to take the train back into Boston, and she offered to drive me to the train station. She said it was a long walk."

"This is important. Did you see anyone outside of your house?"

"It was dark."

"I know it was dark. Did you see anyone?"

Tim was quiet for several seconds, his eyes closed. "No."

"How did you get to Dwayne's?"

"I cut down through the school."

Flynn sat up at attention. "Down the path by your mother's house and into the parking lot?"

"That's what I said."

"Tim, think very hard. I know it was dark, but tell me what cars you remember seeing in the parking lot."

Tim closed his eyes. "There were cars... There was a police car. Patrol car. It came into the lot. No lights, just checking things. I saw it and went part way back up the path until it left."

"Why did you do that?"

Tim looked at Flynn quizzically. "I've been staying away from the fuzz since I was eleven. It's instinct."

Flynn nodded. "Go on."

"The patrol car did a pass around the lot, slowing up for the cars. I think one had a couple of kids in it because they took off as soon as the patrol car went by. I mean, the patrol car didn't stop or anything, it just cruised by real slow. The car – it was one of those really ugly things – like it's got a construction john bolted to it – left real quick. The light never came on in the car, so I didn't get a look at them. Anyway, the patrol car left the parking lot with the little car driving out about a minute behind it."

"How long did you stay up on the path?"

"Just until they left. Then I kind of made a circle around the edge of the parking lot, keeping to the trees."

"Did you see any other cars?"

"Just one more. A couple of minutes later, some fancy SUV came down the road into the parking lot. That's when I picked up my pace."

"Can you describe that car?"

"I didn't see the color, and they all look alike."

"How did you know it was fancy?"

"It had one of those – what do you call them – 'rhino guards' on the front of it. Like they're going on a safari in Massachusetts."

Flynn was now sitting up perfectly straight. *Chuck Mahoney's*

Range Rover had a rhino guard. "See anyone inside the car?"

"It was dark."

"If I showed you photos of SUVs, do you think you could identify the car?"

"Where is this going, Detective?" the attorney interjected.

"Miss…" – he had forgotten her last name, and could focus only on 'Tiffany' – "…Tim may have seen something or he may not have seen something. You don't want to compromise his testimony and neither do I. Don't make a rookie mistake that sends your client to prison. Just listen, pay attention…" Flynn swallowed the last three words he had nearly added, *"and shut up."*

"Tim, I've reconstructed your evening by talking with the people you were with Tuesday night, and I've got a gap of between an hour and an hour and a half that I can't account for. You left your mother's house at ten, but you didn't get to Dwayne's until well after eleven. If you cut through the school, you should have been at his apartment in fifteen minutes, tops. Where were you the rest of the time?"

Tim looked at Tiffany, who was silent, though clearly fuming.

"It's important, Tim," Flynn urged.

"I don't have to say anything."

"Tim, there's a district attorney who is aching to put you in Concord for the rest of your life, and he's going to use that gap to say you went back to your mother's house and killed her."

Tim swallowed. "I broke into a house."

"What?" the lawyer said, sitting upright.

"Where?" Flynn asked.

"On Preservation Way. One of the big houses. I don't know what number. Second one on the right."

"How did you know it was empty?"

"Joe told me."

"Joe Haskell?"

"Yeah. He said there's a girl there who is one of his… well, who buys stuff from him, and she said she and her parents were going away for a week. Joe said it was the second house on the right."

"What did you take?"

"I found about three hundred dollars and a couple of watches. I also took a couple of checks from a brokerage account."

"Do you still have these things?"

"They're in my apartment."

There were other questions, but they could wait. The time line had been filled in and, more important, Flynn had his first link that put Mahoney at Sally Kahn's house on the night of the murder.

Outside of the interview room, Flynn spoke with the young attorney. "Your client will probably have to plead out on burglary, drug possession and a couple of other things, but there's strong evidence that someone else may have killed his mother. My advice – and I strongly encourage you to check with the public defender – is that you let Tim sit tight at least until Monday morning. I may be able to come up with enough evidence to release Tim by then, and all he could do between now and then is to get himself into trouble."

* * * * *

The phone was ringing. Caller ID said it was David's cell phone. Liz didn't want to answer it. She tried out excuses. *I was at the supermarket. I was in the shower.* The phone stopped ringing, indicating the answering machine had picked up. Liz exhaled. Almost immediately, she heard her cell phone ringing from her purse. *Damn.*

"David! Was that you on the house phone just now? I was out in the yard."

"And I ought to be there weeding," he said. "I'm sorry."

"It would sound better if it were the first time you had ever bagged the weekend."

"What if I said I could get home Monday night?"

"I'd say you rigged it so you didn't have to mow the lawn, but I'd love to have you home." *Do I mean it? Yes, of course I mean it.*

"How's the case coming?" David asked.

"Chuck Mahoney and Irina. A regular Bonnie and Clyde. Talking on cell phones just before the murder. Except that Chuck says he never got the calls. Meanwhile, the police are trying to track down Irina in St. Petersburg. You're missing some good stuff."

"It sounds like I'd be in the way. Anything else on her computer?" David asked.

The conversation fell into a familiar pattern. David spoke of business, Liz of the garden and events in town. Liz fully described the meeting with Diane Terwilliger but omitted lobsters with Flynn. So the subjects were safe ones. Perennials to be divided, rock walls to be extended. After twenty minutes, Liz felt she had accounted for her time adequately, the dinner with Flynn obliterated from the official marital record.

After the call, Liz scrolled through Irina's email file in detail, making notes as she went. The messages between Irina and Mahoney were telling about the relationship. Irina's notes were lengthy and romantic. Mahoney's – when he answered – were terse and non-committal. Even after a weekend at Foxwoods – apparently the one at which Sally had photographed the two of them – about which Irina had written three long, rapturous messages, Mahoney had responded only to the first, and that with a two sentence response, typed on his Blackberry, *"Great time. Do it again soon?"*

As to any plot to murder Sally Kahn, there was only the one, cryptic message from three days before the murder. It was the same message Flynn and Patrolman Frankel had found earlier that day:

"Chuck,
Call me when you get this. I think Sally has pictures of us."

Mahoney had not responded to the message.

At 11:30, tired and disappointed that she had found no 'smoking gun', she shut down the computer and turned off the bedroom light. *It has to be there. I just haven't looked in the right place.*

* * * * *

Flynn returned home at 11:30. He saw no lights in his house. Walking softly into the kitchen, he saw the inevitable note on the refrigerator door.

At my sister's for the weekend. Dinner in the fridge.

11.

Sunday

Liz's cell phone rang at six. She had been working in the perennial beds since a few minutes after five. It was within a few days of the summer solstice and the sun rose at a preposterously early hour. The birds had started their morning cacophony at 4:30, and Liz found that drapes and double-pane windows kept out neither light nor sound.

David was full of good cheer. A lengthy conference call the previous evening had produced some sort of breakthrough that Liz did not fully understand, did not follow on a phone call, and was not particularly in a mood to parse. Instead, her thoughts were directed toward an infestation of weeds that mimicked the tender late summer perennials just coming to life under the soil.

And toward the question of who Irina would contact to let them know she had arrived safely in Russia, and where she might be staying. Liz made a mental list of the handful of garden club members with whom Irina was friendly. Russia was wired, Russia had phones. A woman who left the country suddenly would want certain people to know she had arrived safely. Mary Giametti, certainly. The two sat together at every meeting. And there was Iseul Kim, the shy, Korean-born woman whom everyone in the club took under their wing, and whom Irina had made her confidante. If Irina had contacted anyone, if would be these two.

"David, why does your phone work in Europe while mine doesn't?"

She heard the laugh at the other end and was not amused. "We're still on the case this morning, I see."

I don't need the condescension right now, Liz thought.

"My phone has a GSM chip, yours doesn't," he said. "Europe and the U.S. have different cell phone standards. The newer the phone or the more expensive, the more likely that it has the circuitry to work anywhere. But even if the phone doesn't come GSM-enabled, you can buy a SIM card that has the chip – but don't ask me what SIM stands for. It's, like, thirty bucks and available at kiosks at every airport in Europe."

She put aside being miffed about the 'we're still on the case' comment and thanked him. The call ended a few minutes thereafter.

Liz knew Mary was a sporadic communicant at St. Teresa's, but with five masses on Sunday plus a Saturday-evening 'early bird special', there was no reliable time to assume that Mary would be awake and talking on a Sunday morning. But Isuel was a regular at the Congregational Church. Unless she was away for the weekend, she would be at the ten o'clock service.

Which means she would be reachable by phone by nine o'clock, perhaps earlier. Liz went back to her weeding, and to planning what she would say when she spoke with those two women.

* * * * *

Flynn awoke with a sense that today was the day.

At five o'clock, he had worked his way through international directory assistance and had reached an English-speaking officer of the St. Petersburg police. He had explained the need to find Irina and had provided the three names and addresses. His Russian counterpart, a police lieutenant named Droski, had understood the need for speed and had promised him both discretion and a prompt response.

Before six o'clock, he had downloaded and printed photos of as many vehicles he could find with non-standard front grills. If Tim Kahn could pick out the Range Rover, Flynn had the first solid lead linking Chuck Mahoney to Sally Kahn's death.

Before seven o'clock, he had called British Airways in London, going over the head of the regional representative with whom he had spoken a day earlier. Finding where Irina was staying was the first step toward getting her on a plane back to the United States.

At seven o'clock he began his drive toward Belmont, and the Sisters of Charity. Half an hour later, the secluded 1950s-era buildings were around him, sheltered under mature pines.

He entered a familiar building. A nun in full habit was there, reading the Boston *Globe* comics.

"What ever happened to *Dondi*?" she asked. "I used to live for that comic strip."

"There's probably some newspaper in North Dakota that still carries it, Sister Anne," Flynn said. "You could subscribe. I think you just liked it because it was about an orphan."

"That was fifteen years before I took my vows."

"I admit I was always a *Dick Tracy* fan myself," Flynn said. "I guess that means the comics we read are our destiny."

Sister Anne smiled. "You're looking better, John. I was worried about you for a couple of weeks there. You're apparently settling in at your new job. Hopkinton?"

"Hardington. Hopkinton's where they start the marathon."

"Matthew is looking forward to seeing you."

"Then we shouldn't keep him."

They walked to a building that bore the name, "St. Francis" and went in. It was a dormitory, with doors spaced every ten feet. They stopped at the fifth door.

"Matthew, your father is here," Sister Anne said, gently.

Flynn gave the nun a kiss on the cheek and squeezed her hand. She kept walking. "I'll be in the refectory if you need me," she said as she left.

Matthew sat on his bed, attired in a white Polo shirt and freshly pressed khakis. He looked up at Flynn and smiled.

"Hello, Matt," Flynn said. "It's Sunday. Would you like to take a walk?"

He did not wait for a response. Instead, Flynn offered his

hand and Matthew took it. Matthew was thirty-four, but his face was smooth and unlined. Matthew's hair was tousled, much as Flynn's had been at that age, but his coloring and face with a hint of freckles were those of Annie. Flynn walked slowly. Matthew set the pace, walking with a hint of unsteadiness.

There was a picnic table outside of the dormitory. Flynn led his son there, and Matthew sat obediently.

"It's been a good week, Matt. I feel like a detective again." And he told Matthew of the unfolding tale of the death of Sally Kahn. As he told the story, he focused on his son's face. He left nothing out. Not the comments by the medical examiner or even the previous evening's lobster dinner.

"I think you'd like Liz Phillips. She has a daughter a little younger than you. Apparently got married a year or two ago. I only saw a couple of photos, but she's quite a looker."

Hydrocephalus, he thought. It has a name now. In 1978 even doctors called it 'water on the brain', a demeaning name for a tragic... what? Accident? Birth defect?

The hospital said it wasn't their fault. It wasn't the forceps. It happened in the womb, an intrauterine infection. A normal delivery of a full-term male infant. But within days, something was wrong. The head was enlarged. 'An accumulation of cerebralspinal fluids in the ventricles of the brain.' The ventricles had enlarged, pressing the brain against the skull, damaging tissue.

Three decades ago, the concept of shunts to drain away the fluid or antibiotics to treat an inflammation in newborns was unknown. The prognosis from the experts was uniform. Severe neurological damage. Matthew might live a few months or even a few years, but he would never be 'normal'.

Under threat of lawsuit, the hospital and physicians group offered a settlement. Matthew would be placed in an acute care facility where he would receive care for the few months he was expected to live. John and Annie Flynn could put the tragedy behind them and get on with their lives.

And there it should have ended. Except that Annie said, "no." Annie Flynn, two years out of St. Elizabeth's School of Nursing, said, "I will care for my son."

And she did. And Matthew survived beyond the first year and it was hailed as a miracle. But the same miracle that kept Matthew alive slowly drained the life out of the marriage of John and Annie Flynn. After five years, Annie finally acknowledged that she could not provide the twenty-four hour care that Matthew needed, and the Sisters of Charity were contacted.

Annie grieved another year that she had failed her son, but the grief inexorably turned to anger that John had not helped enough. Annie went back to nursing, John slipped deeper into a primary identity not as a husband or father, but as a Boston policeman. And their lives together became lives lived separately.

"So you see the pickle I'm in," Flynn said. "Everything is circumstantial. Everything depends on getting this Russian divorcee to come back to Boston willingly. And I have no leverage."

Matthew sat, looking attentive, and smiled. He had never spoken. It did not occur to his mind that words were possible or expected. And so every week Flynn had come here and sat and talked, or walked the campus of this forgotten corner of the Archdiocese of Boston.

Sister Anne had spoken candidly of the archbishop's desire to close and sell off the facility. "They're waiting us out," she had said one morning a year earlier. "We're no longer in the resources guide. We're not on the web site. Our last new child was six years ago. And once we retire or the last child leaves, Cardinal O'Malley has twenty acres of prime real estate to sell to the highest bidder." In her voice that morning, Flynn had detected equal parts bitterness, defiance, and resignation.

At ten thirty, Flynn led Matthew to the reception area. Sister Anne had moved on to Real Estate. "A triple-decker in Dorchester for seven-ninety-five," she said. "I think I went into the wrong business."

"I don't think so," Flynn said. "From what I can tell, you're in exactly the right business. See you next week."

Flynn did not ask if there had been any change, for there was never any change.

By habit, he flipped through his notes as he walked back to the car. His phone had not rung while he was with Matthew, but it was still early by Sunday standards. Talking through the case had allowed him to put things in a different perspective. He better realized the urgency of the fingerprint report from Norfolk Sheriff's, and cursed himself that he had yielded to Chief Harding's demand that only 'local' resources be used. He dialed the number for the evidence lab and reached a kid who knew nothing about the case.

"Are there any adults working today?" Flynn asked caustically.

"I'm not sure I understand you," the young voice on the other end of the line said.

"Who is the senior officer in the evidence lab today?"

"We don't really have the lab open on Sunday, sir. I'm sure they'll get right on it tomorrow morning, though."

Flynn hung up before he said something that would get reported up the chain of command. All the way to Hardington, he swore that he would never again obey an idiotic order, regardless of who gave it.

* * * * *

Liz stared at the clock, watching the second hand, creating a rationalization. If services are at ten, then you have to be ready to go by nine thirty, and you must have had breakfast by nine, which means you were awake and showered by eight thirty.

Eight fifteen. Close enough.

Isuel Kim, to her relief, was also an early riser, and had been baking since seven.

"I know this is a strange question, but did Irina call you on Thursday or Friday?"

She had. Friday morning. And told Isuel that she was going to

Russia for a few weeks to see her mother, who was ill.

"Have you heard from her since? A phone call? An email?"

No. But it was just Sunday. Irina had been in Russia for only about a day.

Mary Giametti sounded as though she was still on her first cup of coffee. She, too, had received a call on Friday morning from Irina, saying she wouldn't be at the memorial service because of a family emergency. And she, too, had not heard from Irina since Friday, but was similarly unconcerned. "She'll call," Mary said.

Liz hung up the phone feeling vaguely dissatisfied by the answers she had received.

The garden club yearbook didn't list cell phones, but Irina had given the number to Liz at some point during the past year and Liz had jotted it in the margin of her book. She dialed the number. It went immediately to a voice mail box, indicating the phone was turned off – or was out of range.

"*This is ridiculous*," she said to herself, and heard Flynn's words from Saturday. "*...the questions have to be asked officially, meaning they have to come from a policeman... I don't want 'impersonating an officer' added to whatever else is on your rap sheet...*"

"Damn it. She's called someone. And they know where she's staying." This was said to no person, though her cat, Abigail, looked up expectantly. "And how do they know I'm not a police officer?"

She found Irina's wireless carrier on her second try and found that there was a 'law enforcement liaison' office that honored such requests.

"I need all activity since Friday morning – calls or text messages – and I need it faxed or emailed to my home, because it's Sunday morning..."

It was no problem. Things frequently went to home email addresses on weekends. Liz breathed a sigh of relief. And thought it was fortunate that Pastor Allen of the Congregational Church did not hear confessions.

On her way to church, Main Street traffic was moving unusually slowly, but the reason was readily clear. Ten or twelve cars in front of her was a slow-moving flatbed trailer, on which was an oversized, bright-orange backhoe. The trailer was attempting to make the turn onto North Street, and was waiting for southbound cars to clear the road in order to have sufficient turning room.

This was the special excavator Chuck Mahoney had ordered, Liz thought. It's going to Lake Drive to tear out the foundation. Chuck is untouchable. He knows Irina is going to stay in Russia for a very long time. He has no doubt warned her that coming back would be a disaster for her. *He's going to get away with murder.*

* * * * *

At the Hardington police station, Flynn paged through the emails Eddie Frankel had laboriously organized. There was only the one frantic request from Irina to Chuck Mahoney's Blackberry. *"Call me when you get this. I think Sally has pictures of us."* And Mahoney would claim he had never seen it. Or had seen it and didn't care.

Flynn had the photos in question. Irina with Mahoney. Irina with Robert Portman. Photos that incriminated Mahoney in nothing more heinous than adultery. And he had made it clear that he couldn't care less.

His cell phone rang.

"This is Edward Hunt with British Airways in Boston," a clipped voice on the other end of the phone intoned. "First, I don't appreciate anyone going around me on security issues. It wastes times."

"My apology," Flynn said. "I was getting frustrated and time is very short. I'm looking for a suspect and it will only get harder to find her every day."

"Well, you're going to have to look somewhere else. I don't have a notification card for an Irina Volnovich or Irina Burroughs.

She wasn't on that flight."

"But she bought a ticket for…" Flynn thumbed through his notebook. "…BA 612. Boston to London. Connecting to Moscow."

"She may have bought a ticket, but she never checked in for the flight. Sorry."

Flynn knew enough not to vent frustration on British Airways, or to sound stupid by demanding to know what flight she might have taken. He thanked Hunt and hung up.

He was still staring at his phone when it rang a second time.

"This is Lieutenant Peter Droski…"

"Tell me you've found her."

"She is not in St. Petersburg, at least not at any of the three addresses you gave me."

"You're certain?"

"We paid a visit to each address. Each thought she was coming. No one has heard from her since Friday evening."

"Son of a bitch."

"Pardon, please?"

"Thank you, Lieutenant Droski. I'm sorry to have put you through such an effort for nothing."

"We can check immigration for you. Their records are computerized, but we do not have the same kind of quick access you have to such records in America. It may take two or three days. I would be pleased to make such a call."

"Thank you. I would appreciate it."

"My pleasure."

Flynn again stared at his phone. And thought about Chuck Mahoney. And the Cheshire Cat grin when Flynn told him about the interview with the Russian police.

Mahoney knew Irina wasn't in Russia.

And then the phone rang a third time.

* * * * *

Summer services were mercifully short. Coming out of the church, Liz spotted Isuel Kim and apologized for the early call. Then, from the corner of her eye, she saw Jane Mahoney opening the door of her aged station wagon.

"Jane!"

Liz saw her glance up, and then resume getting into the car. Liz ran through the church parking lot, Jane had backed out her car and was attempting to move around other cars to get to the exit.

"I don't have time to talk to you," Jane said. Her eyes were moist, her face tear-stained.

"What's wrong?"

"I don't have time to talk to you. Please leave me alone," she said and rolled up her window. Jane ran up over the curb, across a grass strip, and onto Main Street, the station wagon groaning with the effort.

Liz stood in the parking lot, her mouth open. On Friday evening, Jane had been effervescent and sociable. Thirty-six hours later, her demeanor had completely changed. Something had happened, though Liz could not guess what it was.

She quickly made her own way home and went immediately to her computer. There were the records from Verizon Wireless. She opened the email.

Irina had made no calls to anyone since Friday at noon.

She reached for the phone by her desk and called Flynn's cell phone number.

"John, it's Liz. I think Irina's dead."

* * * * *

They were in the police station, deserted except for the dispatcher. Flynn had quickly described his two calls from the St. Petersburg police and British Airways. Liz had explained that, sexual stereotypes aside, a woman with a cell phone did not put it in her purse and forget about it when she was traveling.

"It's human nature to stay in touch. At least it's a woman's nature. We call or text people to let them know we're all right. Irina's phone isn't turned on. It isn't being used."

Which, they agreed, led them to Chuck Mahoney.

Mahoney's statement said he had taken Irina to the airport.

"EZ Pass," Flynn said. "You can't get out of Logan without paying a toll. When I was at the construction site yesterday, I remember seeing an EZ Pass transponder on the Range Rover."

"You can get those records?" Liz asked.

"We do it every day. The perp tracking device. Except this time, I'll bet there's no toll for either the Callahan or Ted Williams Tunnel."

Flynn called EZ Pass and got a password from their law enforcement liaison. Three minutes later, Chuck Mahoney's EZ Pass transactions were on Flynn's computer screen. There was nothing on Thursday, Friday, or Saturday.

"So where is Irina?" Liz asked.

"Shallow grave is the best bet."

They looked at each other. "Or a foundation," they both said.

"The excavator he ordered was making the turn up North Street when I was going to church a little over an hour ago."

"Jesus Christ. I need backup." He yelled out to the dispatcher. "Who's on duty today? Who's on patrol right now?"

The dispatcher yelled back, "Palmer and Frankel."

Flynn turned to Liz. "Where's an intersection near the Lake Drive site?"

Liz thought. "North and Charles. It's about a half mile away."

Flynn loped to the dispatcher's desk. "Let me talk to Frankel."

A connection was made. "Eddie, it's John Flynn. I need you to be at the intersection of North and Charles in five minutes. No lights, no sirens. You need to be armed and ready. And, whatever you do, don't drive down Lake Drive. You understand?"

Frankel said he understood.

"I'm going with you," Liz said.

"I'm going to arrest Mahoney for the murder of Sally Kahn, and there's a damned good chance I'm going to find the body of Irina Burroughs in that foundation he's crunching into rubble."

"You can take me or I can follow you. I'm not staying here."

"Jesus Christ."

At eleven twenty they were at the intersection of North and Charles.

"Park at the side of the road where he would have to back out," Flynn told Frankel. "Don't get out of the car until I do. I'm going to block any other exit. Liz, please don't get out the car unless I specifically ask you to. I don't think we'll be using guns, but I don't want any chances. Do you understand?"

Liz nodded.

At that moment, a fully loaded dump truck rumbled by, coming from the direction of Lake Drive.

"Call dispatch and tell them to have Palmer stop that truck before it gets out of Hardington," Flynn said to Eddie Frankel. "And don't let the driver make any calls. Mahoney gets no heads up from anyone."

They waited three minutes, then heard the second patrolman report that he had stopped the dump truck on the state highway and had possession of the driver's cell phone.

"Let's go visit Mr. Mahoney," Flynn said.

The two cars drove the half mile to the site of the teardown. From a hundred yards away, Liz could see the large orange backhoe, its flatbed truck carrier, and two dump trucks. She did not see the Range Rover but, incongruously, she saw Jane Mahoney's station wagon. She saw two men running toward the excavator.

"John, that's Jane Mahoney's car. Something's wrong."

Flynn pulled his car in behind the station wagon. Fifty feet away was a tableau. Two men, uncertain of what to do, standing near Jane Mahoney, who stood with stooped shoulders just outside the Plexiglas cabin of the backhoe. Inside was a person slumped over the backhoe controls.

Flynn and Liz bolted from the car simultaneously. Liz ran to Jane, who looked at Liz with bewilderment. Jane's face and blouse were sprayed with blood. Liz embraced her, not knowing why but sensing this was the right thing to do.

Flynn raced to the cab. The man slumped over the controls was Chuck Mahoney. A large knife – the kind used to carve turkeys – stuck out of the base of his neck at his left shoulder. Blood was everywhere. Flynn felt for a pulse but found none.

"Get the EMTs!" he yelled to Frankel. "Knife wound to the neck. No pulse, massive loss of blood."

"He gave me a piece of her jewelry and tried to call it a present," Jane whispered. "The bastard gave me the necklace that slut wore to the May meeting. And he called it a present. He's sleeping with her, he's buying her presents, he's taking her out to dinner. And I get a piece of her jewelry second hand."

"Do you know where she is?" Liz asked gently.

"Probably down in there." Jane motioned with her head toward the rubble of the house pushed into the basement. "I saw him sneak a blue tarp out of the garage last night. He killed her but he kept her jewelry. Probably planned to give it to his next bimbo."

She turned her head up to face Liz. "I prayed all through church this morning. I prayed for guidance. But God didn't answer. And the knife was still in the car when I got out of church, so I guess he was saying I had to make my own decision."

The wail of an ambulance siren was already drawing close. Liz continued to hug Jane, who now was softly crying.

12.

Epilogue

The body of Irina Volnovich Burroughs was, as Jane Mahoney guessed, wrapped in a tarpaulin amid the rubble of the basement of the Lake Drive house. She had died of strangulation. Her luggage had been salted among the debris of kitchen cabinets, appliances, and miscellaneous household goods left when the family moved. Jewelry believed to belong to Irina Burroughs was recovered from the offices of Mahoney Construction on North Street.

The operator of the excavator said that Chuck Mahoney had tossed him the key to the Range Rover and said to enjoy a long drive in the country. Mahoney said he was an expert in the use of the big machine. The operator, who was already getting double time for working on Sunday, was all too glad to get the additional bonus of being able to drink beer and watch the Red Sox on a Sunday afternoon.

The two drivers of the dump trucks still at the site concurred in their version of the story. The first truck had been loaded and sent on its way. Chuck Mahoney was smashing the foundation with the jaws of the excavator in preparation of loading the second truck. Between the noise of the diesel engine and his attention to the task at hand, he neither saw nor heard the station wagon pull up behind the excavator. A woman got out of the car carrying something in one hand, but because she was neither young nor especially attractive, the two men paid insufficient attention. The woman paused only briefly before mounting the steps leading to the cab of the excavator, opening the Plexiglas door, and plunging a knife into Chuck Mahoney's neck. Mahoney apparently never noticed his attacker because he did not struggle with the woman.

The woman then climbed down from the cabin and stood just outside it. The two men rushed to the scene of the stabbing but could agree on no action. The arrival of the police a few seconds later relieved them of any responsibility to intercede.

Chuck Mahoney was pronounced dead at the MetroWest Medical Center in Natick.

It would be Tuesday afternoon before the Massachusetts State Police crime scene unit produced a report on the fingerprint and other physical evidence gathered from the bedroom/office of Sally Kahn. Several dozen fingerprints belonging both to Irina Burroughs and Chuck Mahoney were found on the computer keyboard, monitor, and desk. This was deemed sufficient evidence to add Chuck Mahoney's name to that of Irina Burroughs as the persons responsible for the death of Sally Kahn.

Murder charges against Timothy Kahn were dropped. He pleaded no contest to a charge of breaking and entering of a home on Preservation Way and was sentenced to six months in a drug rehabilitation center.

The lead story of Tuesday evening's newscasts and the Wednesday morning newspapers was of a raid by the Environmental Protection Agency on the premises of Landini Brothers Sand, Gravel & Concrete in Overfield. A simultaneous raid was held at the development site of a 'lifestyle center' shopping complex in Stoughton.

EPA investigators at the Stoughton site found thirty barrels of the toxic chemical Benzapyrene, which was believed to have been illegally dumped there in the 1950s by a long-defunct chemical company. Investigators found ten barrels from the Stoughton site at the sand and gravel company, where it was in the process of being laced into the concrete mix manufactured by Landini Brothers. Tests showed that upwards of sixty barrels may have been disposed of in this manner, most or all of it at the site of a new wastewater treatment facility in Milford. Experts consulted by the Boston *Globe* opined that the sewage plant would need to be completely dismantled and that remediation would take three to five years.

Frank and Phil Landini, the two owners of Landini Brothers were arrested as were three employees believed to be complicit in the transport of the barrels. Also arrested were six executives and managers of the land development company and its site preparation subcontractor whom the EPA said knew of or approved of the illegal removal of materials from a hazardous waste site. The EPA said it had moved swiftly upon receiving information from concerned citizens who had observed suspicious behavior on the part of the concrete company. Singled out for commendation was Dr. Alvin Duclos, Chairman of the Chemistry Department of MIT, who had identified the hazardous material and its probable source.

* * * * *

On Wednesday morning, Chief Amos Harding gathered his full department – twenty police officers and civilian personnel – for a meeting in the department bullpen. Also invited to the meeting was Liz Phillips, president of the Hardington Garden Club.

"A lot has happened over the last several days," he said. "We went fifteen years in this town without a murder. Then, in the last week, three people have died."

Chief Harding paused and cleared his throat. "As many of you know, we initially had a confession to the death of Sally Kahn from her son. We now know that he didn't do it. I think I know why he gave us that confession. I believe he feared for his life. We now know that he saw Chuck Mahoney's car pulling into the high school parking lot the night of his mother's murder. He must have thought Chuck saw him and, once he knew his mother had been pushed down those stairs, he figured being in the Norfolk County lockup was better than being Chuck's next victim."

"As to this Volnovich woman, well, I never met her. And I

don't know if all the stuff in yesterday's *Herald* is true, but from what I can tell, she was some real piece of work. And she didn't do the image of our town any good. This is not some 'Peyton Place on the Charles' and I don't care to see that kind of story about my town on the front page of the paper. But she's dead and it's not my place to cast aspersions on someone who has passed on."

"I don't know what to say about Chuck Mahoney. I've known him since he was a baby and I know both of his parents. Chuck was a good kid who never gave me or anyone here any trouble. Whatever he and this Irina cooked up – or whether she pushed him into killing Sally Kahn or vice versa – well, there's no excuse."

"I've also known Jane Mahoney all her life, and her family goes back in town a long time. As I'm sure all of you know, she's over at the state hospital in Bridgewater undergoing a psychiatric evaluation. I'm not excusing her, but if I were in her place, I might have done the same thing. It's a tragedy all the way around."

Chief Harding paused for a moment. He spoke the next words looking not at his audience, but at his shoes.

"I guess a lot of the reason we cracked this case is because of our new detective, John Flynn. Detective Flynn and I have had some words about his methods, but he did get results. Some of you may have heard me hollering at John. That was – unprofessional of me."

At that moment, Liz glanced over at Flynn and caught his eye. Both of them smiled.

Chief Harding looked up again. This time, his gaze was on Liz.

"But the real reason we're here this morning is that I got a letter yesterday," Chief Harding continued. He held the letter up so everyone could see it. "It's from the Thomas and Felicity Snipes Charitable Foundation. Tom and Felicity haven't been here long, but they've already given a lot to the community – sports equipment for the middle school, for example, plus a lot of stuff they do anonymously. Well, they'd like to establish a contemplation garden here at the police and fire station, and they've given us a check for ten thousand dollars to build it. And they've stipulated that it will be cared for by the garden club and that they'll pay for its annual maintenance."

"Ordinarily, I don't think individual people ought to be paying for things for the police department. But given all that's happened, I think this is a good a way of putting all of these murders behind us. If you ask me, Tom and Felicity may be new people, but they're good people."

Acknowledgements

A book is the product of many hands. Many people have told me stories over the years, and certain of those stories have been retold in these pages. I hope I have fictionalized them sufficiently that no one will be caused embarrassment.

Betty Burgess Sanders has been my wife for 36 years. For the past six years she has also been my editor, telling me when I wander too far off base. Thank you for putting up with me.

Books require endless proofreading, and Faith Clunie and Barbara Provest caught numerous egregious errors that I missed. Thank you for having the attention to detail that I obviously lack.

A circle of readers too large to mention individually read my manuscripts and provide honest feedback that makes them better books. I am in your debt for your forthrightness.

Bookstores are supposed to be a dying business, but they are better at introducing books by unknown authors than any computer or website. BookEnds of Winchester and Wellesley Books are two such institutions that gave me both shelf space and kind words from their staffs, and I am truly thankful.

I have had the pleasure now to speak to dozens of book groups, and to give talks at libraries, senior centers and book stores. Interaction with readers who have read my words provides the psychic fuel that keeps me writing.

Finally, I have high praise for garden clubs. They are remarkable institutions that benefit their communities. My wife is a past president of the Medfield Garden Club, and she is active in the state federation. Through her, I have met hundreds of wonderful garden club members from across the country. Please do not tar and feather her for the plots that I, alone, have dreamed up.